For Fionnghuala, she with the fair shoulders

CONCESSION
Street Secrets

1

May 1868

Alex O'Shea stood with a crowd lined up along Wellington Street, listening to their exclamations when the guards fired their guns as if they were trying to level the Parliament building with their bullets. For a moment, he felt off balance, shocked, as if he had been transported to a battlefield. Smoke tickled his nostrils. He would need to meditate on what, if anything, this ceremony meant for the new confederation of Canada. His article would be due early the next morning at the Kingston *British Whig*.

He decided to take a stroll into the grubby parts of Lower Town. It would be a good setting for the next scene in his novel. Who had killed the curious policeman, how, and why? To sell his book, the answers needed to be sensational, like in *Lady Audley's Secret*. At heart, he wanted to be a detective, because he believed he had devilish mysteries inside that he needed to explore or else go mad. His detective resembled himself.

He had another reason to go to Lower Town. He knew that women of all ages sold their bodies there. On previous trips to Ottawa, he had spent a few dollars groping and coupling in back alleys.

With the smell of gunpowder in the air, he started off toward Sappers Bridge when he came across a curious sight. Everyone was ignoring a woman dressed in black at the edge of the street, her hands clasped over her ears and her veil drawn. Did she not realize the gunshots were ceremonial? Black was an ominous colour, but he was curious.

"Madame, may I be of assistance?" he asked.

She was shaking, and he assumed she did not hear him. He touched her shoulder, hoping to get her attention. She lowered her hands, but she would not look at him.

He repeated his question. Her answer was long in coming. It could have been a case of excessive grief or a ploy to sell her body to him. "Do you know where Concession Street is? I seem to have wandered away from Father's house." She had a sweet, eloquent voice. Who could she be mourning, a mother? A husband? Perhaps she was living with her father because of her husband's death, but how could she not know how to find Concession Street, only a ten-minute walk away? Was she hysterical?

She pulled back her veil and looked up. Her face was beautiful: lush lips and eyes with a fantastical depth that reminded him of his mother's eyes. Her skin seemed like an ocean-swept pearl, or was it sickly white?

He decided the girl was only fifteen or sixteen, but he still wanted to take her in his arms. If this was a paying proposition, so be it. He offered to show her the way. Her smile was radiant despite a foiled effort to get to her feet. Perhaps she was ill. He told her she could hold his arm.

"I'm afraid Uncle George may see us, and we will be in trouble," the girl said as they took the first steps among the dispersing crowd of gentlemen in formal suits and woman in wide skirts. She stumbled, but he held her up.

He assured her that he could explain the situation to her uncle, although he wasn't at all certain. Her uncle sounded like a rough man, but Alex couldn't leave her in her current state.

"Uncle George lives with us now that Father has passed away. He was in the United States and never ever came to see us. Now he and my sister, Maddy, run the sawmill."

They proceeded slowly along Sparks Street, which was much cleaner than Alex recalled from his last visit—hardly any horse droppings and no scatter of garbage or shreds of old clothing. He wondered if Ottawa had made a special effort for this day, the celebration of the monarch's birthday during the second year of confederation, or if sanitary improvement was a regular showpiece of the capital city. Kingston was still up in arms about not being picked by the queen as the capital. In fact, he was relieved not to be living in a town dominated by the public service or the lumber industry. He made a joke about Ottawa's "dead wood," but the girl did not understand, even after he explained it.

She leaned more heavily on his arm. He loved the pressure of her slight body. As they came upon Sally Street, he suggested they rest on a bench near the Wellington Street Market. She was fascinated by the sales at the vegetable and flower stalls.

"I have never been here before. Thank you for taking me, Mr. . . . ?"

"O'Shea . . . Alexander. I find it surprising that you live so close by and yet have never been to this market. Have you just moved into the neighbourhood?"

She looked up at him, her skin white as a ghost's and looking as if she would disappear if he touched her. Her dreamy eyes seemed enchanted. They were his mother's eyes. Could she be a spirit? He had heard Ottawa had ghosts.

"Oh, no, I was born in our house. I have read about markets and always wished to go to one." She smiled like a child. His tongue was tied. There were so many mysteries about this girl that he did not know where to start.

He rose to his feet, and the corners of her mouth went down. "You're leaving me?"

"I'll be right back. Don't worry; you can watch me the whole time." He was over his head and needed to extract himself. And yet, it was totally unexpected, an adventure to distract him from dark thoughts.

He returned with a bouquet. She looked sad and miserable but took it in her hands. "These are for me?"

"Yes, I thought flowers might brighten your day, Miss . . .?"

"Oh, they're so beautiful. I have never seen them before." She stroked the petals with her fingers as if they were alive and might respond by purring like a kitten.

"Why, these are common daisies, and those two are lilies. I'm surprised they're new to you."

"I have read about them in books. Sometimes ladies are called Daisy and Lily."

He watched her face and hands as she admired the flowers and could not help recalling a painting of a little girl by Sir Joshua Reynolds, "The Age of Innocence."

"There you are, Miss Mary!" a man said so loudly that the girl dropped the flowers. Alex jumped to his feet, feeling guilty that he should be seen trifling with her by the dreaded George, if this was the man. He was bald, his forehead wrinkled, and he wore a tie and a formal black suit that was too large for him.

"Benson, you need not shout so," Mary said. He had to be a servant, probably the butler.

"Miss Baker had me out looking everywhere for you. Her orders are that I bring you home immediately."

"Very well. I'll return," she said as Benson crooked his elbow for her to take. "But Mr. Alexander shall escort me while you lead the way."

"You know very well that Miss Baker will not be pleased, and besides, I'm sure Mr. Alexander has other business that needs attending." He looked at Alex, his eyeballs shifting sideways and his jaw tightening. A silent message: *Go away, or I'll knock you down.*

"Do you have a little time, Mr. Alexander? My sister Madeline would like to meet you, despite what our servant says." Mary looked defiantly at Benson.

If Alex walked away, he knew he would never meet her again. Her eyes mesmerized him.

"I do. My train leaves for Kingston in a couple of hours."

Benson exhaled loudly. Then he turned and strode away, stopping to check if they were following. Mary took her time collecting the flowers she had dropped and then accepted Alex's proffered arm.

Along the way, she dawdled, much to Benson's irritation. She was fascinated by every stone-and-brick house and office, plants in flower boxes, the large doorways, ordinary things. When Benson stopped to say, "Miss Baker may well have summoned the police by now," Mary laughed at him.

She asked Alex about Kingston. He told her about the Saint Lawrence River and the harbour, Queen's University, the old buildings in the town, and the penitentiary. Her eyes sparkled at everything he mentioned, and she kept saying, "Oh I should like to see that! I would draw a picture," until, finally, he asked if she was an artist.

"I used to draw. Maddy and I had a teacher who helped us."

"I would like to see your drawings—and ones by your sister as well. Ottawa is a marvellous place for sketching. Parliament Hill, the Ottawa River."

She looked vacant when he said this, as if she did not recognize even the ground where she stood. "I'll show you some, but I'm sure they are not good . . . of ordinary things, like the chairs in our house. My sister has not kept her drawings."

He had come this far on a whim. He wondered how this girl could be so naïve. Was the Concession Street destination a madhouse? They were on Concession now, and Benson stood in front of a heavy oak door with black iron studs.

The stone house was somber. It could well be an institution. Benson expected him to deliver his charge and be on his way, a wise thing to do. Alex released Mary's hand from his arm, but she tightened her grip.

Out the door came a portly woman, perhaps close to Alex's age, twenty-seven, wearing a low-cut, wide-skirted scarlet gown, a jewelled necklace around her neck. Benson and Mary were cowed by her. Despite her weight, she was handsome, with blue eyes and long, coiffed hair. She pulled Mary away from him. Alex tipped his hat to her. She gave him a scathing look. "What has gotten into you, child?" she said to Mary. "You know very well that you're not to leave this house. Look at you, in that old mourning dress! You disgrace our household."

"Maddy, I'll make a scene right here on the street if you don't invite Mr. Alexander in for a cup of tea after all he has done to help me."

Madeline's eyes travelled up and down Alex's body. His friend Eliza had said he was a decent-looking man, upright and strong. However, people usually stayed clear of him, because he lacked spontaneity and humour. Nevertheless, he must have passed the examination. "Very well then," Madelaine said. "You're welcome to come in, Mr. Alexander."

"It's O'Shea, Miss. Alexander is my given name." He was wary of her, especially of the way she had looked at him, as if he was on sale.

Benson held the door open, and Alex followed the ladies, feeling like a lamb entering the chute for shearing. It was mouldy inside. Did the family not believe in the benefits of ventilation?

In the salon, Mary pulled him over to a large, purple, upholstered chair. He said he would be just as happy sitting in one of the hard-backed chairs, but Mary refused. "No, you must sit in Father's chair, as it is the most comfortable." She looked like she would cry if he declined. Madeline did not object, so he sat on the cherished seat and felt himself sucked into cushions that emitted the odour of stale cigar smoke.

"Benson, please see to the tea, and Mary, go change into a normal dress. The blue one is nicest."

Mary ascended the stairway like the child she was, so familiar with her home. Madeline looked at Alex with a crafty expression that he had only seen once before on a magician who had made a rabbit disappear. Was he being tricked? "Please, excuse my sister. She's still mourning the loss of our father, who died a year ago."

That explained it, a depressive state brought on by mourning.

"She is very young to have lost a father . . . and a mother?"

"We lost our mother when Mary was a baby, but she is not as young as you suspect. She is twenty-two."

He was speechless. Twenty-two?

"Mary has not matured like other women and cannot let go of her grief. I think the life of a recluse would age most people, but Mary remains a child waiting for Father to come home, so she can sit on his knee."

A maid entered with tea and biscuits, and Madeline flicked her finger at a side table and then toward the door—she was quite the commander. He wondered if she and the absent Uncle George were a match for each other or if she ceded the crown when he was around.

"Does Mary have friends or a craft to distract her? She mentioned drawing . . ."

Madeline flinched. "So, she told you about drawing, did she? What else did she tell you?"

"Very little. Mr. Benson met us by the Wellington Street Market."

"I see. There are no secrets here, but I worry sometimes if Mary has spun a tale or two. She frightens the servants by such behaviour, although I see you're made of sturdier stock." She rose and poured tea in white-and-dark-blue teacups decorated with oriental flowers. "These were made in Worcester. Father brought them back from a business trip to England."

She was acting like he was an intimate friend. Her bosoms were quite wonderful, from what he could see of them, and that was quite a lot.

Mary appeared on the stairs, struggling with a load of canvases.

"Don't you fall!" Madeline shouted.

Alex rushed from his seat to relieve her. One drawing slipped out of her grasp and tumbled down the stairs. Mary pouted like a little girl but cheered up when he retrieved it and showed her it was undamaged.

"Bring them here, and I'll select the ones that Mr. O'Shea will see," Madeline said.

Mary rushed over, and he followed. When she was relieved of her burden, Mary turned to him. "Mr. O'Shea? I'm confused."

"My first name is Alexander, but you may call me Alex."

Mary led him back to the big chair, sat on a padded stool nearby, and looked up at him with wonder. "Can you stay for dinner?"

"No, I have to catch the train today and be at work in Kingston tomorrow morning." He wondered what would happen if he could stay on. Would the uncle that Mary had mentioned come home and throw him out? He wished he could stay. With her long, golden tresses and blue dress, which had a high lace collar, Mary looked like a little girl dressed up for a birthday party, or the way her mother would have looked in her youth.

"Here, you may start with these," Madeline said, interrupting his reverie as she handed Mary some drawings.

Mary moved the stool, so she was down below at his side, and handed up the first sketch. "This is the very chair on which you're sitting."

It was detailed, and the creases in the fabric resembled a mouth with evil eyes. It also seemed muscled, as if it could squeeze the life out of someone sitting in it. Alex blinked, and it was an ordinary chair, blinked again, and the malicious character returned.

"Well . . .?" Mary asked.

"It's interesting."

Mary pouted. "That means you don't like it."

"He does not need to like it," Madeline said.

He could not disappoint Mary. "No, no. I like it, because it's so alive. I want to see more. Please." In truth, he did. This was a mystery. How did the hand of such an innocent young woman render such sinister portrayals?

As he examined more of her drawings, he saw Mary watching his face, ready to cry with every crease of his brow and to laugh joyously when he was amused. Mary confirmed that all the drawings were of objects in the house. But wood, iron, china, and cloth all turned into the same personality, sometimes angry and other times merely mischievous. Mary talked of the light that came through the windows when she did some of the drawings and of the flickering candlelight that illuminated others.

After she had shown him the selected drawings, he took out his pocket watch. "I must be off. Thank you, Miss Baker, for the tea and you, Mary, for the art exhibition. You're very talented." He stood, and Mary looked into his face with such longing that he thought he would remember her for a long time.

"It was a pleasure to meet you, Mr. O'Shea," Madeline said.

"Maddy, can I please ask Alex to write to me? Just short letters. I never get letters. And I should so love writing to him."

If Mary was twenty-two, why did she have to ask her sister?

"You may. Mr. O'Shea, my sister has no friends, and it would be a favour to us. Please stop by again for tea if you're in Ottawa. Let us know when you're coming."

"Very well. Here's my card."

At that moment, Benson announced George. He looked like a monster, his thinning hair awry after he took off his hat, the blackened hole where his eye used to be, and his scarred face. Alex held his breath and glanced at Mary, who shivered, and Madeline, teeth clenched and brow furrowed. When George was introduced to Alex, he merely shook his hand and then excused himself to go to his room. Alex took his leave.

✢

The face of the innocent maiden looked in through the windows of the train on the way to Kingston. The face brought to mind his mother, the expressions he had seen on her radiant face when he and his mother went out for walks on starry nights, and she pointed out the constellations and planets. It was the wonder in her face that he loved to see more than the glory and mystery of the orbs in the sky.

That fateful morning just before Christmas when Alex was ten, his mother wanted to go into town to buy him skates. His father warned that the ice on the river might be too thin to cross safely. Alex looked woeful. His mother said his old skates were too small. Alex would be so sad when his cousins came over for Christmas to skate on the pond. His mother's charms overwhelmed his father, as usual. A big, strong man, he had cut down trees to clear the land and built the house and barn by himself. He was always patient with Alex. Now he, like the rest of the family, no doubt looked forward to a holiday and going over to his brother's place for Christmas Eve and inviting them to their house for dinner on Christmas Day. Father offered to go himself, but Alex's mother said she wanted to buy cloth to make presents. She would bring along Alex's little sister, and Alex could stay behind to feed the chickens.

Father hitched their horse, Blackie, to the sleigh. Alex was so happy that he jumped for joy. Skating with his cousins! Could he learn to do figure eights the way they did? They were older, but he usually caught up with them.

His mother gave Alex a kiss and told him they would not be long. His last sight of her smiling face was when she looked back and waved at him as they were nearly halfway across the river. Then he heard a loud boom. Could it be thunder? He saw a huge slab of ice tilt sideways along a crack, his father leap off, still holding the reins and hoping to lead Blackie back onto flat ice somehow, and then him slipping, along with the sleigh and horse, into the water. The slab righted itself with only Blackie's head showing in the crack, neighing and then going silent.

Alex ran part way out onto the river, heard more rumbling sounds, and then fled back to shore, where he cried and shouted for a long while.

His mother haunted him always, and now he had seen her eyes in someone else.

2

"Come on, Batch, we have an edition to crank out," Tom Hughes said, shoving Eliza's hand away from the printing press, so he could look inside.

Eliza wished she could shed that name, "Batch." Her schoolmates had called her that, because she was tall, her voice was like a man's, her jaw square, and her muscles larger than those of other females. Now she could not shed the name, even at her workplace. She didn't want to wear fashionable hoop skirts, because she believed she would appear to be a guardsman dressed like the queen and knock down objects from the shelves in the cramped printing room of the Kingston *British Whig*.

Hughes was a reporter. He had been a thorn in her side ever since her father, who she called "Pater," brought her in to help him set type. She caught on quickly, and after Pater died, Hughes fumed when they offered her work for half wages. He said she was taking a job that rightfully belonged to a man who needed to provide for his family. He watched her constantly, waiting for a mistake he could report. The present moment was no exception. Did he sense she delayed fixing the press, so her friend, Alex, who had been late that day, wouldn't be in trouble?

She shoved Hughes aside. "Now, you get away. I heard Mr. Barker tell you to work up tomorrow's shipping news. I'll have this running in no time."

Still hovering behind her, Hughes lit a cigar and blew smoke toward her. "That wire you got at the general store will never work. It'll just damage the press. Women can't do the job."

"Though I'm always in haste, I'm never in a hurry," she said, knowing it would infuriate him.

"How dare you quote the revered Wesley to me! You're an inferior devil who should never have been entrusted with this work."

She turned to face him. "Women are better than men at some things. I can typeset an entire page ten times faster than you. Now go away before I hit you!"

"Ha!" Hughes stuck out his weak jaw but backed away from her glare nonetheless.

Eliza imagined that Alex had gotten too engaged in writing his detective novel while in Ottawa and came home knocking back whiskey. He had arrived late to the office, puffy eyed and foggy minded. Immediately, he was called in by Mr. Barker, the editor, whose baritone voice sounded unusually annoyed. Alex's article on the queen's birthday was to be on page three of the *British Whig*.

"It's ready to try," Eliza said finally, engaging the machine and watching the pages she had set prior to the breakdown coming out.

Hughes scoffed. "I doubt it'll last the day."

She made her right hand into a large fist. Hughes cowered. Soon everything was printed, except for the third page. She waited, setting type for advertisements to appear in the next day's paper. Alex rushed in, carrying his manuscript, which was all marked up by the editor. Hughes seized the opportunity to go out for tea, by which he meant downing pints at the Royal Tavern.

"What happened?" Eliza asked. "Normally, Barker lets your work pass right through."

Alex shrugged, lost in thought rather than looking chastised. "I didn't sleep last night. I'll read the article aloud while you set it. That will be faster."

Eliza wanted to ask him more, but he started reading immediately. She smelled the stale whiskey on his breath. Twice he lost his place, and she caught him up on it. Barker came in and looked down on them like Moses from the Mount. When at last Eliza finished the typesetting, she had to work the press.

"Can we walk after work?" she asked.

"Please, forgive me, but I have to stay late to make up for today and—"

"I know, Mater will be expecting me." Her mother hated the name "Mater," but Eliza insisted on it. Bachelor and Mater. Mater the master. Just the two of them in the household now and no prospect for change. However, her friendship with Alex made her life as a woman worthwhile. He was the kind of person who had no friends, just like her. When she first came to the office, the two of them went from exchanging pleasantries to walking out together, exchanging books, and revealing some of their personal histories to each other. She held back one secret about herself that she feared would revolt him, and she had a notion that he was hiding something as well. If he ever kissed her, she would have to confess.

She knew that Alex felt insecure and might leave. He wanted to be a fiction writer. A reputable journal had printed one of his mystery stories, and two of his articles had been published in England in Charles Dickens's *All the Year Round*.

As Eliza approached her mother's house on Sydenham Street, she saw the patches where paint was peeling off the shutters and the weeds were overtaking the plants. Her mother expected Eliza to dedicate the next two weekends to painting and gardening, because Mater was incapable of such tasks, and they had no money to hire a local lad to do the work.

"Here, where have you been? Have you picked up the post?" Mater sat at the table, bent over and wrinkled. She knew very well that Eliza had been working, but she always cross-examined her regardless.

"Yes, Mater."

Mater saw an envelope in Eliza's hand, a seed catalogue. "There will be a letter from Paul, and I insist you read it to me immediately." Mater had spectacles that no longer sufficed for handwriting and small print. She always dressed in her best clothes of times past, when Pater was alive.

She waited, like a dog for a bone. Just for form's sake, Eliza looked through the pages of the catalogue and then said she needed to visit the loo before reading. Her mother harrumphed.

In her bedroom, Eliza looked through old letters from her brother Paul, a former gunner with the British Navy who had died six months earlier. She picked out one from when he was stationed in Scotland, not long before the news came of his being swept off a ship and lost at sea. Mater had repressed that news. She was losing her memory.

Eliza read the letter Paul wrote about a trip to the seashore with a young woman and her family.

"Oh, I would so love to meet her. I'm sure she's the sweetest, most beautiful girl in the British Empire. All the girls fall over each other for him, but he knows to pick only the finest," Mater said before asking her to re-read the letter.

"I need to put the chicken in to roast and peel the potatoes," Eliza said.

"Just peel the potatoes and boil them with the chicken. I like them that way," Mater replied.

Eliza knew what would happen next. While the food boiled, Mater would say the same prayer she did every night for Pater's soul and Paul's safety and then, when Eliza served the tasteless provender, Mater would chase the food around her plate with a spoon, because she was going blind. She would ask Eliza to give an account of herself while out of the house and then say, "I hope a man doesn't have his eye on you. You know that wouldn't be proper."

"Why is that, Mater?"

Mater shook her head the way she had since Eliza was a little girl. Why did Mater remember her secret when she had forgotten pretty well everything else? The secret was Eliza's earliest memory.

She was four and having a bath, playing with a little wooden boat her father made her. Her mother approached her, saying, "I should have done it before. I should have . . .." She reached between Eliza's legs and felt the appendage that was down there and the slit below it. "In your unmentionable, you will be a woman below and a man above. You don't want people to call you a freak." She began pinching Eliza's nub, which Eliza had playfully named Freddy. Her mother's fingernails dug in, and Eliza screamed and squirmed, but her mother persisted. There was blood.

"I need the scissors. Don't go anywhere. It will hurt and heal. You'll be better."

Still screaming, Eliza climbed out of the bath and hid under her bed, wedging herself in. Mater shouted at her to come out, but Eliza just screamed for her father. She stayed there until she heard him coming home from work.

As she sat and watched Mater's head nodding, the scene replayed itself over and over again, as it had many nights. Finally, Mater agreed to retire to her bedroom. The routine was for Eliza to wash the dishes and write a letter. Her letter must be to Paul from Mater, and she would be obliged to read it to her the next morning before she went to work.

She would not write that letter. Instead she wrote to Alex, telling him how much she loved him. The next morning, she would hold this out and pretend it was a letter to Paul, recite the same boring missive that Mater loved. Before leaving, she would reread her letter to Alex and then rip it up.

✤

"So, who killed the curious policeman?" Eliza asked the next evening. Wagons passed by, pulled by horses sagging after a day's work. She was walking with Alex down to the harbour. It was a calm, warm evening. He had been proceeding distractedly, seeming to have developed a geological interest in the rocks along the shoreline. Eliza wanted him to tell her what lay so heavily on his mind. Was it his novel?

"I haven't got that far in the novel," he said.

"Did a black cat cross your path while you were in Ottawa, or did you spot only one magpie without seeing its mate?" she asked, taking up their old way of joking with each other, familiar with his superstitions.

Just then, a stranger approached on the walkway, the sun in his eyes, possibly someone from America, across the river. "Good evening sir and . . . and . . .."

"And missus," Alex said sternly.

The man tipped his hat as he scrutinized Eliza.

Oh yes, Eliza thought, *I'm an odd one. I look exactly like a man similar in age to Alex, except taller.* She wore one of the old dresses that had come down from her granny. Her hat had no flowers or other decorations. Yet Alex had defended her. He knew she was a woman with feelings.

He picked up a flat stone and threw it into the harbour. It skipped across the water four times before sinking. Finally, he looked at her. "Eliza, I can't dismiss my passion."

She saw the hunger in his eyes. Was his passion for her? She wanted to throw her arms around him, but he turned away.

"What happened in Ottawa?" She felt like dropping to the ground. She was not the object of his passion. Yet that look of his... if only someday he could gaze at her like that.

He told her of his encounter with the two strange sisters, one the essence of simplicity, beauty, and purity, the other a high-fashioned woman who controlled the household, and an uncle who looked like an ogre. Perhaps the strict sister protected the innocent one, but they were shrouded in mystery. The younger one seemed like a mermaid. Eliza wondered how he felt about the older one.

"I'm mesmerized," he said, pulling at his hair on both sides of his head.

Feeling uneasy, she patted his back. "Don't let it worry you. Tomorrow morning you will wake and smile at your little adventure. What's more, any further meddling with that family sounds dangerous to me." She feared for him. She looked out at a steamer on the river, then down at her dowdy dress, tried to straighten a wrinkle.

"You're my best friend, Eliza, and what you say is wise, but I need to make up my own mind. While I'm held in the grip of this fantasy, I'm driven like a fiend. Last night I wrote a letter to the wounded one, Mary. She needs my help."

"You make her out to be the original Angel in the House!" she said, smarting as she thought of all the letters she had written to Alex and never sent.

"These passions awaken my spirit. I want to help her. That could repair a broken part of me." He looked as guilty as a boy who had raided a garden.

"Your obsession over these sisters is beyond my ken."

"It's beyond mine as well. You must give me a few days to untangle my thoughts and feelings. My impulse to go and protect Mary will probably go away."

"You have a novel to occupy your spare time. That's where the great mystery lies."

He nodded. "That's true."

They walked part way toward downtown, shook hands, and then Alex left. Eliza never had the courage to ask him to kiss her. She walked farther along the path, knowing that Mater would be hungry and outraged.

If she were a complete woman, she thought, Alex's words would have wounded her.

3

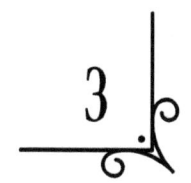

The morning rain made the Baker house look even more like a madhouse than it did when Alex had seen it two weeks earlier. The door-knocker sounded like bones rattling together.

"Sir, it's early to come calling," Benson said, closing the door behind him and facing Alex like a sergeant of the guard.

Alex took out his pocket watch, the brass tarnished, not polished like when he found it in his father's effects. He was five minutes early. Perhaps the family was at church. He did think 9:30 on a Sunday morning was an unusual time to be invited. Had Mary not consulted with Madeline?

"I'm here at the request of Miss Mary Baker," he said.

Three times he told Eliza he would never again enter this house of misery, and three times he had responded to Mary's letters. In her fourth letter, she pleaded with him to come immediately, and he felt his heart being pulled out of his body by invisible chains.

"I'll take my leave of her like a gentleman and explain that my work will keep me in Kingston," he had said solemnly to Eliza. He could tell she doubted him. This was the first thing that had ever come between them.

Benson continued to block his entry. "Your return to this house is unwise. There are matters I must discuss with you. Come away with me." Benson was soft on his feet, like a panther.

"Is someone ill?" Alex had heard frequent stories about the outbreak of measles and influenza, but this year the great epidemics, like cholera and typhus, seemed under control. Could Benson be leading him down Concession Street toward the Ottawa River, because the house was quarantined? Perhaps disease was why Mary had sent him such an urgent message, but none of the usual warning signs were posted.

Benson led him into an undeveloped lot, where birds picked at piles of stinking garbage. So, Ottawa kept its main streets cleaner than Kingston, but it did not clean up hidden miasmas like this.

"There is no change in the house or to those inside," Benson said. "But may I tell you something in confidence? If you reveal it, I'll lose my position." He stood like a soldier at attention, eyes watching any move Alex might make. He wore no hat, and the rain ran down his face and onto his collar.

"Yes, of course."

"You should go from here and never return. There is evil in the house, and it will draw you in." His expression was changeless.

Alex thought of Mary's drawings. Was it evil he had seen in her rendering of everyday objects or something her tutor taught her to do? Could the tutor have done sinful things to her?

"Benson, what the blazes do you mean? Is someone in the house malevolent?" If so, it must be George—both women seemed wary of him.

"There is, yes, but I can say no more."

"You can't just warn me without a shred of evidence or at least a word of explanation." If it was George, then he wanted to protect Mary and Madeline from him.

"I'll say no more. If you insist on coming, you cannot say I failed to warn you."

The impetuousness of the man! Servants were easily dismissed. A word or two with Madeline, and he would be gone.

Alex walked toward the house. Benson marched past him and opened the door for him to enter, then looked down at the stone threshold, watching Alex's feet cross it. Alex already suspected there was a secret in the house, and now he wanted more than ever to uncover it. This was more important than imagining who shot the curious policeman in his novel.

Benson took his wet hat and coat and shook them before hanging them up and announcing Alex's arrival. Mary came running. What a bright and splendid face she had, more than ever the pre-Raphaelite vision. She wore a green dress that looked new, with lace that encircled her pale, delicate throat. "Alex, you're late, but I knew you would not fail to come."

She led him indoors, her hand so frail in his. Had she lost weight since he last saw her? Madeline sat at an oak desk in the drawing room with stacks of paper on top and other documents rolled up in pigeonholes. She motioned them to be silent as she examined a document, drew lines through some of the sentences, and wrote notations. Then she rose to shake his hand. There were ink stains on her fat fingers, a stark contrast to her stylish gown.

"I see I'm disturbing your letter writing. I had in mind asking Mary to accompany me on a stroll, but, due to the rain, might we take tea in the salon? Perhaps she can tell me about her week and I can tell her mine." He did not want Madeline to be his arbitrator when he broke the news to Mary that he would not be returning. Mary could continue writing to him if she wanted, and he would reciprocate if he had time, although that was unlikely.

"I'm not writing letters," Madelaine said. "My work is to keep accounts for the mill."

"Oh, congratulations. That . . . that is very responsible work—"

"For a woman, you mean to say."

Alex began to sweat under her pinning glare. Her hands landed on her hips, and he looked down, avoiding her large, confident bosom. Had she caught him looking the last time?

"It is responsible work for anyone," he said, "but there are difficulties that women encounter, and it is noteworthy that you have overcome them. How do they respond to you at the mill? I ask this only as one who writes for a newspaper."

Madeline did not respond, appearing cross and uninterested.

"Oh, Shorty brings her loads of paper and takes back her work," Mary said.

"Shorty?"

"A clerk," Madelaine explained. "I work here at the house. The arrangement goes back to when Father was alive."

At the mention of "Father," Mary sniffled, and Madeline scolded her for it. He thought this was the right time to take his leave. He had been thinking it would be more humane to speak to Mary in person but, upon reflection, decided a letter would be best. He clasped his hands together and looked from one sister to the other. Madeline stuck out her wide chin, and Mary bowed her head. He gave Madeline a thin, veiled smile. Madeline spoke before he could talk of departing.

"Mr. O'Shea, I would like you to do a great favour for Mary. I don't know how you have done it, but she has been rising out of her despair ever since your first visit. Don't disappoint her." Madeline said this with measured words, akin to a command.

"Why, yes, if it is in my power." For Mary's sake, he could delay his farewell.

"Very good. You see, Mary has brought out her easel and drawing pencils for the first time since Father passed away. She wants to draw a likeness of you."

The easel stood in a corner of the room, like a soldier at ease. Mary rushed over to it, flashing a smile at him. "Oh, please, Alex. It would give me such joy."

He hesitated, recalling the evil representations Mary had drawn of the household furniture. If she made him into a ghoul, how would that help her?

"Oh, please, Alex, do! You have such a virtuous face. I'll give you the drawing when I'm done, and you can show it to your father and mother." Mary gestured with her pencil for him to come forward. He could not resist, although the mention of his parents hit him like a slap.

"Perhaps we ought to go to another room and not disturb Madeline?" he said.

"No, no, you will be required to stand in silence, and it pleases me to see Mary at work again," Madeline said. Having Madeline on guard was uncomfortable—as if they were children who might get up to something naughty.

He stood about ten feet away from the easel. Mary came over to position his arms. Her hands flitted around like chickadees. How could he ever have thought she might be a prostitute when he first spotted her?

"What expression should I have on my face?" His head was ordinary, nose of medium size, skin light in colour, brown hair barbered recently. He wore his normal slight smile. If she said "angry," he would refuse.

"Just as you are. Smile a little more. Now that's perfect."

And so the morning passed. Mary worked slowly and carefully, glancing at him with pretty, curious expressions, asking if he was tired and wished to sit on the sofa to rest. Madeline's pen scraped at a fast rate. On occasion, she muttered curses, and other times, "bloody George" and "stupid George." When Alex suggested that both model and artist could use a break, Mary demurred for herself, saying she had to make some touch-ups, but she did call upon their maid, Victoria, to bring tea.

As Alex waited for the tea, he took out his pocket watch. He had only an hour left before he had to catch the train to Kingston. The time passed as if he were in a trance, but now he had to say goodbye forever and break the poor girl's heart.

He stood and spoke about his departure. Both women approached him, Mary wringing her hands and Madeline holding her pen like a dagger. "Next time please inform us of the length of your visit," she said.

"I'll not be able," he began, about to carry out his mission to part for all time, but Mary tugged on his arm and dragged him over to the drawing. He held back the rest of his statement and examined what she had produced. He was surprised that the drawing was all on one side of the paper. What did she intend for the other side? She had drawn an outline of his body and worked in fine detail on his hair and the top half of his face. His eyes were kindly, more so than he imagined them to be in life. Mary looked up at him, still holding his arm tenderly, her expression similar to the one on his mother's face before she died.

"Do you like it?" Madeline asked.

"Yes, but it's too perfect. I'm not so handsome."

"We're all harsh judges of ourselves. Now tell us when you'll come back, so Mary can continue the work. I daresay she will set her drawing materials aside until that happens."

He turned to Mary. "Now you've made a start—"

"I only make one drawing at a time, Alex. Say you'll come back soon, please."

Caught in the crossfire of the overbearing sister and the innocent, needful sister, what could he do but assent? He said he would return for at least a full day at the end of the following week. He resolved that, when Mary finished the drawing, he would depart for good.

Before leaving, he encountered Benson, who looked the way a doubtful guard must when releasing a repeat offender from prison.

⁜

A week later, a maid who would not make eye contact with him answered Alex's knock. Mary hovered behind her.

"Mary, come and sit down," Madelaine scolded. "Remember the proper way to receive a gentleman. Let Victoria take his coat." She was sitting on a chair in the salon. He might have left his coat in Kingston; the day was so hot.

Mary backed away, chastised and embarrassed. Madeline gave him a slight nod, and Mary, watching her sister closely, imitated her. Once again, Madeline sported a fashionable gown, violet this time, and Mary wore the same old-fashioned dress with lace coming up to her chin.

They led him to the drawing room. Madeline sat down at her desk, and Alex and Mary hovered.

"May I bring you tea or a cold drink?" Victoria asked.

"Water only, thank you." He glanced around the room, curious about the drawing on the easel, facing the wall.

"Mary has been hard at work while you were away," Madelaine said.

Mary turned up the corners of her lips and nodded, looking up at him. She patted his arm but pulled away when he touched her hand. He caught Madeline observing them.

"Mr. O'Shea, you may go and see what Mary has done and resume your position, so she can continue," Madeline said. "You'll excuse me. I have a great load of work today because of a fire in the lumber yard."

"Was it arson?" he asked, the newspaperman in him showing.

"No one knows. The yard was neglected." The angry way she said it made him curious.

"Why? Don't mill workers regularly monitor the supplies?"

"You would think so, but now I must . . .." She was angry, no doubt with her uncle George. She took down a paper from one of the stacks on the desk. He wondered why, in this large house, she did not have a private office.

Mary led him to the easel and turned it awkwardly. She had indeed been working, not on his image but on a strange fruit tree in the centre of the drawing, towering above his head. Its roots spread out like gigantic veins. He knew that tree, but from where? He searched the caves of his brain, a tree in nature or in a book?

"Please, Alex, let's do what Maddy says and go back to where we were before. I want to keep working on your face." He carried the easel for her to where it had stood on his previous visit. Mary rewarded him with one of her special smiles, which took him back to his mother. He thought of how he would like to have that smile available to him more often. Every night perhaps? It was a shameful thought. In her mind, Mary was still a child, and he did not fancy living with a child for a wife. He doubted he could ever educate her in the realities of the adult world if Madeline had failed to do so. And he had his own bouts of depression, which would make him a poor mentor.

The maid brought in the tray with a decanter of water, glasses, and a plate of biscuits. When Madeline was not looking, Victoria raised her eyebrows and smirked, looking from Mary to the tray.

"Victoria, inform Cook that Mr. O'Shea will be dining with us at midday and dinner," Madeline said. He thought of objecting, saying he had work to do in his hotel room prior to his departure on Sunday morning, but Madeline's tone was so decisive that he decided to obey. While Mary drew him, he could think about the curious policeman—he told Eliza that he would unveil that mystery to her when he returned to Kingston. It couldn't be the robber, because that was too obvious. Perhaps—his thoughts were interrupted when Victoria left the room, causing a question to come to mind.

"Is Benson away?" he asked, wondering if the man had been fired for warning other visitors that evil lurked in the house.

"Why do you ask?" Madeline said, her back to him.

"Oh, an idle thought. I'm used to him being here. He's not ill, I trust."

"No, he's with George on a business trip to Montreal," Madeline replied.

He decided to ask nothing more, just let Mary explore his face with her eyes. Where was he? The policeman was onto something sinister, but Mary's eyes distracted him. They moved ever so slowly down his face, her hand filling in details, shading his nose, his mouth. The strange thing was that he felt her fingers on him, molding, creating. How could this be when his mother had made him? Ever since she died, he kept blowing apart like a haystack in a tornado.

His thoughts were interrupted by Madeline going to the door and shouting for Victoria. When she arrived, out of breath, she went to remove the tray.

"You remember?" Madelaine asked. Shrinking, Victoria put down the tray. "Sorry, Miss Baker, the dusting." She took a feather duster down from a rack near the fireplace and set to work. The room did not look dusty to Alex, and no dust flew into the air as she swept. He thought servants did that kind of work only before the family had risen or gone to bed.

He watched Madeline's stiff, rapid steps as she went to the door.

"Alex?" Mary said, holding a pencil in the air.

"Oh, I'm sorry. Your subject is unruly, looking away from you. May he approach the artist?"

Mary nodded, and he came up and admired her work while she kept an eye on him, looking for signs of disapproval. None were needed. His face and neck were nearly done, but it was too perfect a visage, as if he was an angel, innocent, content, not the face he saw in the glass when he shaved. After his first visit, seeing how she had rendered the furniture with malevolent characteristics, he expected at least a sneer on his lips.

"Does Madeline ever let you out of her sight?" he whispered, thinking that Victoria was a spy for Madeline. She noticed them standing together and moved farther away.

"Only when she's asleep," Mary whispered.

"Miss, the tea is cold, but the biscuits are still there. You had no appetite at breakfast. Here, let me bring them to you," Victoria said, setting down the duster and going for the tray. Just then, Madeline returned.

"Take the tray away, and help Cook with the lunch. We'll be ready to eat soon," Madeline commanded.

At lunch Mary refused the chicken, beets, potatoes, and sweetmeats. She allowed Victoria to serve her a half piece of bread and a tiny amount of salad. She nibbled and, for the most part, looked down at a spot on the table just above her plate. Madeline sat at the head of the table, ate heartily, and asked Alex, as a reporter, if he knew of any major goings-on in the "Mother Country."

He was tempted to counter by saying that Canada, since the previous year, was no longer a child of England. Instead, he found himself saying, "There's not too much stirring in England now. You no doubt have read that the House of Lords recently banned public hangings."

"What? I thought they were more civilized than us. If the public doesn't see justice done, murders will double or triple," Madeline said, making a savage cut in the air with her knife. Mary looked like she had just seen a ghost. He went on to explain that hangings would continue inside prisons.

"No good, no good," Madeline pronounced.

Mary had set down her utensils and made no effort to resume.

"Mary, I see that you have no appetite," he said. "I trust you're well?"

Mary didn't respond, merely slumped in her chair.

"Mary rarely eats at lunch. She has a large breakfast and then reserves herself for dinner, although sometimes she passes on that meal as well. You see she has a narrow waistline, as is the mode in this modern age."

Why had Victoria said she did not eat at breakfast? Mary was narrow at the waist, and all of her that he could see was too thin. She looked as if she would break into pieces if she fell over. Could she be one of those fasting girls he had read about? Mary resumed her regard of the spot on the table.

"Do you and Mary frequent playhouses or readings at literary societies?"

Mary bit her lip, the look in her eyes begging him to stop.

"No, it is not our passion. I may take Mary to the next public hanging though. Now, Victoria, bring on the dessert and coffee. Mr. O'Shea's time is precious." He wanted to insist that Mary speak for herself, but clearly that would place too much stress on her. She refused cake but accepted a cup of coffee. He heard her slurping—no one had taught her how to drink in company. Could he be that teacher?

After lunch he proposed that they go for a walk by the river. Mary might bring along her sketchbook, as there were many sights that would inspire her. Mary said not a word but looked at Madeline. "Of course, it should be the three of us going," he added quickly. "Do you not need some fresh air after working at that desk all morning?"

Madeline shook her head. "I must reattach the chain that binds me to my job. Today is July fourth, and the Americans are having their holiday, but Canadians are hard at work. Of course, what you're doing here is work of another sort, inspiring Mary to draw again."

"I'm sorry to hear you're so busy, Madelaine, but Mary, let's go out for an hour, and then you can resume making me immortal."

This drew no smile from either sister. Mary looked only at Madeline and, once again, bit her lip. Madeline crossed her arms. "The main purpose of you being here is to help Mary recover her artistic form. I presume you will not be able to return tomorrow? No? Well then, behind us we always hear, 'time's winged chariot drawing near.' We will have time for conviviality at dinner."

He swallowed his objections, amused by the irony that Madeline knew Marvell and that the only "mistress" in the room was herself, and she was far from coy. Madeline led the way back to the drawing room, where they resumed their positions. While Mary drew, Alex worshipped her face the way a Catholic might adore the virgin mother's. One moment she seemed puzzled and glanced by turns at the drawing and at him, and then her face lit up, and she propelled her hand.

"There," she said at last.

"You've finished?" he asked, walking toward her but not so quickly as Madeline, whose head blocked his view when he arrived.

"It is a very worthy rendering of the theme we discussed," Madeline said.

"What theme is that?" he asked.

"Innocence," Mary replied.

Alex knew he was not innocent. His sins were manifold. Ever since his youth he had thought devils might come and claim him for their own.

He expected his entire figure in the suit would be completed, but only the face looked out at him, and it was, indeed, an angel's face, a primal innocence. Not his real face. He kept his mouth shut and figured it out: the drawing was of Mary, her innocence transposed onto him.

Victoria came in with afternoon tea.

"Leave the tray, and we'll serve ourselves," Madelaine said. "Please, don't interrupt us."

"Yes, Mistress, I'll not forget," Victoria whispered. Looking down, she sped out of the room, closing the door softly behind her.

Madeline took a cup of tea to the desk and resumed her work. Alex sat on a divan with Mary, poured her tea, and tried as many tricks as he knew to get her to eat a biscuit, to the extent of eating several of them greedily and proclaiming they were the best he had ever tasted. She laughed as if he were a dog clowning around. She had a nibble and then growled at him like a puppy.

Madeline took a watch from a desk drawer and looked over at them. He refused the hint. "Why did you choose the theme of innocence?" he asked Mary, keeping his voice low.

Mary stiffened. "I started drawing you . . . and then Maddy and I talked about what it could mean."

"What it could mean? I thought you were just practicing, starting to draw again."

Mary opened her mouth and then closed it.

"Is innocence the theme because your other, very good, drawings are frightening?" he asked. "Was there something—"

"Mr. O'Shea, Mary saw you as innocent, and I encouraged her to keep going with that as a theme," Madelaine said. "There's nothing more to it. Your discussion is distracting me from my work, and I'm sure Mary will be disappointed if she doesn't get more done during your visit."

Mary jumped up and ran to the easel. Alex moved slowly, unhappy to be under orders.

"There's one more thing," Madeline said. "Mr. O'Shea, would you mind removing your shirt? Mary needs experience drawing musculature—professional artists include it in their works. She is too timid to ask you herself, and she asked me to make the proposal to you."

Mary looked down, blushing. Madeline trained her eye on him, as if he were her employee.

"I didn't expect this," he said, wondering if he should take umbrage and depart immediately. Eliza would have advised him to leave, because they were using him as a tool. And yet, were those tears on Mary's cheeks? Poor child, he would do anything for her.

"Very well, but don't expect to see many muscles. I'm the wrong man for that." He walked to the divan, pulled down his braces, and removed his shirt. Admittedly, it was hot in the room, and this half-nakedness was comfortable, but he was embarrassed that he did not sport a single hair on his chest.

Mary kept on drawing. Two times he tried to make her laugh by flexing a muscle like a strongman, but she merely looked nervously over at Madeline until he resumed his pose. When Madeline said it was dinner time, he got dressed. He had no interest in examining the drawing, nor did he receive an invitation to do so.

"Victoria, bring Mr. O'Shea pen and ink as well as notepaper from my desk," Madeline said at dinner as she continued her angry disquisition on the sawn lumber industry, its market risks, and the despoliation caused by fire.

"Is it necessary?" he asked, puzzled.

"You agreed to write an article on the topic for your newspaper."

Did he? He was only vaguely aware of her babble, but he nodded to pretend her points had registered. Instead, he had been sneaking glances at Mary.

As Victoria served, Mary shook her head at the beef. She permitted Victoria to place a small potato and a spoonful of jellied fruit on her plate, but she refused everything else. When Alex pleaded with her to take a roll, she relented and selected the smallest one. She glanced up nervously from time to time and caught him watching her chase the serving around in a circle with her fork.

Alex looked up when Victoria set the writing materials beside his plate. "Unfortunately, we've got enough articles on industry for this month—"

"And yet you agreed without saying that before," Madeline said. He was making her cross. She had caught him out.

"Oh, I meant to say that the *British Whig* has run these kinds of articles on the lumber industry, but I'm not the man who wrote them."

Madeline straightened in her chair. "Just write down what I say. Your editor will see it is a rare topic, how a woman guides the ship during a crisis while the captain sleeps."

"Ah, yes, that may make a difference," he said. He understood enough about the editorial policy of the *British Whig* and other daily newspapers to know they would have no use for it. Nevertheless, he scribbled notes as Madeline talked, still shooting glances at Mary, who put a tiny spot of jelly into her mouth and ate it so slowly he thought Madeline had time to dictate two articles before her younger sister would swallow.

The dining room door flew open, and George Baker, followed by Benson, stomped into the room. He seemed annoyed to find Alex with his nieces. He pointed at Madeline. "You and I need to talk in private."

"The fire is your fault," she shot back. "You hired idiots to keep an eye on the stack. No doubt they were your boozing companions. That's why I told Shorty to fire them all. The next crew will come to the house one by one, so I can interview them."

George's one eye looked at her as if she was a Confederate militiaman on the charge. "You're out of your league, Miss, firing my men. I meant it when I said we need to have a private talk. The drawing room."

"We left that room in disarray. How about the salon, if you insist on meeting immediately?"

George grunted his assent and marched out. On her way, Madeline told Victoria to take the drawing into Mary's bedroom. Then she asked Benson to watch over Mary, in case she had any of her "odd spells."

Mary gave up any further attempts to eat and looked at Alex with her heavenly blue eyes. "Did you enjoy your dinner?"

"Why, yes, I'm happy to be with you. Madeline's story about female captains of industry is interesting, but my employer will not likely print it."

"Just introduce her to him. Madeline is impossible to resist and . . .."

"And?" It was going to come out, but Benson cleared his throat, and she stopped. He was the one who had suggested there was evil in the house. If only Alex could get Mary alone, without Benson hanging around like a prison guard, he might discover the sinister secret!

"Benson," he said, trying a stratagem, "we had some fifteen-year-old sherry earlier. I believe it was the end of the bottle. Could you please find another? Miss Mary and I could each use a glass." Luckily, Mary did not reveal that she had only water earlier.

"Sir, we can wait until Victoria returns. I'm sure she will not be long."

"No, I'm afraid our mouths are watering for that delicious potion," Mary said. "Go now, please. You're familiar with the wine cellar, and it won't take you more than a minute." Alex was pleased she mimicked his expression of command.

Benson grunted, and they heard his quick footsteps once he withdrew from the dining room.

Alex moved his chair closer to Mary. "We may only have a moment alone for me to talk to you," he whispered. "Will you risk slipping out of the house tonight when everyone is

45

asleep? I'll wait, no matter how long it takes, even until the sun comes up tomorrow."

"Why?"

"There is a secret in this house, and it frightens you. I want to help."

Mary looked down. Tears fell from her eyes. He shook her shoulder and said she must hurry to answer. Still she sat, a frozen, weeping angel.

"I'll try to come. There is a secret. Father started doing horrible things to poor Maddy—"

She stopped when Madeline barged back in, looking as angry as a harpy. Alex moved away from Mary.

"What in damnation is going on here?" Madelaine asked. "And where's Benson?"

Mary shivered. Alex did not want to answer and was relieved when Mary said, in her quivery voice, "Alex was helping me get something out of my eye. I think it's gone now. Benson left to look for a bottle of sherry."

Benson chose that moment to return, bearing a bottle.

"Is it enough that I have to deal with an irate and panicky uncle who doesn't know how to run our business and, on top of that, to discipline a disobedient servant?"

Alex seized the moment to stand and declare that the time had come for him to return to his hotel room. Madeline took no notice, still roiling in anger. Mary rose and gave him her hand as well as an affirmative look.

⁘

After his abrupt departure, he went back to Russell House and fortified himself with whiskey. He glanced at the notes he had taken. He might edit Madeline's story and submit it, though the editor would almost certainly reject it. Why try? Because Mary said Madeline was a victim. She needed help, just like Mary.

He turned to his notebook and began writing random notes on the investigation following the death of the policeman in his novel. They made no sense, and he could not continue it, not that night. For now, all he could do was to try and save Mary and, if possible, Madeline. Was this honourable, or was he being driven by the base motive of bodily passion?

Returning to Concession Street, he watched the lamps being turned off in the Baker house. The street was deserted. The tall houses seemed to be leaning over to conspire with each other. He stepped in horse manure and used a pocket handkerchief to wipe it off. He risked walking under a streetlight to read his pocket watch, 11:58. Eleven and fifty-eight added up to sixty-nine, an evil number. He continued to stare at the house until it became midnight. No doubt Mary had fallen asleep or lay shuddering, frightened by his proposition. It was ludicrous of him to have devised it.

A cab came up the street, and the driver stopped to ask if he needed a ride—low fares at that time in the morning. He dismissed him politely. The house was dark, and he needed a few hours of sleep before the long train ride. Yet, he had said he would wait all night if necessary.

He could not mistake sudden movement at the front door. Someone half-opened it. There was a loud cry, and the door slammed shut again. As he ran up, he heard bolts closing and Madeline shouting. He could not distinguish what she was saying, but afterwards came George's baritone voice. "What in tarnation is going on here?" Alex could not make out anything further.

He grasped the knocker and almost began slamming it down on the door but then stopped. What good would his intrusion do? Mary had probably confessed his role in drawing her out of doors on an assignation. Madeline and George would vilify him.

This would be his last visit to the Concession Street house. His haste to expose the secret had worsened Mary's situation, and her keepers would have nothing more to do with him. He had fallen into the valley of temptation, but from now on, he must resist and put his shoulder to the wheel of Good.

4

Eliza saw that Alex, on the Monday after his return from Ottawa, shut himself away as if he was in a prison of his own making. He had a quick meeting with the editor, sat at his desk, sifted through papers, and wrote, not making eye contact with her. When Hughes stepped out, she went to Alex and laid her hand on his shoulder. "How are you, my friend?"

He looked as if he did not recognize her. What had happened? He had bags under his eyes and whiskey on his breath. His silence was even more alarming. "What's wrong?" she asked.

"I don't want to talk about the weekend. Ottawa is over. I never want to go back there again, and now I need to concentrate on this article."

She went back to setting type. Both stayed late that day. She put on her coat after Hughes left and was about to go out to the street when Alex came over. "Look, I'm sorry for being rude. Can we have a drink together?"

She didn't think he needed another drink and was still bothered by his behaviour. "I'm sorry," she said, "but I have to go home and make supper for Mater. She'll be starving by now."

"Well, may I at least walk you home?" He was a sad puppy.

"That would be lovely. Thank you."

Once on the street, they both placed pennies in the outstretched hands of beggars, who sat in their rags, backs up against the stone foundations of the office buildings. They talked about the summer heat. She took off her coat, hung it over her arm, and handed it to him when he offered to carry it.

As they came up to the Christian Brothers School, he suggested they take a detour, even though it would make the walk longer. She wondered if the place evoked fearful memories in him—he attended it as a boy. She had heard of the harsh treatment that some lads received. She had not made any such connection before, but now that she thought of it, Alex held what the church would call heretical views. He and she had talked often of evolution and the questionable existence of one God, the Creator. It came naturally to her, as Pater had avidly followed the debate in England over Charles Darwin's theories, and he had a collection of books by Darwin, Huxley, and other evolutionists that he encouraged her to read.

Eliza talked about Hughes, how he was getting more irritating, interrupting her work with his Wesleyan strictures and snide comments. She did not tell him about how, on Saturday, when Alex was away, Hughes asked if she was a man in disguise.

"Hughes has powerful acquaintances at the Methodist Church. I guess he thinks he can get away with anything, but one day, I'll teach him a lesson. I'm through tolerating bullies," Alex said.

Had he been bullied by the Baker family, and now he wanted to strike back at a surrogate? She did not want to probe, because his mood was delicate, especially after he suggested the detour around the school.

They continued their silent procession even as the traffic calmed when they turned northwest on Division Street and then west on Jenkins Lane. The houses, one-storey cottages essentially, were shabby but Eliza's less so. She had painted the exterior and thinned the hedge. Anything was better on her days off than sitting by the grumbling Mater.

"I would ask you in, but Mater would be disturbed by my having a male friend." She had to speak up because of the clanging of Eagle Foundry, less than a block away.

"Why is that?"

She had woken him from a trance. "She'll be afraid of losing her favourite slave, even if I tell her there's no danger of that."

Alex raised his eyebrows. "Eliza, one day you will find a man who wants to take you away with him, not to make you his slave but because he will love your goodness and attractions."

No one, not even Pater, had ever said something so kind to her. She examined his face to see if a smirk was hidden there. No. She blushed. "You have been contemplating your novel."

"Yes, you're right. My novel. I'll be getting down to work on it starting tonight and continuing every hour except when my best friend has time for gloomy, old me."

"I'll always be here for you."

"Come here, my little friend. You with the brave heart," Alex said, giving her a hug. Little friend indeed. She thought how much taller she was than him, and she wished she could bring him in to meet Mater as a beau. Wouldn't that be a shock!

Eliza had always thought the grinding and banging of the foundry was hard and cruel, but now it sounded like sweet music.

❖

Two weeks later, Eliza contemplated taking a complaint to Barker about Hughes's treatment of her, prophetic denunciations, little pinches when no one was looking, and then shocked, innocent expressions on his face when she protested. Alex was again in a world of his own, writing for the paper and working diligently on his novel, though he took an occasional walk with her.

When Hughes left early one day, Eliza went over to Alex. "Let me ask you the great question, who killed the curious policeman?"

"I haven't quite got to that chapter yet, but if I said it was another policeman, would you be surprised?" He had a smile on his face. She felt encouraged.

"That would surprise me. All signs pointed to the bank robber."

"They would."

"Ah, yes, and so that's what happens in mystery novels? The last person you suspect is guilty?"

"If you didn't read all those history and poetry books, you would know that's the way it works in mystery."

She wasn't sure about that. Just now she was reading *The Ring and the Book*, poetry by Robert Browning that Alex had given her as a present. It was about a murder trial in Rome in the late seventeenth century—poetry, history, and murder.

"I must have missed the clues in the pages you gave me to read," she said, hoping he would offer more.

"I planted the clues subtly. The secret is not revealed until the end."

Alex returned to his work of the day, a digest of European news. Secrets, Eliza thought, the policeman in Alex's novel was not alone. Life had so many secrets—who killed who, what was happening in the Concession Street house, what colour of pantalets women wore, the secret she had under hers.

The rain came down as she went home. She plodded and splashed. The bottom half of her father's Macintosh resembled a wall of mud. It was her favourite garment. Before she met Alex, she had fantasies about running away from Mater, dressed as a man.

At home she removed her boots and threw the coat on the mat. It was odd; Mater had sharp ears and usually marched out to present her with a list of demands and deficiencies, and she would be appalled by the muddy mess at the door. But the house was silent except for the foundry

53

noise and the rain pattering on the roof. She had a few glorious minutes to read Browning before she started cooking.

The dinner Mater had ordered in the morning was boiled potatoes, fried liver, and onions. Eliza began by getting a fire going in the stove. Then she went out to the street pump to get water. It was a quiet street, and near the pump, a young man and girl were embracing. Although she paid no attention to them, they stopped and whispered. When she turned toward home, carrying two buckets of water, she heard the young man say, "Lor', I'm glad you don't look like that," and the girl burst into giggles. For a second, Eliza halted and considered going back to teach the young man a lesson. However, Mater must be hungry, and she had not started to prepare the meal. Peeling potatoes and onions were second nature to Eliza, but she hated the thought of touching the liver, cutting it into bloody pieces and smelling it as it fried.

When she got inside, Mater still had not called out for food. When the meal was ready to serve, she went to Mater's room to wake her. But Mater was not there, and the bedclothes had not been disturbed since Eliza made them up before leaving for work in the morning. She went to her own bedroom. No Mater, but her papers were scattered about, her diaries pulled down from a shelf. What? A terrible thought struck her. Ever since she became demented, Mater claimed to be unable to read. Could that be a falsehood? She went to the drawer where she had hidden, under gloves and socks, the letters from her brother Paul. They were dog-eared by now, and Mater, or whoever had ransacked the room, had discovered them. She found some of them in the litter on the floor.

She ran through the house, looking in cupboards and finally went out to the back of the house. Mater was not in the toolshed. If she had strayed, she couldn't have gone far.

The only place Eliza had not checked was the privy. She knocked on the door and then tried it, only to find it was locked from the inside. She shook the door, trying to grasp it and pull with her fingernails. Then she ran to the toolshed and grabbed Pater's crowbar. She had to damage the wood before getting leverage, but at last, with one great heave, the door flew open, and Mater's suspended body swung out. Eliza took two steps backwards. Then she tried to lift her. Mater was as cold as a stone and nearly as stiff. She pushed her aside to get into the privy, ignoring its stink and the smell that came from Mater, who must have released her stool after carrying out the act. In the darkness of the privy, it took some time before she discovered what Mater had done. There was a hook above the door that Pater had used to hang his coat when he came to do his business. Mater had tied a noose around her neck, climbed onto the privy seat, leaned over to attach the rope to the hook, and then jumped down. Her feet were just above the floor. Did she panic and have second thoughts? Eliza saw no sign of that, such as scratches or splinters under Mater's fingernails.

On the floor, fouled by Mater's excretions, was a paper. Truly, Eliza ought to leave that for the doctor, who would cut Mater down. However, it looked familiar, and she had an idea what it would be, so she reached down and removed it to examine before destroying it. Yes, it was the short letter from Paul's commander, informing Mater that her son had been swept overboard during a great storm, that he had given his life for country and queen and would be remembered. When she read that letter to Mater shortly before Christmas the previous year, when Mater had expected him to come home on leave, she sat glassy-eyed, silent as a stone, and refused any of the consolations Eliza offered. When Eliza said they must arrange for a funeral and a monument to him, Mater said, "What? He'll be back," and continued her abstinence from speaking and hearing about it.

A few weeks later, Mater had surprised her by asking that she read the letter they just got from Paul at Gibraltar. Thus, the charade began, with Eliza reading the old letters that Mater suspected had just come in and required a response. Eliza ought to have destroyed the commander's letter.

Was she responsible for her mother's death? No, she refused to convict herself.

❖

The visits by the doctor, policeman, and undertaker were torturous. They peppered her with questions and looked disgusted when they cut Mater down and carried her ill-smelling body to the bed waiting for her inside the house. Eliza supplied a blanket to place beneath her, so she would not soil the bed all the way through—not an ordinary blanket but the tartan travel rug Mater and Pater brought back from their honeymoon in Scotland.

When she was alone, she closed Mater's door, cleaned up the scatter in her own room, threw out the dinner she had prepared, and lay on her bed, wondering what would have happened if she had returned earlier. What if she had looked for Mater immediately upon entering the house?

Her sleep was neither deep nor long. She woke in the night and remembered a dream of running along the seashore, searching for something or someone, accompanied by a fierce dog that barked as she ran. She wore the shoes and suit of a man and reached up to straighten her hair, which had been cut short. As a girl, usually upon waking in the morning, she daydreamed about this kind of escape into the guise of a male. Love for her father and for Alex kept her from carrying it out. The barking dog made her think of Mr. Barker, so she wrote a letter to him, saying her mother had died suddenly, and she could not come in to work.

When the town woke after eight o'clock, she went out on the street and found a boy who perked up and looked trustworthy when she offered him a United States dime to take the letter to the newspaper office.

By midmorning, when she was eating a hearty breakfast of eggs and potatoes, she realized that a difficult task lay before her. She had told the undertaker there was no need to send women to wash Mater and dress her in burial clothes, that she would take care of it herself. A terrible mistake, or was it? A worm of curiosity wriggled inside her and grew into a cobra. She rushed to prepare hot, soapy water. Mater's room smelled like the Black Hole of Calcutta. No one had opened a window, so she did now, gulping the outside air that refreshed even though it smelled of smoke from the foundry.

Inch by inch she pulled down the sheet covering the body. Mater's eyes were half open. Eliza thought the doctor had closed them. She pressed gently on the cold face, expecting the eyes to be like robin's eggs, but they were more like dough, and she pressed and held until the lids were shut. Continuing, she removed the sheet entirely. Mater was wearing her brown day dress. Eliza would dress her in society clothes, not the modern fashion but the ones she wore when Pater was alive. She would pick the dress that was in the best condition and make sure it had been washed recently.

So far, these were simple matters. Now she was about to carry out a depraved act. She could still go to the undertaker's and pay for women to wash and dress her. She took three steps back from Mater, feeling something whack her on the back of her head as Mater used to do sometimes. It was only a broom handle she had disturbed in her retreat. She imagined Mater sitting up and screaming for her to get out of her room. However, there was no turning back. Damnation was already visiting her.

Returning to the bed, she lifted Mater into a sitting position with one arm and, with the other, pulled up on her dress, unhooked the back, slipped the sleeves out of her arms, and lifted it over her head. Very awkward. She now lay in underlinen. Eliza searched in Mater's drawer and found a scissors that she used to snip through the next layer, taking great care not to cut the skin. These she pulled out from one side, and now Mater lay wearing only her pantalets. An evil voice inside her said, "Rip those off now! Do it and learn! You may have caught it from her!" She resisted, even though her hand was attracted to them like iron to a magnet.

She lifted Mater again and washed her neck and back. When she set her down, she paused on the breasts, washed them, and felt them with her hands. Why were Mater's large and Eliza's only small hills? Mater had given birth to babies, and Eliza had heard that suckling enlarged the breasts, but by this much? Five of Eliza's would fit inside hers.

She washed the legs. The back of them were fouled by her excrement and urine. She lifted them and pulled them apart, putting them back to rest on fresh towels.

Now came the part that, if there was a God, would send her directly to hell. She had seen female genitalia in paintings, but they were dimly represented, a little, dark bush of hair usually. Neither Pater nor Mater had enlightened her on this topic. She might have asked a doctor, but Mater never allowed a doctor to examine Eliza, even when she was sick. Mater kept asking her if blood was coming out down there. She had said no. Mater had nodded and said, in response to her questions, sometimes a person gets a cut down there, especially if they play with glass or a nail. It had never occurred to Eliza to play with such dangerous things down there.

God be damned. She believed in evolution and did not think there was a realm just above the clouds where the dead, who obeyed all the commandments for all their lives, wore haloes and sang hymns. She needed to know. Knowledge is God.

As she placed the scissors next to the skin to cut open the pantalets, she was struck with a thought. Rape is evil. Although her mother was a rotting corpse, she would be doing the one thing, without her consent, that would be the most outrageous act ever done to her. Eliza dropped the scissors and ran outside, down the street to the pump, worked the handle like a madwoman, and scrubbed her hands under the cold water. When she stopped, a woman she did not know was standing there with a bucket. The woman looked away, as did nearly all people who saw the freak.

Walking back, she realized she could not leave Mater the way she was when the undertaker arrived. She went back into the room, almost expecting to find the body with its legs together again. She turned it over, the head facing away from her. She picked up the scissors and quickly snipped the pantalets and pulled them off. She washed the buttocks and then, making sure the cloth was balled up in her hand, reached under and cleaned the genitalia.

She dried the body and lifted it to remove the soiled sheet and towels, then set it down, still on the stomach. After pulling a clean pair of pantalets onto the corpse, Eliza could stomach turning it again. Working methodically, she dressed her in clean underlinen and a dress, covered her with a sheet, carried out the soiled clothes, and washed the floor.

"Mater, there's nothing more I can do for you," she said, closing the door and sinking into a chair.

5

After work, Alex ran all the way to Eliza's house. She did not answer his knock. He entered and saw her rising from a kitchen chair, looking at him as if he was a housebreaker.

"My friend, have you been sitting there all day?"

"No, I did . . . things. They came to take Mater's body away."

"I'm so sorry. I hope her pain didn't last long, and a doctor gave her something soothing at the end."

She looked down at the floorboards, as if searching for a lost pin. Alex went to her. He gave her a long hug, his eyes filled with tears. When he held her at arm's length to see her face, her eyes were dry.

"Eliza, it's not your fault. I'm here to listen. If you bottle up what's worrying you, it will hurt all the more."

"You're not the one to talk. I know how you have bad memories of the death of your parents and sister, but there's something else. I think it has to do with Christian Brothers . . .."

He had trouble swallowing. "I'm out of breath from running, but would it help if I told you a secret?"

She put her hands on his shoulders. "We're best friends, Alex. If I speak of my secret wounds, can you do the same for me?"

She had hit his weak spot. He had never told anyone, and yet he relived the attack at Christian Brothers almost as much as he had his mother's death. For a long time, he thought he had been claimed by the devil, and he worried his presence might have doomed Mary. It was irrational, but there it was. Eliza gave him a little shake.

"Very well," he said. "I'll go first. Let's sit together. You're right about Christian Brothers." They held hands as he told her he had always been alone after his family's death. Their priest advised the attorney to arrange for the sale of the farm and to use the proceeds to educate young Alex in a Catholic setting.

At Christian Brothers, Alex kept away from other boys and studied harder than anyone else. His mother's death lay on him as the greatest sin a Christian could commit. He aspired to be the most devout pupil. Schoolyard games did not interest him. At first his schoolmates teased him, but he never fought back. Eventually, they lost interest in him.

He felt glorious when he went to confession, and the Father said that he, out of all the boys in the school, was the most fit to take up Holy Orders. Shortly after that, in the classroom, the Father caught some of the boys at their foolery and lectured them, saying they would be punished the next time and that they should be more like Alexander. He should be their model.

He wanted to confess that he was the greatest sinner in the school but was afraid it would destroy his reputation. He wrote out his confession and put it under his pillow.

When he returned from the library, he came upon boys gathered around his bed and one of them distorting his confession to the wild laughter of the others, saying Alex caused his mother's falling from a trapeze and landing on his father and sister, killing all of them.

Alex had never fought back, but in that moment, he was on fire and wanted to slay them. With his arms made strong by farm work, he threw two of the boys to the ground, kicked one when he tried to get up, and punched another who intervened. Finally, they pinned him to the ground and pummelled him. He heard the Father ordering them to stop. It was the one who told him he had been selected. After questioning all of them, he took the attackers away for corporal punishment.

"Poor Alex, you weren't responsible for what they did. After standing up to them like that, didn't you get more respect?" Eliza asked.

"Well . . .." He paused to think about how much of the rest he could tell her. "No, quite the opposite."

Alex described how he kept saying his prayers aloud, including some days later when he was urinating in the lavatory and heard footsteps behind him. *Someone's waiting his turn*, he thought. He was not deterred from praying. Suddenly, someone grabbed his arms and twisted them around his back. He realized there was more than one of them. They did not allow him to see them, pushing his face to the ground. They beat him until he was almost senseless and then told him to keep quiet or they would kill him. The claimed to be devils sent to avenge his sins. He started to shout, but someone banged his head on the floor and repeated the warning.

They took turns hitting him, and he began to think the voices, in truth, belonged to devils. When they left off, one of them, in a harsh, low voice, told him not to turn his head as they returned to hell, or they would come back and do it over again. The devils laughed evilly on the way out. *That's what devils do, laugh*, he thought. Despite all his prayers, God had not saved him. He never believed in God again.

"Oh Alex, what a horrifying memory! I understand why you thought God deserted you, but those were the brats who were punished for beating you up in the dormitory."

"Part of me realizes that's true, but the helpless, hurt feelings keep coming back, no matter what I do."

He had not told her the worst part, how they tore off his breeches and spread his legs wide, how they burrowed into the hole where he defecated, and how he felt searing pain. How the thrusting went on and on until there was wetness—was it blood? How it started up again as he felt another devil enter him.

She hugged him. "Now you've told me, and you're a better friend than ever."

"I'm glad to hear we are. Now your story," Alex said, holding her out again.

"I feel as guilty as a murderer for my mother's death. She hung herself. You know how her memory had been failing, and she believed that my brother, her favourite child, was alive?"

"Yes, but there was nothing you could do, just as I could not have ordered my parents not to go out on the ice. It's not your fault."

"You were a boy, Alex, and not at a responsible age. I could have covered all traces of my brother's death, and I could have been here sitting with Mater right now."

"You took neither your brother's life nor your mother's. You'll recover from this after you're through grieving. It's natural."

"So, it's natural? Other things are not."

"What things? You're bothered by something else. Now that we're in the confessing mood, please tell me." Alex had hit the mark. Another secret.

"Alex, your friendship means everything to me. If I tell, you will spurn me."

"I'll do no such thing. Tell me you murdered your mother, and I'll keep quiet about it and still be your friend."

Eliza looked frightened, as if her mother's ghost had just entered the room. "I'm . . .." she faltered. He waited patiently. "Mater told me that I'm deformed, part female and part male." She looked at him. He looked frightened.

"Why did you pay any attention when her mind was going? You're not deformed."

"It was when I was a little girl, and Mater wanted doctors and everyone else to keep away from me. I do have a part of me . . .." She blushed, unable to continue.

He hugged her and felt her sobs. "You may be anatomically different than the average woman, but difference is not a problem. If we were all cast in identical molds, humanity would be boring. I care for you, my friend."

She held him tight, and for a moment he found it hard to breathe, such was her strength.

"You need food and sleep," he said. "Why don't you sit on the rocking chair while I cook for you? I'll keep you company tonight."

"You will? Isn't there a risk to your reputation?"

"My reputation? Usually the lady worries about her own."

She laughed and then sat down on a kitchen chair, informing him that the rocking chair belonged to Mater, and she could not sit there, not yet and perhaps never.

While he prepared sausages, potatoes, and beans, all quite fresh in the larder, he kept an eye on Eliza. What kind of world did she inhabit now? One with both parents and her brother dead, only one friend, and work at the newspaper? Not a very populated world.

This led him to think about his own world. The newspaper meant little to him, the novel not much more (he had exaggerated his progress on it). He had a single friend in Eliza. He gazed out the window and imagined Mary peering in. Oh, why could he not have been man enough to break into the Concession Street house, carry her away, and run to some place where they could invite in Eliza and hide from the world?

"Something's burning," Eliza said. It was the sausages that he had not turned over during his reverie.

"That's what you get when you have a man cooking for you," he said, waving at the smoke with a towel and vowing to keep an eagle eye on the rest of the cooking.

"No, the great chefs are men, my friend." Eliza rose from the chair and came over to scrape the char off the meat.

The noise from the foundry died down. At one point, she looked at him, and he returned her gaze. He held her hand, but she took it away.

At dinner he was surprised that she ate heartily and quickly, rather like Madeline. Her manners were good enough: she did not get food on her face, eat with her mouth open, or belch like many of the diners at public houses, where he often dined. She seemed lost in her own world as he, afraid of having another vision of Mary, talked about the newspaper. She responded by saying "yes" or "no" and looking down at her plate.

He needed to get her away, however briefly, from this house of the dead. "Look, it is a beautiful day, and dusk is still an hour away," he said at the end of the meal. "We could go out for a walk. It will do us both good."

She looked around as if her mother, though dead and carried away, demanded her presence. "If you wish."

"I do. Where would you like to go?"

"You choose."

For him, the outside, however rundown the neighbourhood, was fresh and like having a mass of cobwebs wiped off. Old folks sat on doorsteps. Workers were returning home.

He asked Eliza if she would like to come to his rooms, where she could spend the night in his bedroom while he slept on a settee in the writing room. "No, thank you, Alex," she replied.

He led her south down Division Street. She agreed to rest her hand under his elbow. The cobblestones and the shrubs were resplendent in the sunlight. There were hardly any passersby and those who did come along may have looked at them as an odd couple, but they kept quiet. They continued south on Barrie Street until they reached the ordnance land and Murney Tower. A troop in red uniform marched there, so they were prevented from going directly to the water.

"Pater used to bring me here," Eliza said. "He worked for the *British Whig* when that Martello tower was built, in eighteen forty-six. Everyone was worried that the Americans, who were battling the British in Oregon, would attack farther east. Have you ever been inside it?"

This is encouraging, he thought. *She's found something to take her mind off her mother.* "No," he said.

"You go over a dry moat to get in the door and then climb up to the top, where there are four windows facing the harbour, called caponiers, which have holes for rifles, and a cannon that can roll out and shoot at invading ships. Pater thought it a marvel. He said it made us safe."

"Did he frighten you, talking about an invasion?"

"No, I believed we were safe, and when I grew up, I wanted to be one of the soldiers manning the cannon up there."

"A girl soldier?"

She paused. "Girls and boys have strange fancies. I used to have some about the steamers going up the river." She pointed to a steamer going by.

"What kinds of fantasies?"

"That I would get on board one of them, and it would take me to faraway lands, where I had never been." She looked so longingly out on the river that he thought it would be a small enough thing for him to do. He still had a portion of the money left from the sale of his father's farm. The funds had taken him to England to finish his education. This would be a good way to spend the rest.

"Let's go, Eliza. I can afford to take you and anyone you want as chaperone on a grand tour of Europe."

She opened her mouth and looked at him, as if struck by lightning. "What are you—"

"Before you say another word, let me explain. After your mother's funeral, you can inform Barker that you need a month off work to attend to your mother's affairs and to mourn for her. He's an understanding man. I'll ask him for a month's leave to finish my novel, and away we'll go."

"Will he let us take that much time off? That leaves only Hughes."

"It would be a good thing. Hughes will demonstrate what an idiot he is, and there are always others to step in while we're away." He might indeed work on his novel while away with Eliza. Or he could think of what should come next in his life. Writing, yes, but not doing the same old thing at the *British Whig*. And he would get rid of his obsession with Mary.

He did not realize that Eliza had stopped, and he was walking ahead, until she called out to him. "Alex, it's too generous. How can you? I'm an embarrassment."

"I'll hear no more of that. Are we friends or not? Yes, well, let's go. How far have you gone on the steamer before?"

"To Montreal, but—"

"To Montreal? Is that all? I'm talking about London, Dublin, Edinburgh, Paris, and Berlin. One thing, the chaperone will have to keep mum about this afterwards, so Barker doesn't find out."

"As far as the chaperone is concerned, I have another idea," she said, coming up to him. He could see she had warmed up to his proposal. But what could her idea be? He asked her, but she merely shook her head.

"Later," she said.

Dusk having descended, they returned to her house. She was as quiet as she had been on the way there. He insisted on spending the night in the rocking chair just outside her bedroom door, saying it would be wrong to sleep on her mother's bed after she had so recently occupied it. Eliza brought him a pile of blankets and bade him goodnight.

During the night, he caught snatches of sleep and remembered a dream of straying into Eliza's bedroom to climb into bed with her and finding that she had turned into a beautiful princess. This dream clashed with another he had about Mary's face, her thin body, and her innocence.

⁂

The next day, Alex went to the post office. It was rare for him to receive mail other than a few literary journals, so he blanched when he saw the handwriting on the envelope handed to him by the clerk—Mary's.

Once out on the street, as horses clopped by, he opened it. Inside were two pages, one from Mary in wobbly handwriting that said, "Dear Alex, please come as soon as you can. I miss you. Your Mary." The other was from Madeline. She said it was unfortunate that he had departed during a family quarrel. Both she and Mary were concerned, because he had not written and probably misunderstood the situation. He remained a valued friend. In her concluding paragraph were sentences that made him stagger: "Mary is unwell, and I'm worried about her survival. Evil George is to blame. It does not behoove me to say more on paper. When you come, I'll explain."

The devil was at play again. He had an evil, one-eyed face.

6

Someone knocked on Eliza's door at nine o'clock. Only one person might come so late. Sure enough, Alex stood on the step, reluctant to come in, even though, four nights earlier, he had slept at the house, and the previous night, he had come to tell her that he had booked tickets for their trip.

"Caesar, you never stood on ceremonies," she said, resuming the hilarious time they had on the previous night mutilating Shakespeare. They had promised not to play this game on the journey.

"I'm no Caesar, but you may well be Calpurnia," he said, smiling thinly as he came in. Why did she feel gloomy clouds entering with him? It had been a clear, sunny day.

"Have you come to warm Mater's rocking chair tonight, because she'll be put under the ground tomorrow? It would be a kind offer, typical of you, my best friend, but I have come to terms with it and expect to sleep soundly. Tea or coffee? Come in and sit down."

He stood on the mat inside the door, his face dark in the dusk, which had now settled. She brought over a lamp.

"I'll not be able to come to your mother's funeral tomorrow."

"I don't mind. Barker would be annoyed that two of us took the day off anyway." That was a lie—she had counted on him to come.

"There's more."

"The trip is off?" she asked, not liking like his hangdog look.

"No, only delayed until I sort things out, and then I'll reschedule it." He had not looked her in the face since he came in.

"You mean to sort out things in Ottawa."

"I don't know how long I'll be away, a week, maybe more. Barker believes I'm attending my uncle's funeral and that my aunt needs help temporarily. I'm telling you this falsehood, knowing you will not betray me." His lips were stretched thin in a way she did not like.

"Something troubles you, my dear friend. Tell me about it."

"You're my best friend as well, but I have nothing specific to tell you. I leave early tomorrow on the train and need to pack tonight."

"Think back to when you got me to speak of my troubles. I'm here for you. Just sit for a little while and talk." He stood as if his feet were fixed to the mat, pulling in deep breaths and letting them out slowly.

"I'm sorry, but I have to go now. Tomorrow I'll think of you," he said, turning and going away into the night. He walked slowly, as if each step was a new worry in his mind. Perhaps, if she had some whiskey to offer, he would have stayed. She made a mental note to buy some.

"Jesus Christ!" she repeated three times when he was well out of earshot, no doubt making her mother turn upside down in her cheap coffin at the undertaker's.

⁂

When Eliza returned to work on Monday, Barker made a point of coming out of his office to say he was sorry for her loss, and he hoped that, with no family members remaining, she would be able to cope. "I assure you, Miss Malkins, that your job here, that you do as well as your father ever did, is secure."

While the editor was in the pressroom, Hughes looked like he was the hardest-working man on earth. He had already grumbled to her that he would have to do the work of two while Alex was away.

When Barker returned to his office, Hughes yawned like a tired jackal. "So, Miss Milkens, where is your sweet, little partner in crime? How could you let the dear boy go without taking you along?"

"Mind your own business," she said.

"Oh, but it is my business when the darling duck flies off, and I have to carry on with his leavings. What's more, you know perfectly well where he is, because you're on intimate terms with him. Such goings-on should be confined to the wedding bed."

She was tempted to go over and hit him, but he would no doubt run to tell Barker, and the word "secure" still rang in her ears.

7

Alex noticed the spot of food on Madeline's dress front and her trembling lips. How unlike her. She grasped his arm. It was the first time she had ever touched him.

"George put us in danger, and we need to be armed," she said.

"You have guns?"

"A pistol. Father had it in case intruders broke in. You did not see Victoria holding it behind her back when she let you in tonight. Her father trained her to shoot. I have no idea."

He never expected George to turn into a madman. Would he forcibly enter his late brother's house and harm Madeline? "But," he began, about to suggest she exaggerated the risk.

"Alexander, please keep your voice down. Mary needs her sleep. She has suffered the most."

"What? How could that be? You had the quarrel with him."

He was Alexander now and not Mr. O'Shea. Would he ever be Alex?

Madeline swallowed several times and took deep breaths. "I'll not varnish the facts. In the middle of the night when you were last here, Mary took it upon herself to go down to the street door. She stumbled in the dark and woke us up. George was the first to get to her, and he dragged her to his room. I tried to stop him, but he pushed me down and yelled so even the servants could hear, 'She will never again bring down disgrace on our house and our mill!'"

"Oh God, what did he do to her?" He hated to ask. George must have ravaged her. Horror upon horrors—like the attack in the Christian Brothers? Mary was weak. How could she survive this?

"He flogged her until the clothing on her back was in tatters and covered with blood."

The image of it was like a kick between his legs. "Why didn't you get the gun to stop him?"

"I didn't know where Father kept it. Now that we have it, we're slightly safer, but George is an expert marksman, and he has a collection of pistols and rifles. I tried to comfort Mary after he let her go. I had to see to her wounds. We stayed in Mary's room with the door locked until Victoria knocked to let us know that George had gone. I also had the locks on the front door changed."

"Madeline, why didn't you send for me that night? I would have come immediately."

All this time she had held his arm. Now she enfolded him in a hug. When she released him, she blinked, and tears dropped to the floor. "Alex, our dear friend, we would have lost you. In your rage, you would have fought George. He would have shot you and claimed self-defence."

"But he has no right to injure your sister. I would have informed the police of his brutal crime and brought an officer to arrest him."

"They would not believe an outsider like you against the word of a mill owner and would insist on Mary being examined. She would not have allowed that. We wanted to let time pass, so you could cool down before coming to see us."

She was right; he felt like bolting out of the house to pursue the devil and beat the life out of him. "What's to be done? The two of you are prisoners here with only Benson and Victoria to protect you."

"Benson has gone over to the other side. He thinks his bread will have more butter there. George no doubt bribed him. Today I saw Benson spying on the house." She looked lost. What an odd reaction for her. A moment later, her face hardened, and she stepped away. "If you ever need the gun while you're here, it's in my desk drawer in the drawing room. Things may get worse as I start my counter-attack."

What a remarkable woman, the kind who might lead a revolution heading into the twentieth century. Alex felt guilty that he had suspicions about her when Benson warned him about evil in the house. The evil one was a man after all.

Madeline seemed impatient for him to respond. He didn't know what to say. "I was just thinking how amazing you are. What kind of counter-attack?"

"George thinks he is the sole operator of the mill and that he can force me out. I have a surprise for him, a lawsuit. He owns only a minority share, and I have documents that he desperately needs to stay afloat. Mr. Ditchling, my lawyer, is examining them. Not many days from now, Georgie will be heading south once again. His only way to cheer up will be to whistle Dixie." She smiled triumphantly.

Alex took out his pocket watch, a quarter to ten. "I apologize again for arriving so late. You have given me much to think about tonight."

"No, don't worry. You wasted not a minute in coming to see us, and I understand that trains get delayed, especially when a cow gets on the track. Poor cow."

"Yes." He had explained this when he arrived. Empathy for a cow—there were depths in Madeline he had never seen before.

"One last word on Mary," she said. "You better sit down for this, and I'll get you a whiskey rather than more of that insipid tea Victoria served."

He already knew about Mary's lack of appetite, anxiety, and inability to sleep without medication. That villain George had savaged her, on top of all the suffering she had endured already because of her father's death. Was it the American Civil War that made George a monster? He deserved to be shot.

The whiskey Madeline brought him was more than generous—at least four fingers. What was she going to tell him? She took a long swallow from her full glass and smiled at him. Was she trying to seduce him? He sipped the whiskey. It was smoky, high-quality stuff, probably imported from Scotland.

"What are your feelings for Mary?" she asked.

He swallowed more whiskey. "I care what happens to her. She is a sweet, innocent, young woman who deserves to be happy."

"Do you want to help her be happy?"

"Yes, if I can. It's difficult, because I don't live here. My work and other duties keep me busy." He felt weak, certain she could see through his vagueness.

"Do you love someone else?"

"No, I don't."

"In that case, I must tell you something about Mary. She is too shy to tell you, but she confides in me."

"If it was told to you in confidence, then you ought not tell me."

"This is different. I'm sure Mary wants you to know. She loves you. Every day she dotes on the drawing she has nearly finished. It's the first drawing she has ever made that glows with positive energy. You'll see tomorrow morning the look on her face when she finds you're here. It is love."

He thought of the contrast between those powerful, twisted drawings of household furniture and the platonic rendering Mary had made of his face. Was she dying of love for him, and he had not realized it? Did he have love for her in his heart? What about poor Eliza back in Kingston? If he went away, would she make another friend? He drank the rest of the whisky as Madeline watched.

"Another?" she asked.

"No, I have to weave my way back to Russell House. Thank you for confiding in me."

She kissed him, then shook her head slowly as he backed away, bowed formally, and turned to go.

⁌

The next morning was windy with scant drops of rain. He arrived at 9:30, right when Madeline had requested. Mary's lovely smile rewarded him as she stood behind Victoria, who double-locked the door once he was inside. Madeline joined them in the drawing room, and they sat down to tea and biscuits, none of them with much to say other than formalities.

"Mary, why not try one of these?" Alex asked as he started on his second biscuit. "They're still warm. Cook must have made them this morning."

Mary pinched her lower lip and glanced at Madeline. "Please, for me," he added, smiling as gently as he could, trying to hide the squall raging inside him.

She picked up the biscuit and, examining it like a stone that could be an old Indian arrowhead, crammed the entire thing into her mouth. She grinned like a mischievous child. Alex held his breath as she masticated, her cheeks bulging and pulsing. He was ready to lie her down and reach into her mouth if she choked. At long last, she opened her mouth, raised her teacup, and drank. He exhaled, and Madeline clapped. "Well done, little sister, but it's not the most ladylike way to eat."

"I'm aware of that, Maddy," Mary said, selecting another biscuit and taking a nibble.

When Alex looked at Madeline, she smiled and nodded slightly. Did this mean Mary's survival depended upon him? But who did Madeline design for him—Mary or herself? Were the two of them to care for Mary, as if she were their child?

"Alas, I must leave the two of you alone. At eleven I have an important appointment with Mr. Ditchling. I expect not to return before one o'clock." As Madeline rose, Alex watched her smooth, heavy movements.

"Maddy," Mary said, "why can't Mr. Ditchling come here instead of you going there? You told me it's not safe—"

"There are too many documents for him to bring here. I have no fears, but just to comfort you, my darling, Victoria will accompany me. Alex will protect you." She gave Alex a look that told him to remember what was hidden in the desk.

"Why don't you take along the object in the drawer?" Alex asked. Mary looked mystified.

"Oh, two women out on the street in the light of day are perfectly safe," Madeline replied. "There is no need."

Alone in the house with Mary! He was astounded, a whole new level of trust. His reservations about Madeline continued to melt away.

Once Madelaine left the room, he talked to Mary about his novel—how he started writing the story after reading, in 1865, an account of the confession of Constance Kent to a crime she committed at Road Hill House in Wiltshire, England, in 1860. Everyone in the country house knew more than they were willing to tell. So, a house was the crime scene in his novel. He invented a curious policeman who seemed to be on track to solving the crime when he was mysteriously murdered. He did not tell her that now he sometimes thought his novel a useless piece of trash. What was he doing?

Mary's eyes grew larger and larger. He meant to interest her in something other than the hell she had experienced. They heard the front door slam shut and the locks turn, Madeline and Victoria departing. Mary began to cry and shake. "Please, don't tell me more."

He was ashamed. No one else was in the house. It was improper, but he reached out and hugged her anyways to comfort her, stroking her long, silky hair. He used to play with his mother's hair that way. "Mary, dear, what you could use is fresh air. Let's go for a walk down by the river. There's something I want to ask you." Yes, he would make her his wife if it meant saving her. He wanted to propose outside, not in that jaded mansion.

"Please, Alex, may I finish the drawing? It's my greatest wish." She straightened up, looking at him with her deep, blue, innocent eyes.

If his family returned from the dead and asked him to do one thing for them, would he deny them? His proposal had to wait. Somehow, he felt relieved.

"Certainly. I never thought I would become a work of art, but you're succeeding in doing it, my dear." His blandishments made her look like she would start crying again. He glanced toward the wall, where the easel stood with the drawing on it. "Let's look at it before we start," he said, stepping toward it.

"No, please," Mary said, pulling him back. "It has to be a surprise. Otherwise, I can't finish it."

She had worry lines on her face, and he could not deny her. He took up his old position standing while Mary moved the easel and sized him up, as if reckoning his height. "Could you please remove your clothing, like you did last time?"

"Oh, yes, expose the musculature that I don't have." He laughed as he tore off his coat, tie, and shirt, leaving them on the floor where he stood.

Mary looked askance at him. Could this be too embarrassing for her, or did she worry that Madeline or Victoria might come home early?

"No, I'm embarrassed," she said in response to his question. "I'm trying to draw you in a Renaissance style, when artists worshipped the human body, thought it the closest someone could get to the divine."

His sweet, shy Mary. She knew more than he thought. Had she and Madeline rehearsed this line before he came or, more likely, had she learned it from her tutor?

"You want to draw me without any clothes?"

Mary closed her eyes and nodded. "Yes," she whispered.

"No problem. I understand the reason. In truth, there's nothing immoral about it."

Mary looked away while he shuffled out of his shoes and pulled off his trousers and undergarments. When she glanced in his direction, his naked figure made her turn pink, as if she were the one in the nude. He could not help imagining how thin and frail her naked body would be and then worried that desire might cause his member to rise and embarrass them both. He slapped his cheek.

"What was that?" Mary asked.

"A fly."

She nodded and began to sketch. A peek and a longish period of drawing. Another peek and then the same. Over and over. Time passed slowly. He would have looked at his pocket watch, but he did not want to move if it broke her concentration. He heard that many natives did not want to be portrayed or have their photograph taken, because it would steal their spirit. What did Mary want from him? His body? Its "musculature"? Surely not. He was a little flabby, though not like the men he had seen out near the river who worked in the lumber industry. His spirit? He had stopped believing in such things after his mother was taken from him.

He wanted Mary more than ever, not as a naked body but as his mission. He had been a confused pilgrim, grasping at this and that, failing, falling back on drink. Protecting Mary would be his reason for living, his salvation. It might atone for his mother's death. Perhaps, after all, there was such a thing as spirit.

A knock at the door interrupted his reverie and made Mary jump and drop her pencil. "Whoever could that be? It's too early for Maddy," she said in a shaky voice, hauling the drawing to face the wall. He pulled on his trousers, stuffed his underwear and socks into his pockets, threw on his shirt, pulled up his braces, and put on his shoes. The knocking continued, louder now.

Mary threw her arms around him. "Don't answer. They'll go away."

Before he could reply, the knocking resumed in a way that sounded as if someone had set about damaging the door. He held Mary's hand as he went to the desk, opened the top drawer, and found the pistol. He had a rudimentary knowledge of how to use it. He told Mary to stay out of sight when he opened the door and not to let anyone see her through the windows, even if it meant crawling on the floor and hiding under a table. Speechless with fear, she attempted to stop him, but he gently pushed her away and down to the floor. With the revolver tucked into his waistband behind his back, he turned the latches on the door.

With a scowl on his half-blasted face, George Baker was the most frightening person Alex had ever seen. His fist had been raised to pound once more, and Alex thought it would immediately descend upon him. Instead George lowered it and sneered. "You're the new butler here, eh? Or has she snagged you into her web? Some kind of businesswoman is she if she don't open the door when I come as arranged." He wore a rumpled black suit that seemed less natural for him than the work clothes he had been wearing when Alex saw him last.

"If you refer to Miss Baker, she is not at home, and you're not welcome here," Alex said. Behind George stood Benson, his arms crossed.

"Wait a minute! I've seen you before. Benson, who is this man?" George asked.

"He is Mr. O'Shea, a friend of Miss Mary. He has visited several times before."

"Then why in the blazes are you blocking my entrance? I came to see Madeline at that vixen's call, and I mean to have it out with her. Step aside. I own one-third of this house."

"No, you will not enter," Alex said, pulling out the pistol and levelling it at George's chest, watching his arms, so he could pull the trigger before George knocked the gun away.

"Sir, come away. We can write to Miss Baker when she returns," Benson said, the only calm person around.

George sneered again. "What do you mean? She's here. Come out of hiding, Madeline Baker! How dare you play tricks on me." His good eye glared at Alex like a pirate's.

"I should shoot you for what you've done. You're a scoundrel!" Alex shouted, losing control.

"Uncle George, please, please, go away. Father would have been enraged at you if he was alive," Mary pleaded. Alex almost turned his head to look at her, but that would have been folly.

George's face softened. "Dear Mary, is your sister truly absent?"

She must have nodded, and Alex loosened his grip on the pistol.

"Where is Victoria?" George asked. "Call her to come out."

"She's with Madeline," Mary said.

"What? She left you alone with this person, who she no doubt enticed into being the new daddy? How outrageous! She ought to be dragged out, have her clothes torn off, and be stoned in public." The monster inside George returned, and he stamped as he raged. Alex was convinced he would have breathed fire if he could. Passersby stopped to watch the drama.

"So help me, I'll kill you." Alex tightened his grip on the pistol, his finger itching to pull the trigger. If not for Mary's cries, he would have fired.

"Sir, I must insist," Benson said, putting his large hand on George's shoulder and pulling him back. Alex took the opportunity to slam the door and close the latches. He heard George bellowing, but there were no more knocks on the door, and no stones were thrown through the windows. The sounds from outside eventually quieted down.

He put the gun on a table and went to Mary, who still lay on the floor. She was white and took short, quick breaths. Her pulse raced. Was this hysteria? So much had been written on the topic, but it had never interested Alex before. He felt Mary's stomach and then rolled her onto her side. Her corset was so tight, it was no wonder she had fainted. He checked his pocket watch—at least thirty minutes until Madeline and Victoria would return. Scooping Mary up—she was as light as a fairy—he carried her to the salon and set her down gently on a soft settee, face down. He felt through the fabric of her dress the places where her corset was attached. Wriggling them from outside did nothing, and he could not undo the latches by reaching down behind her neck, because she wore a tight silk collar. Only one way—from the bottom.

Wasting no time, he pushed up her dress, then the petticoats. Lightning struck when the thin, bare flesh of her buttocks was exposed. He was told most women did not cover up down there like men did but had temporarily forgotten this fact in his haste to save her. He turned away and continued by feel, stretching the tight fabrics that covered her until he reached the cords. As he undid them, he felt the skin on her back, a mass of scar tissue. Had George done this? He should have shot him while he had the chance!

It seemed like more than thirty minutes had passed after he loosened the corset when Mary finally began to move.

As quick as a pickpocket, he tried to straighten her clothing. It was futile, of course, because she struggled to sit, clutched her dress to herself, and looked at him as if he were a phantom.

He explained what he had been trying to do. She looked at him with a dull expression and then, to his surprise, kissed him on the lips and left to go up to her room to straighten her clothing. He remembered having left the pistol near the door and carried it into the drawing room to return it to the desk drawer. The easel intrigued him. Even with the attempted invasion, Mary had taken the time to turn it to the wall. If he went over now, that would be a breach of trust. He sat and thought about what George had said. Why had he used endearments when he saw Mary? Had he come once again to satisfy his gross desires? And then, when he found out Alex was alone in the house with Mary, why did he explode and ask if Madeline had made him Mary's new daddy? Only a couple of hours earlier, he had admired Madeline for protecting Mary from George and for her honesty. Now he was confused. He needed a drink, so he took a large glass of brandy from the cabinet.

His pocket watch indicated fifteen minutes after two. He heard Mary coming, and he ran to the foot of the stairway, but she said she needed no help.

"You have taken a fright and look pale. Since we ought not, after all, go outside, let's repair to the kitchen for something to eat. I, for one, am starving," he said. Exactly the opposite. Only drink would satisfy him, and it was only Mary who needed sustenance.

In the larder lay questionable hunks of meat, but a raspberry pie showed more promise. A small table was in the middle of the room—obviously used by servants during earlier times when the owner of the house was wealthier. He cleaned its top with water and soap, dried it, and invited Mary to sit. She looked around like an explorer who had come upon a land never before discovered.

"Maddy used to come down here in the nighttime to eat," she said.

"Did she? That surprises me when there were servants in the house to bring food to her."

"No, it had to be a secret between her and me. We talked together a lot when everyone else thought we were in bed. We chipped . . .." Mary turned red. Something had slipped out that she wanted to keep inside. "It was a long time ago," she concluded.

She would not say more. What could explain Madeline's behaviour? Was her father a disciplinarian who wanted his daughters to be thin like Mary?

He set out two large pieces of pie. "You may start while I make tea for you and pour myself another glass," he said.

Mary sat but did not pick up her fork. It took him a while to stoke the fire. Then, while waiting for the kettle to boil, he sat beside Mary and ate a forkful. "Mmmm . . . so good. Cook is a magician. Please, go ahead and try it."

Mary picked up her fork and broke off a tiny portion at the point of the pie. "That's a triangle," she said.

"Very good. And now for our next lesson. How can you make a triangle disappear?"

Perplexed, she set the fork on her plate. He was about to plead, but she got a sudden daring look on her face and popped the tiny piece of pie into her mouth. He got her to eat a little more.

"Mary, wouldn't it be fun to keep playing little games like this? Right now, we are servants sneaking some of the master's food. It never tastes better," he said. Whatever were the sinister secrets of the Concession Street house, they emanated from George or Benson or the ghost of the late Mr. Baker. Not Madeline, as she wanted to protect Mary. Not Mary. She was innocent. She had been a victim, and only Alex could save her.

"You wanted to talk with me about something?" Mary asked, perhaps to divert him from his tricks to get her to eat.

"Yes. Outside would have been better, because now we may be interrupted by your sister's return. But here goes. You must think about it; do not answer me immediately."

Before he got down on his knee, he had a blinding vision of Eliza shaking her head. If she was telepathic, he sent her a message back to forgive him and remain his friend. But down he went. "Dear Mary, will you do me the honour of becoming my wife?"

⁜

Alex thought Madeline seemed out of sorts when she returned. She rushed into the kitchen, the drawing room, and upstairs. Mary sat upright and smiled as if she was hiding a birthday present from her sister.

"George came here," Alex said. "He said you had called him for a meeting, and he was irate that you were away."

"What nonsense! I'm not going to meet with that villain except in front of a judge. He must have known I was away, and he wanted to punish Mary."

Alex saw her rage mounting. What would Madeline have done if she had been the one holding the gun?

"Mary must have been scared. Is that why she's sitting there looking hysterical? Was George as violent as usual?" Madeline asked.

"He was angry and loud. I had to threaten him with your gun to get him to leave."

"Oh, why didn't you shoot him and end our troubles? It would have been self-defence." She made Alex feel like the dunce in the classroom.

Madeline rushed over to Mary and held her, squeezing a few tears from her eyes. She rocked her back and forth. "You're safe now, my dear," she said, as if she was Mary's mother. Mary, who had been glowing after accepting Alex's proposal, cried. Her greatest bond in life was with Madeline.

"Alex, it was indiscreet of me to say that I wished you had used the gun, but you don't know how dangerous and insane George has become. He is always armed. It's a wonder he didn't pull out a gun to shoot you or have that traitor Benson do it. Do you know there's a tiny gun called a Derringer that he could hide in his pocket or sleeve?"

They returned to the drawing room, and Madeline sat at her desk, flipping through papers she had brought back with her. Alex felt like a conspirator, sitting on the divan and whispering with Mary while occasionally catching Madeline keeping her wary eye on them. At dinner Mary nibbled happily and took part in the table talk, which was totally unlike her.

As soon as Mary began yawning and blinking, Madeline called Victoria to help her up to bed. Alex shook hands with Mary, feeling odd, because he had touched more than her hand that day. On her way up with Victoria, she turned back. "Maddy, could Alex sleep in our house tonight and during the rest of his visit? I would feel so much safer."

"I'm not utterly opposed, although people might talk—"

"That's true," Alex said. "You live on a busy street, and you must be careful of your reputation." The house continued to feel weird to him. He wanted to get Mary away from it.

"Oh. . .." Mary moaned.

"Well, I can offer this to you. I'll be here early in the morning, and during the night, I'll stand guard on the other side of Concession Street to ensure all is well. Miss Baker, place a candle in Mary's window if there's an emergency and you want me to come in."

"You'll lose so much sleep," Madeline said.

"I'm a light sleeper. In a pinch, I can stretch out tomorrow for a nap on the divan. Now I must leave."

"Come with me for a moment," Madelaine said. "You need something to protect yourself if you're out on the street."

"What is it?" Mary asked.

"Do you want our friend to be safe?"

"Yes, of course."

"Very well. Goodnight, sister. I'll be up to see you before you go to sleep."

Mary looked at Alex as if she had rosebuds in her eyes. Then she slowly mounted the stairs.

Alex knew that Madeline was about to loan him the gun for his duties on guard outside. He wanted to tell her that he did not trust himself with a weapon, but it was hard to disagree with her.

✥

Near the end of the week, peace returned to Baker House. Alex arrived in the morning, exhausted from his night patrols. He slumped on the divan in the drawing room, reading to Mary and keeping an eye on Madeline at her desk. When his eyes started to close or he tripped on his words, the ladies sent him off for a nap on what had been Benson's bed in the servants' quarters. At meal times, if Mary did not eat anything else, Alex teased her into pecking at morsels of cake.

On Friday he whispered to Mary that it was time to inform Madeline of their engagement. She became like a shivering mouse about to be brought before the cat. Alex cleared his throat and began formally, "Miss Baker—"

"Excuse me, Mr. O'Shea, I must review two last clauses before signing this document. As you know, I'm hard at work protecting our interests." So, he was no longer Alexander to her. Mary pulled on his arm. He kept her standing with him, waiting while Madeline signed the document with a flourish and folded it into an envelope.

"Mr. O'Shea, can you do me a great service? Mr. Ditchling needs to receive this letter urgently, and I can neither spare the time nor trust the messengers—"

"I would be pleased to take it immediately after our discussion."

"Thank you. I would send Victoria, but in these dark times, she is too frightened to go out by herself. I wonder sometimes if that evil man is truly our Uncle George. An imposter may well have stolen the letter that was sent with Father's testament. Now, you have something to say to me?"

Alex's face reddened, and Mary stood rigidly, looking down at her hands, which she had made into a little nest. As Alex told Madeline, haltingly, about the pledge they had made to each other, Mary nodded in affirmation, afraid to meet her sister's eyes. When Madeline said, "I'm surprised and utterly delighted," Alex had the impression that she wanted to slam her fists down on the desk and hoot in derision at the two little babies.

"In Kingston, we will escape everything that haunts Mary and makes her ill. You, Miss Baker, are welcome to visit and stay as long as you like."

Madeline looked like someone had just slapped her. She bore down on Mary. "Sister, did you agree to this?"

Mary nodded and cringed as if she was confessing to a dire crime.

"Mr. O'Shea, you have my blessing in becoming my sister's husband," Madelaine pronounced. "However, with respect to her residence, you must realize that she has lived in this house for her entire life. The shock of being transplanted to a new place and away from my side will be too great for her. In her enthusiasm, she may have gone along with your plan, but you don't know her like I do. However, you do know her health is delicate."

Mary wilted. Alex twisted his mouth to the side. "Do you not think, my sister-in-law to be, that another locale, away from your threatening uncle and the site of your father's death, would be healthier for her? I'll watch over her and bring her back to visit if you're too occupied with your affairs to come to us." How did Madeline get such power over Mary? They seemed like master and slave.

"She may be equipped for such a transition later, in two or three years, but as her protector since the death of our parents, I'll not permit her to be removed immediately. You, sir, may reside with her in this house once you're married. It is a big house, and the two of you will enjoy privacy. I'm sure, with your journalistic talents, you will find employment in this town."

She had thrown down the gauntlet, and Alex was furious. He could not catch Mary's eye. Unable to defend his argument, she remained silent. "I suggest we defer the topic of our residence until a later time," he said angrily.

"Yes, I agree that would be best," Madeline replied. She seemed confident that, when Alex returned to Kingston, she could ensure Mary would remain faithful to her way of thinking. How did she do it?

8

Eliza wondered what those crazed sisters had done to Alex when he showed up unshaven, with bloodshot eyes and shaking hands. Hughes watched her every movement, but she had to find out. She set down the type and heard Hughes singing his favourite hymn, "How Can We Sinners Know," and tapping his feet on the floor as she went over to Alex.

He had his head lowered, ostensibly concentrating on documents, and she leaned close to whisper in his ear. "You're down in the depths today. Why?"

He looked her in the eye, his face like a dog's that had forgotten its training. He did not have time to say anything as Hughes came rushing over, nudging them aside, so his face was between theirs. "Oh, it must be devastating news, and the star reporter, me, must be part of it. Has our prime minister been assassinated?" Hughes smirked.

"This is none of your business," Alex said. "It's personal."

"And you're no gentleman," Eliza said, giving Hughes a push in the ribs.

Hughes made a mock show of being offended. "Were you a man, Batch, like the way you look, I would invite you to meet me at sunrise with pistols." He went back to whatever trivial work Barker had assigned him, guffawing.

Eliza turned her head close to Alex's and heard him whisper, "You'll find my news quite startling. I'll tell you on our walk home tonight." Couldn't he give her a clue at least? Now his mouth was sealed.

"Summer love is such a sweet, sacred thing," Hughes said. He got to his feet just as Eliza left Alex. "Tea time for me," he continued, but as she approached him, quite prepared to shove him again, he uttered, "Oops!" and fell to the floor, his arms flailing and his hand pressing against her groin.

On the floor, he wriggled with glee. "You're always spilling oil. It's supposed to go into the machine, not onto the floor." Eliza could see no oil under his feet and told him so.

Could Hughes have felt her nub? It was covered by a dress and undergarments, but the force of his groping had almost knocked her over. Hughes rose nimbly to his feet.

"I must say, I must indeed say, that today's news is world shaking. Astounding! The lightning of the Lord will strike down."

Eliza made a fist and shook it at him.

"No fisticuffs necessary. I retract my challenge. Now I must depart for my tea, leaving you two lovebirds alone in this inky nest. It occurs to me, however, as a parting salutation, that if she is he, could you, Alexie, be she? It's just too confusing for my little brain, and I can only picture—"

He was interrupted by Eliza throwing a haymaker of a punch at his nose. It bled profusely, and Hughes covered it as he bent over, howling. Alex moved Eliza aside and threw

Hughes at the typeset shelf. Hughes went down with the lead type falling upon him. He wriggled, looking like a cornered rat.

Barker steamed out of his office. "I heard a crash in here. What the hell is going on? Hughes?"

Hughes looked at the editor like a picture-book martyr. He lifted his hand from his nose, showing his bloody mess of a face. "They beat me up, sir, for no reason at all. I told them the pressroom was untidy, oil on the floor, dangerous. Sir, they've always had it in for me. My friends, especially in our congregation, know I'm an honourable man, and these two are just jealous."

"Can you get up?"

"I may be able to rise with great effort." Hughes grabbed at the shelf, pulling more type down, got to his feet, wobbled.

"You two could have helped him," Barker said. "Now, Hughes, take yourself off to the hospital, and come back when you're fit. You other two, come to my office."

Neither Eliza nor Alex sat down when they were in the office, although Barker sat behind his desk and sighed deeply. "Editing a newspaper is not supposed to be like this. I may have to do this run all by myself. O'Shea, I'll start with you. What's your explanation for such violence? Your job hangs in the balance."

"He insulted Miss Malkins, not once but repeatedly. Enough was enough."

"How did he insult her? Tell me his words."

"No, I'll not reveal them. He's a scurrilous wretch, no matter how high his connections, and I'll no longer abide his presence."

Barker shook his head, then turned to Eliza. "Miss Malkins, you will give me your version of this sordid event."

Eliza did not respond, just shook her head and looked steely eyed.

Barker got up and turned his back on them. He looked out his window, as if the result of his query could be found out on the street. Eliza watched Alex, but he did not look at her.

Barker sat down again, picked up a pencil, and used it as a drumstick to enunciate his words. "Mr. O'Shea, your work as a writer of news and as my sub-editor has, until recently, been outstanding. I used to worry I would lose you to one of the big city newspapers. Having said that, you have acted in a rash way that no newspaperman ever should. Without an explanation from you, I have only Hughes's words to fall back upon, and so—"

"Sir, I was the one who broke his nose!" Eliza shouted. "Mr. O'Shea merely came over to protect me. You must not fire him. I'm the one who needs to go."

Barker's eyes widened. "You? I was about to pardon you, but now it's out of the question. I have no choice but to sack you both."

At once Eliza and Alex went toward the door, but Barker's face softened. "Miss Malkins, this blow comes at you just after the death of your mother. Do you understand why I can't keep you on here?"

"Yes."

"I can give you a good recommendation to help you find work elsewhere. I'm aware of your personal circumstances, of the loss of your father, mother, and heroic brother. I owe this to your father."

"Thank you, sir."

"Mr. O'Shea, I can't make you the same offer, but I can say this: I'll not warn other newspapers about you. If I'm asked for an opinion, I'll say you're an adequate reporter. To both of you, please leave immediately, and take your personal effects with you. When you see the light of day, you will reform your ways, and I wish you good fortune when that time comes." Barker picked up a quill and turned his attention to a notepad on his desk.

⸭

They walked toward Eliza's house, the sun heating up the roads and buildings they passed, the streets quite empty of traffic. She kept an eye out for horse and dog waste like a ship navigator; Alex would have stepped in them as he vented his wrath about what had happened and how that "bastard" Hughes had come out on top. Eliza worried if he was thinking also about what Hughes had said about her being a man. Did he no longer want to associate with a freak?

"I was the cause of the altercation, and I injured him. You heard what Barker said about your talent. If you go back tomorrow and plead with him, I wager he'll take you back," she said, interrupting his invective.

He stopped and looked around. What did he expect to see? They were alone in front of a carriage barn. "It's you that worries me. What will you do now? You might have kept silent and let me take the blame. I don't mind—"

"Being dismissed? Why? You're a born reporter. I wish I could do your work," she said, feeling guilty that he was heading back down the road of gloom that overtook him from time to time.

"It makes no difference, because I planned to resign today anyway. I'm moving to Ottawa."

"What? Because of those sisters?" Her worst fear, Alex held in thrall like a prisoner, worshiping the sisters as if they were saints.

"Yes. I'm getting married," he said, taking hold of her hand, which she promptly withdrew. She couldn't look at him, not now. Her dream about him crumbled like an old brick wall.

"To which sister?"

"Why, to Mary, of course. She's sweet and innocent and needs my protection. I think she will die if I'm not there to cheer her up and induce her to eat. When she has recovered, she will be the perfect mother for my children," he said defensively, as if he was making himself believe his own words.

"And you will be living in Ottawa rather than here . . . with your bride?" He might as well be away.

"Yes, for the time being. We will live in their house, because she wants to keep on being close to her sister. I would like us to move out of that house eventually, say a year or two."

She had nothing to say. No amount of convincing would change his mind. She should be congratulating him, but that would be like wishing someone a good trip as they headed into the Inferno. *Alex, why throw yourself away like this?* She made a secret wish that the weak, little, conniving sister would die before she could destroy his life.

"I have two more things to tell you before I go to pack up my few worldly goods. Eliza . . .." He took her by the shoulders to turn her face toward his. "You're my best friend in the world. I want to keep up our friendship. I'm devastated that we will not be able to travel together to Europe, as I promised. Someday, when I make more money, I'll invite you to travel with Mary and me. Please, visit me in Ottawa. Come for the wedding—it will only be a small affair. Consider moving to Ottawa and visiting us at our house."

"Do you think that strong-willed sister you told me about will let me take one step into her house? Wake up, Alex! You're dreaming." She pushed his hands away, swept the hair out of her face, and exposed her square jaw.

"No, you're wrong this time. Think it over. I'll write to you. I'm sorry if I made you—"

"Jealous, just like a woman? Hysterical?"

"I didn't mean that. You're a wonderful woman." He held out his arms to hug her.

"Good luck, Mr. O'Shea," she said, walking away stiffly, like a man.

9

Someone peeked out the corner of a drape on a front window of the Baker house. Alex heard the latches sliding open before he could knock. The door opened slowly. He expected to see Victoria, but Madeline stood there, looking all around on the street, holding the handgun he had returned to her before going home to Kingston.

"Alexander, quick! I don't know how to use this."

"Is something wrong?"

In response, Madeline dragged him inside. The snap of the latches sounded like a series of mousetraps going off. Once she finished, she became erect and formal. He rubbed the dust off his feet, watching Mary, who seemed cross. "Why didn't you come last night like you promised? Victoria's sister is sick, and she's away, leaving only Maddy to protect me."

"I got in late and was too groggy," he lied, the only excuse that came to mind. In fact, the train was on time, but he was so tormented by doubts that he needed to go to the bottle. He wished he could talk with Eliza. Now she was far away and did not want to be his friend any more. What exactly had Hughes felt when he groped her? How could that make a difference in their friendship? Why had he committed himself to Mary? He did not desire her body. He wanted to protect her innocence. It had been too hot in his hotel room. He had gone outside and wandered over to Lower Town. There, he paid a woman for her body. Would he ever be faithful to Mary?

"Alexander, let me take your coat, so you can sit and talk with Mary while I make tea. I hope you had breakfast. Cook is out shopping, but I can bring you something from the larder." This was different, a domesticated Madeline Baker!

"That is kind of you, but I broke my fast at the hotel and am capable of hanging up my own coat. I have another suggestion: let's call each other by our familiar names, Madeline and Alex." He smiled, but judging from Madeline's reaction, he had breached her protocol of command. He had to take a stand with this Napoleonic woman.

"Maddy! Call her Maddy," Mary said. He looked at his fiancé, in many ways still a child.

"Very well, Madeline and Alex it shall be." Madeline spoke with the firmness of a schoolmarm. "You know the closet where you can hang your coat. When Victoria returns, you must let her take it. It is an insult to the house to refuse." She strode off toward the kitchen.

He sat next to Mary on the divan. She looked as if she wanted to hug him or do something improper before the wedding. She seemed even more a wisp of a thing, her fingers bony and her waist so small he thought he could span it with his two hands and a third, if he had one. She had dark circles under her eyes.

"Are you well, my darling?" he asked, trying to soothe her. She lowered her head, and he dared to place his hand on her upper arm and to pat her. Her little, silken body, perhaps he could learn to enjoy it.

"I missed you," she said.

"And I you. I don't plan to travel out of town again."

She was pleased and reached up to pat him. She was like a sweet, little bird locked up in a gilded, covered cage. He had to get her away from this house, from whatever ghosts haunted it. Also, he feared his own Christian Brother ghosts would move in. He suspected something happened to Mary while he was away. Her mood had become dreamier than he had ever seen. She was not about to confide in him. Madeline might tell him, after Mary went to bed.

"Have you been drawing?" He thought this topic would engage her in something positive. Instead, she withdrew her arm.

"No," she whispered.

"I'm sorry to hear that. Drawing makes you feel good. By the way, the last time, you didn't show me the drawing. Can you take me to see it?" Perhaps if he admired it, even if the image of him was unnatural and embarrassing, she might cheer up.

"No, we won't unveil that until after we're married. It's my wedding gift to you." Her voice was steadier now, and she said this as if rehearsed.

"Well, that will not be long from now. I'll go and arrange the marriage tomorrow. Is early October too soon?"

"No, no, that is good."

"Wonderful. Let's go out for a stroll, and you can bring along your sketch pad. There are still some flowers in bloom. The trees are dressed in their autumn finery."

"No."

"Why?"

"Because . . . Uncle George might be there."

Had George come pounding on the door a second time? Was that what this was all about?

"Mary, I can take the weapon along to protect us. George is afraid of me, and you will be perfectly safe."

"He might . . . oh, Alex, I don't want to talk about him."

"Did George come and hurt you again? I'll not let him get away with it."

Bunching herself almost into a ball, Mary told him that George had not returned.

"He whipped you once. Tell me, Mary, I have to know, did he do anything else?" If Mary confirmed it, he would beat George to death, chop him into little pieces, burn the mill around him . . ..

Mary slipped onto the floor, but he was relentless. "Tell me!" he shouted.

She shook with fright and something else . . . shame?

"He touched me," she said the way an actor would say her words on stage. Had Madeline given her these words and forbidden her from providing the obscene details? But her few words said it all. She need say no more. He did not know where Madeline had put the handgun, perhaps in the kitchen, but he wanted it immediately to hunt down George.

Madeline came in with the tea tray. "Mary, get up. You're having one of your fainting spells." Madeline leaned over her. Mary moaned and stirred but kept her face down, hiding her tears. Madeline looked at Alex, and he had no chance to disguise his anger. She must have thought they had a lover's quarrel, but, like a diplomat, she refrained from confronting him. "Mr. O'Shea—sorry, Alex—could you please go into the drawing room while I loosen Mary's corset? She has fainting spells."

"Have you called in a doctor to examine her?"

"No!" came a squeal from under the bundle that was Mary.

"She refuses to be examined. She will be fine, knowing you're back." Madeline patted the top of Mary's head, as if she was a dog.

He went to the drawing room, closed the door, and walked around, recalling how he had exposed his naked body to Mary there. He saw no sign of the easel with the drawing. Madeline's desk had a pile of papers on it, as usual. He was curious. What happened in this house? He opened the drawer that had once held the gun and, to his surprise, the gun glinted at him, freshly polished. How did Madeline get it back there, with the kitchen on the far side of the salon and no other doorways to the drawing room, other than the one he entered? He closed the drawer and prepared to sit patiently, but curiosity drew him on to check the other drawers. Only stationary in the next two, but in the last one, he found an old book. Its cover was water damaged and unreadable. He opened it carefully. He had never heard of the book, *La Nouvelle Justine ou Les Malheurs de la vertu*,

Tome Huitième, by Marquis de Sade, published in 1797 in Holland. A bookmark well into the volume revealed a scene of a naked woman being tortured by a man and another woman. Quickly, he returned the book to the drawer and resumed strolling around the room. Was this the kind of literature that Madeline read? Could she understand French, or was she merely fascinated by the illustrations? Perhaps the explanation was simple—an old desk, owned by her father, and she had let the book stay where he left it.

The library adjoined the drawing room, and he strayed into there, peering at the books, many of them ancient, on shelves that ran to the ceiling. On the top shelf, he spied a line of books that might be companions to the odious volume he had handled. He moved a ladder, made for getting to the top shelves, stepped up, and took off the first book in the row. Yes, volume one of the same series, nine on the shelf, a space on the shelf for volume eight, the one in the drawer.

"Alexander?" Madeline called.

He climbed down in a panic. With no time to move the ladder, he picked a book at random and pretended to be immersed in it when Madeline entered the library.

"Here you are. Did you find something interesting to read?" she asked, glancing at the ladder.

He tried to shift her attention. "Yes, quite a collection here. How is Mary?"

"More composed now. You may return. What are you reading?"

He handed her the book. She raised her eyebrows as she read the title. "Herschel's A Treatise on Astronomy. I didn't know you were interested in the stars."

"Oh, yes, it's a practice of mine to go out at night to look at the stars." He had gone out with his mother to do that. He was flooded with memories and guilt.

"Well, when we're no longer threatened by George, you can take us out walking at night and point out constellations," she said, glancing at the ladder again.

"Speaking of George . . . ."

"No, not now. Mary is anxious for you to return. When she's asleep, we can talk."

Madeline stopped at her desk, and he went on alone.

Mary sat up straight on the divan, skin whiter than usual, blue eyes following him as he came in and sat next to her. He poured two cups of tea. He tasted his, lukewarm and over-steeped. Mary sat like a statue, looking at him.

"Look," he said, trying to brighten the mood, "Madeline brought us these biscuits you like so much. How about having one?"

She scowled. "I don't eat."

"What do you mean?"

"I mean I'm not hungry." She looked cross again.

She would not let him take her outside, and she did not want to talk about drawing. She did not seem interested in discussing the wedding, she had no friends to invite, and she did not have any desires for special clothing for the wedding day. He tried to engage her in where they could go for a holiday following the wedding. She looked puzzled, stumbled on her words, and said George might be anywhere outside the house. Finally, he told her about one night when his mother took him out for a walk under the stars. He was deadly afraid that there might be a bear behind every bush, and he held on tight to her hand. "Look! Quick, make a wish," his mother had said, pointing up. He saw a falling star and made a wish. He did not tell Mary that his wish was that he could be with his mother forever.

A tear rolled down Mary's nose and dripped onto her dress. Others followed. He grabbed a napkin and caught them. He had not told her what happened to his parents and little sister. Now he never would.

❖

"Goodnight, dear Mary. May you have a sound sleep," he said as Madeline supported her arm and led her up the stairway.

"Promise me again you will come early in the morning," Mary said.

"Yes, I have promised three times already, and only a cad would break his word after that," he said, trying to make light of it.

"But will you be safe outside? Maddy, order him to stay in the house." This too she had repeated during the day.

"Alex will be perfectly safe. Now come on, my dear, you're dropping," Madeline said, pulling her up the stairs. "Alex, help yourself to wine or spirits from the cabinet in the kitchen. I'll stay with Mary until she falls asleep."

In the kitchen, he was tempted to look inside all the cabinets, but on his first try, he found one housing two bottles of wine that Cook brought up for their use from the cellar and also a wide selection of spirits. He took out a decanter of brandy, found two glasses, and carried them into the salon. Staying clear of Father's sinister chair, he poured himself a stiff drink and sat on the divan, where Mary and he had spent their drab, mostly speechless day.

His rage with George no longer burned like a fuse about to set off a barrel of gunpowder. He was confused, primarily about Mary, her pallor, and her refusal to bring him into her confidence the way she had the last time he saw her. She ate little, often lifting the fork near her mouth and then setting it down again, as if something had just come to her mind. His priority should be to get a doctor into the house to examine her rather than taking revenge on George. Also, what about the erotic book in Madeline's desk and the remainder of the collection in the library? Temptation almost drove him to revisit the library and examine all the upper shelves, but Madeline would almost certainly discover him there, and this time, no excuse would save him from her ire. A good decision he realized as he heard Madeline's steps on the stairs.

"Is Mary asleep?" he asked.

"Oh yes, dancing with the fairies. It doesn't take long. As soon as you two are married, I must teach you."

She accepted the glass of brandy he poured for her. Twisted thoughts came to mind—the wedding night, Madeline in their bedroom giving Mary lessons.

"If I may ask, what's your secret?"

Madeline frowned but then brightened with a kind of recognition. "Oh, it's simple enough. She drinks a small glass of wine with drops of laudanum, which I administer.

115

Then I read her a bedtime story from books that she has kept since childhood. She's asleep before I reach the end."

"I have heard of laudanum. Isn't it dangerous?"

"Not if it's controlled, like any other drug. It's a wonderful medicine that you should try if you feel anxious or can't sleep. Even Mrs. Beeton recommends it in her famous book, Household Management. I can show you."

"What if Mary accidentally—"

"Wakes up and takes too much? I'm not a fool. I keep it locked in a cabinet in my room. I take it also. Speaking of laudanum, we're nearly out. Would you mind going to the Davidson and Daniel Druggists on Rideau Street to buy some for us? I have tried other chemists, but they're often out of stock, as it's such a popular medicine, and for good reason. Six bottles will last us a long time. They are tiny bottles, only an ounce. I would go myself, but with Victoria away, Mary would become hysterical about George attacking me."

"Yes, I can go for you. Do I need a doctor's letter?" He did not know much about laudanum, other than that there were instances of women overdosing.

"You don't need a prescription. Even a child can buy it. That reminds me, there's something you need to do, or Mary will never eat." She went over to the desk, withdrew the pistol, and handed it to him. He was about to speak when she put her hands to her lips and lumbered away, up the stairs. The gun was loaded. He had not liked having it in his possession during his last visit. When Madeline came back down, she was carrying a belt-like object.

"This is Father's holster. We may have to make a hole in the belt to fit it around your waist, as he was rounder than you. Always have the handgun with you, and show Mary you're wearing it. You'll be amazed how it will lift her spirits."

"Very well." He set the weapon and holster on the tea table, unwilling to stand and be fitted for wearing it. She took a deep drink of brandy and eyed him speculatively, as if he were a horse on auction. He wanted to ask her a host of questions; the gun was a distraction.

"Madeline, please tell me now, did George do something to Mary while I was away? She seems to be ill because of her fright."

"Mary has always been an invalid, but yes, George wrote me outrageous, threatening letters, saying that if we did not cede our interests in the mill, he would break down the door, beat us, and burn down our house."

Her eyes were dark and forbidding. She downed the remainder of her brandy, and he poured her more. He felt rage building again, but, like a mantra, he remembered the soothing sound of his mother's voice when he was little and had gotten into a fight with another boy, "Keep calm, Alex. Your worry will go away like a bad dog."

He had to break the staring match. "Why didn't you go to the authorities with those letters?"

"I know his handwriting. The letters were written by someone else, and they were anonymous."

"Benson probably wrote them. We can catch him at his game and have him locked up too. Where are the letters?"

"I had to burn them, because Mary found them in my desk when I was upstairs, and Victoria neglected her duty to watch over her. Alex, you should be glad you weren't here. Mary's little fainting spell today was nothing compared with that." She looked repentant, but what would Mary have thought of that book in the bottom drawer if she had indeed been rifling through the desk?

"Mary wants our wedding to happen as soon as possible. I told her that I would go tomorrow to arrange it. My first thought was a church, but Mary says she wants it to be at this house, because she's afraid of George. Her fear is so great that perhaps it would be better to have the wedding out of town. What do you think?"

Madeline scowled and shook her head. Was she opposed to the wedding?

"Should we delay the wedding while Mary heals?" he asked.

"I'm surprised to hear you say that. Do you not understand how urgently Mary wants you?"

Alex was taken aback. Other than as a kind of parental protector, in what way did Mary want him?

She drew out a small key that she used to unlock an old oak wardrobe that stood nearby. She lifted something out that was covered by a sheet—it had to be Mary's drawing.

"If that is Mary's work, please don't reveal it. She said it is her present to me, and she will give it to me on our wedding day," Alex pleaded, amazed at Madeline's audacity.

"That was her excuse. You must see it if you're to understand Mary and proceed with your wedding plans. Alex, she is no saint, despite your vision of her. Please, get out the tripod." It was collapsed inside the wardrobe. Madeline stood with her arms wide, embracing the drawing while he set up the tripod. Then she set it down and exhaled.

"You have been mistaken, so very wrong about Mary's love for you," she said as she lifted off the sheet.

He could not believe it. He closed his eyes, opening them again to realize it was no mirage. He recognized the original painting that Mary had imitated, William Blake's *The Temptation and Fall of Eve*. He had seen it years earlier while leafing through Milton's *Paradise Lost*. In the original, Adam was beside the tree, back turned, looking up at the heavens or at the upper branches of the tree, ignorant of what had happened on the other side. But in Mary's version, he looked straight out, utterly innocent, his naked body enhanced somewhat with larger muscles. The tree was the same. He recognized it as the poison tree. In Blake's painting, a huge serpent was wound lasciviously around Eve, and she looked it in the eyes, conversing. In Mary's . . . but it could not be hers.

"That's Mary. Who drew that?"

"I did," Madeline said.

"You drew that without her permission? This is outrageous!"

"Calm down, Alex. She asked me to draw her. At first I resisted, but she demanded, said she would stop eating entirely, and so, as usual, I gave in to her demands. If you're wondering, yes, that's her. She modelled for me."

In the drawing, Mary was on her hands and knees, one arm bloodied, gazing at Alex in awe. She was skin and bones, her back scarred. She looked . . . hungry? At her side lay a bloodied knife and the serpent cut into pieces.

"This revolts me. Who twisted Mary's mind?"

"It wasn't me. You still don't understand, do you? Even with all the evidence in front of your eyes. This is symbolic. That dead snake is George, and Mary is free of him. It's her greatest wish. And she wants you not just spiritually but physically. Women are like that, even ones who parade around and say they are 'Angels in the House.' She's dead afraid you will reject her body, because she has been violated, and here she is showing you her desire. Are you man enough to accept Mary as she is and do something about George, or do you want to put your tail between your legs and hide?" She pointed at Alex's penis in the drawing while saying the last part. Then she turned to him, her face angry, her large bosoms thrust forward.

It was hard to draw breath and face her. "I need time to think about this," he said, then started to walk away.

"I'm not finished yet," Madeline said. "Mary is right to be afraid of George interrupting the wedding. From what Mary says, he hates you as much as us. As far as I'm concerned, ignore my wishes. If Mary wants something, she is not easily persuaded to change her mind. Have it at the house, and stay on here after the wedding. You'll not get her to move to Kingston."

She seemed less surprised than he expected when he told her that he no longer worked in Kingston and that he had come to Ottawa with the intention of staying, establishing himself, moving after the wedding to a rented suite, and eventually buying a house.

She weighed her words. "You'll not get Mary to budge from this house until that madman is out of the way. She will become hysterical. Neither will I let her go if you're planning to go to work, leaving her alone each day. Did she tell you what he did to her?"

Her rage became infectious, but he had enough sense to want to hear her version. "No," he lied.

"That monster tortured and violated her. Her own uncle! Is that not enough for you to go out and take your vengeance on him?"

"Yes," he said, more quietly than she wanted to hear.

Before he left, she insisted he try on the holster. She had him wait while she took a lamp and went to the toolshed outside. She returned with an awl and punctured the belt, so it fit perfectly around his waist. He left feeling less like a western gunfighter and more like more like a boy who had lost his way since his mother died.

❖

Alex rushed to Davidson and Daniel Druggists, weaving in and out of the many pedestrians on Rideau Street, having spent more time than he wished with Methodist Reverend Hawkins, who agreed to come to the house to administer the wedding vows. What a talker! An encyclopedia of marriages going back to Bytown days. He obliged Alex to listen, despite his mention of pressing errands. Alex paid him his fee, and then he had to listen to Hawkins explain in detail why there should not be a photographer at the wedding, as it would deter from the solemnity of the event. Finally, at the door, Hawkins told him how church funds had dwindled despite his best efforts. So, Alex gave Hawkins another five dollars, just to get out.

His worry, of course, was Mary. How would she be on the wedding day? How could he either get George out of town or move away with her? Killing George would solve one problem but create another—his own hanging. He did not like the idea of walking about Ottawa with a concealed weapon. So, he left it in the hotel room. He needed to retrieve it on the way back to Concession Street though, because Madeline might ask him to produce it.

Davidson and Daniel's was a small establishment that did good business, judging from the number of customers in the queue. He considered leaving the errand for another day or going to another chemist, but Madeline would not approve, and for the time being, all hail Madeline. Once again, he thought about his dilemmas. What to do about George? How to get Mary out of that house? How to earn a living in Ottawa? His inherited money was running out. Back came thoughts of Eliza. How would she bring bread to her table? Was she in danger from Hughes?

He saw a container on the shelf with a snake on its label, a bad omen.

"Sir?" a long-faced, bearded man said from behind the counter. Alex had been holding up the queue while his mind circled the moon.

He stepped forward. "I would like six bottles of laudanum, please."

"Six? Do you realize what you're asking for? One bottle has between five and six hundred drops. Six bottles would last you years."

Alex heard a buzz from the people lined up behind him. "I know nothing about laudanum. This is an order I'm picking up for two friends, regular customers of yours."

"May I have their names?"

He thought children could buy this drug. Could Madeline have made a mistake by asking for so much?

"Miss Madeline Baker and her younger sister."

"They are not regular customers. What is your name, sir?"

This was confusing. Who made the mistake—Madeline or the chemist?

"My name is O'Shea. I'm about to become a resident of Ottawa."

"Welcome to Ottawa, Mr. O'Shea. And you're staying . . .?"

"At Russell House." This was irritating. The chemist wrote a note in a memorandum book. Why?

"Mr. O'Shea, I'll fill your order." At last. He reached up to a shelf and took down six small, brown bottles and wrapped them in brown paper. "If these are new users, they should only take a few drops a night," the chemist said as he counted out Alex's change. "If they've been using laudanum for some time, they may proceed as usual, but absolutely no more than thirty drops."

Alex thanked him and hurried away with the package.

10

"Eliza! Hurry with the toast; our Harry is hungry," the lady of the house shouted from the tiny dining room, from which Eliza had removed a sack of dust and crumbs during the day.

"It's coming up," she said. The stew and dumplings bubbled on the stove. No mention had been made of toast. She set the stew aside and opened the lids on the stove, sliced two pieces of bread, put them in the mesh used for toasting, and held it over the flame. At least the kitchen had an appealing smell, unlike the rest of the house. Moments later, she took out the toast, placed it on a plate, and carried it into the dining room, barely large enough for Mrs. Keogh and three children, including the baby. The little boy, Harry, seized both pieces and spread drippings on them. Mrs. Keogh rolled her eyes. "Will dinner be ready soon? My Donald will be coming in the door any time now."

"In five minutes, Madam," Eliza said, comprehending the woman's anxiety. She had hired Eliza at the tiny wage of fifty cents a week, to be paid every two weeks. Eliza became the do-it-all person—maid, cook, babysitter, and "handyman," the latter something that the previous maid could not do and which pleased Mrs. Keogh, because her husband never had time. Eliza arrived at 7:30, right after Mr. Keogh left for work at the harbour, and she left at 6:30 p.m., just before he came home. She was told that the last maid had a "misunderstanding" with the master. She wondered why this poor woman, so afraid of her husband, had looked Eliza up and down before hiring her. Could the master have been forward with her predecessor, and the mistress felt safer now with a maid who looked like a man?

She was running late, because the toddlers had a fight with each other, and she needed to care for the baby while Mrs. Keogh took a dose of laudanum and had a long nap. Eliza did not fear the master. If he made advances toward her, she would bop him on the nose. But more likely, he would retreat from her. Now she did not rush, as her curiosity about Mr. Keogh had been raised. In any case, the stew needed at least five more minutes before she could put it on the warmer and depart.

During her brief recess for lunch that day, she went to the post office and received a letter from Alex. She read it on the way back, almost bumping into passersby. As she listened to the stew bubbling, she read it again. He implored her to come to his wedding, "It will be a very small, informal affair held at the house on Concession Street. I would like to have a friend with me. Please say you will come." He said nothing about finding work in Ottawa, only that he was soon going to spend more time writing his novel. Eliza decided to send him her best wishes and regrets—she didn't want to go, and there was no getting time off work. A lingering fear of Alex throwing himself into the clutches of those Baker women remained with her. She doubted she could keep her mouth shut at the wedding when the vows were being said, or if she could get her hands on those sisters . . ..

She had ignored the demands shouted her way from the dining room—Mrs. Keogh dare not leave her children, because hostilities were sure to resume—and now came the slamming of the front door and a deep, loud voice saying, "Dinner ready? I'm plain starved."

Eliza walked casually into the dining room, bowed to the master, and said she would serve the dinner immediately. Keogh, a tall, scrubby man, looked her over like she was a circus performer. "Who's this then?"

"This is Eliza, our new servant. Remember, I told you—"

"Ugly as sin. Are you sure that's a woman, and nothing improper's goin' on here?"

Eliza returned to the kitchen. He followed her.

"Don't you dare turn your back on your master! Where did you work before that you're so rude? Perhaps you were a pimp; you look like it."

She said nothing, only untied her apron and set it on a side table.

"You deserve a swat," he said in high anger. She smelled the yeasty odour of beer on his breath.

"I can give better than I receive," she said, pushing him out of the way. His eyes were like a bull's seeing a red cape. She ignored him. He was a bully and, therefore, a coward.

Mrs. Keogh and the toddlers were frightened. The baby bawled.

"I'm sorry, madam, but I resign my position here," Eliza said and then steamed out the front door, slamming it behind her. Only then did she think of the wages owed her, a paltry sum, thirty cents.

❖

She was a failure as a woman and a worker. She might as well put herself out of her misery, like Mater, unless a miracle came along.

Some of Pater and Paul's clothes were mixed in the stack she intended to take to the used-clothing man. She dared herself to try on a suit. Mater would have found it sacrilegious, but she was no longer around to chastise her. She sorted through the clothing until she found Pater's Sunday suit. She selected a white shirt and did not look for a tie, as it would be too complicated for her to knot it. After she shuffled off her clothes, she whispered, "Bless me Pater," and dressed in his under and outer clothing. The clothes fit her well—they were about the same height, although he was thicker around the waist. She found his Sunday top hat on a shelf and stuffed her hair up into it, though some locks remained sticking out. Except for her hair, someone who seemed every bit a man looked out at her from the glass. She smiled and then made her face look angry—scary person there. She liked it, the lightest she had felt since Mater's death. It was something she had wanted to do ever since Mater informed her that she was a freak, but anchors had always held her back: Pater, Mater, Alex.

In a daze, she let herself, mirror in hand, wander into the kitchen, take the shears out of a drawer, sit, and begin snipping at hair that had never been cut.

It was frightening to go out like this, but there was no way around it. Eagle Foundry called to her. She took off the suit and put on Pater's gardening clothes.

She approached the foundry like a devil seeking his lair in hell. At her house, the foundry could always be heard banging, and its smoky smell would often come her way if the wind was right. She had never been inside, but now she walked up as if familiar with the place, opened a wide sliding door, and stepped inside, struck by the heat and sparks in the huge pot of molten metal. Hellish indeed.

"What do you want here?" a muscular man asked. He had charcoal dust on his face and wore something like a bowl on his head.

"I would like to talk to the top man."

"Would you now? The boss is over there raking those two fellows over the coals for spilling brass. I'd stay away from him until he's free," he said, speaking from experience.

"Thank you. I will."

"You from around here?"

"Yes." She didn't want to feed his curiosity.

"Odd. I don't remember seeing you before, and I was born here."

"Yes. Same as me." She shrugged. Just then, the boss glanced their way, causing the man to say, "Oh, oh," and rush away to another part of the foundry.

Clearly, the two workers being disciplined were not doing well. They went from waving their hands and shaking their heads to pointing at each other, to open-palmed supplication. Finally, they hung their heads and, muttering, strode past her and out the door.

Behind the boss, a huge cauldron on chains tipped to divulge some of its fiery contents. She walked up to the boss, holding herself upright. "Sir," she said, confident of her voice, aware that it was just slightly lower than the one she used as a woman. "My name is Paul Malkins, and I'm looking for employment." She had papers in her late brother's name, and the knowledge of his death was not well known. Before her mother's memory became jumbled, she had pleaded with Mr. Barker not to put up a notice about Paul in the *British Whig,* as it would wound her. He agreed and generously asked her if he could help in her time of grief and told her he was about to increase Eliza's pay.

"You a gardener?" the boss asked, noting her gardening clothes.

"No, sir, I was in the British Navy and have just resigned, coming to the aid of my aging mother, who lives near your foundry. Unfortunately, I was too late. I arrived just after she passed away." She did her best to look like a prodigal son.

"So, you're accustomed to heavy work? Good. Let's try you out. Come with me."

She followed him toward the great furnace and its sulphurous, metallic fumes. She stoppered a cough. Next to the furnace, it was stifling. There was a pile of smoking stones and grit. The boss ordered one of the workers to bring over a bucket and a shovel.

"Here," the boss said, handing her the shovel. "Scoop off a full bucketful of this slag as quickly as you can, carry it out through the door, and empty it into the slag heap. Then come back."

The tin bucket was large. She found it hard to wedge the shovel into the slag—she had to put all her weight into it. Her work was not helped by the sight of the boss taking out his pocket watch and consulting it. Finally, she put in the last shovelful.

The boss shook his head. "More can fit in. It should be overflowing."

She dug out another shovelful. But oh, was the bucket heavy. Had she ever carried something of such a weight? *You can do this, Eliza or Paul or whoever you are now*, she counselled herself, and then she headed off with it. The handle felt like it was cutting her hand in half, and she kept thinking, *One more step, run, so you can get this cutter off your hand*. She headed out the door and turned, so she was out of the boss's sight. The slag heap was some distance away, but the watch was ticking, and she needed to return at a respectable time. *Throw away the temptation to dump the bucket near the door, and go back in.* She staggered to the slag heap and emptied her load.

Losing no time, she rushed back into the foundry. The boss was talking to another worker when she came up and set down the bucket. "Oh, the bucket test?" the other man said, chuckling.

"Yes, and not too bad, Malkins," the boss replied, taking his watch out of his pocket and examining it again. "Mr. Watts here was nearly a half minute faster, as I recall." The two men laughed. She tried to keep the anger out of her expression and merely look curious.

"Sorry, Malkins, that was just a test. We fill up a cart to make that trip. But carrying a bucket to the heap is a test for all the new men. We can give you a trial of one week at starting wages and then see where we go after that. Sydenham here will show you what to do."

"What's the starting wage?" she asked before the boss walked off.

"Fifteen cents a day, six days a week. That goes up to twenty-five cents if we keep you on."

If they did indeed keep her on, she would get as much in two days as she would have received as a maid in one week. It would keep flesh and bone together during the winter.

After the day of labour, pleased with the boss's comment that she was a "fast learner," she returned home and washed the grime off her face and hands, then changed into one of Paul's suits. It was a little tight on her, but she was in no position to be fussy. The only food she had in the cupboard was stale bread, and in the larder, the bacon had gone rancid. With the meagre means left to her, and with the market closed, all she could afford would be a cheap meal in a public house: bread, cheese, and a glass of beer. She also wanted to find out what it was like to be in a public place as a man.

The weather had been hot and dry for late September. The elderly lady across the street was out watering her flowers. Eliza had seen her numerous times before but did not know her name. As she started walking east, the woman hailed her in a raspy voice, "Sir, can I ask you a question?" A question, just what she did not need. "Sir?" the woman persisted until Eliza came over.

Dusk had arrived, and the woman kept hailing her closer, saying her hearing was "fuzzy." When Eliza got up close enough to see her wrinkled face and balding head of wispy grey hair, the woman started and held her hand to her mouth. Had she discovered Eliza's secret?

"Perhaps you should go inside your house and lie down," Eliza said.

"No, I thought I saw a ghost," the woman said, still shaken.

"A ghost? I can assure you, madam, that I'm no ghost, unless you saw one sitting on my shoulder." She smiled, feeling somewhat relieved.

"Where's the woman who lives in the house you came out of, Margaret's daughter?" The old woman was timid now. Mater never mentioned anything about this woman or any of their neighbours, for that matter. Did Mater roam and mingle during the day? It would be worthwhile finding out.

"As you may know, Mrs. Malkins passed away recently. Her daughter moved to Toronto to find work there."

"Oh, Margaret said that girl was simple and became violent if anyone came near her, so we all stayed away. I doubt anyone will hire her in Toronto. Poor thing. Poor Margaret, having to look after her for all those years." She said "us," so it must be all the ladies in the neighbourhood.

"But, you . . . I'm sorry to be so shattered . . . you look just like . . . .." Now the woman's fear returned. Did she suspect who Eliza was?

"Who, Mrs. . . . ?" Eliza smiled and tried to remain calm.

"Salter. My Bill has moved on, and just my daughter, her husband, and me live here now. I might as well say it: you remind me of the dead boy, Paul, the child Margaret cherished."

She was stunned. Mater must have shown her a photograph of Paul, the apple of her eye. Mater had lived until her last day with the fantasy that Paul was alive and thriving.

"When did Mrs. Malkins tell you that her son died?"

"It was that sad fact that made her . . . die that very day."

Now it was fully dark, and Mrs. Salter backed shakily toward her house.

"My mother was confused at the end, was she not?"

"Your mother?" she screamed, now apparently dead certain Eliza was a ghost.

"Yes. My sister, Elizabeth, told me about that after I returned from abroad, only a week too late. I'm Paul Malkins." She took the woman's arm to help her into her house. Mrs. Salter shook it off and whimpered all the way, at risk of falling. At last, when she had gone indoors, Eliza resumed her walk toward the market, nervous about her thin disguise and how she would have to bear it like a man. What other choice was there?

❖

On the Sunday after her first week of work, Eliza looked at herself in the mirror. Her hair was scraggly, the result of the hasty and maddened cut she had given it before she went out looking for a job at the foundry. How would a more commercial head of man's hair look? She combed and snipped, only guessing at what was happening behind her head. She tried looking stubborn, the way many men at the foundry looked.

She donned Pater's Sunday suit. With a shirt, vest, and coat, she did not need to tie the band of cloth over her breasts that she wore at the foundry. They were small anyways. After dusting Pater's top hat, she took a good look at herself. She might pass for a banker. Too bad she didn't have a cane.

She went out, swaggering a little and catching the eye of her neighbour, who must have wondered what was going on in the house now. She strolled past the foundry, its piles of waste still smouldering in the rare quiet. Continuing south, avoiding the church-going population as much as possible, she made her way to the harbour. She looked at the boats on the river and wished that Alex had been able to take her on a voyage to Europe. He had looked puzzled when she said she would not need a chaperone. Her idea was to dress up like a man, just as she was now, although she would tuck her hair under a hat, so she could turn into a woman again. How would he have reacted? She would never know. He kept writing to her, letters that encouraged her to visit him in Ottawa. But before long, he would be married, and from the sound of it—he never provided much detail—in a complicated situation with the family. He had his own challenges in life. Having a freak like her tagging along would be a dreadful mistake, for him and for her.

❖

On payday the men marched out of Eagle Foundry with renewed vigour and pleasure. Eliza had been keeping to herself, but she knew some of the men by name. A small cluster of them blocked the gate, discussing where they would go to celebrate. O'Rourke, a loud Irishman, stood close by. As the group moved on, he put his arm around her shoulder. "Come along, Malkins. We're off to the Leitrim Inn to drink ourselves into eejits. That'll soften you up." He pulled her along with some force. She decided to join them for one beer.

Just outside the gate were women, some holding babies, conversing with or waiting for their husbands. Some men handed over their pay. A lean woman with a green scarf over her head ran up to O'Rourke. "Sean, our little one be so very sick with fever. Don't you go out and drink away the money like all those other times. Come home and help. Franny has gone to call the doctor."

"What have you done, woman? We don't have money for that quack. Tell him the child has taken a turn for the better, and he can go away. And who's looking after Patrick while you and Franny be away?" He was swollen with rage and waved for Eliza to move on, but she held her ground.

"Mor be looking after them."

O'Rourke exploded and hit her in the face. She fell. Eliza hurried over and asked if she was hurt, taking out her handkerchief to staunch the blood coming from the woman's broken lip.

"Malkins, take your hands off that eejit, who leaves her sick little 'un with a nine-year-old 'un." He grabbed at Eliza's shirt, tearing it.

She rose and stared at him. "Take your wife home, and look after your family."

His eyes burned like coals. He wound up and took a swing at her. She saw it coming and moved aside enough that it only grazed her ear. She returned the blow, and down he went. "Do you want more?" she threatened, standing over him. O'Rourke's wife cried, and Eliza was about to comfort her, when more than one set of hands grabbed her and threw her to the ground, ripping off the rest of her shirt.

They pinned her arms down. O'Rourke was up on his feet, bleeding profusely from his nose. "What's this?" he said, laughing. He pulled down the band she had fastened around her chest. "Well, I always thought he was a ponce, but look you, a she-devil invaded the foundry."

"Leave her, O'Rourke. She won't be coming back," one of the men who had pinned her down said. Both released her, and she tried to cover up.

O'Rourke chortled and spit blood on her. He took some pennies from his pocket and threw them at his wife, who kneeled with her head down. The men went off laughing. Eliza got to her feet and offered some of her pay to Mrs. O'Rourke. She took it gladly, thanked her, and fled the scene. Eliza took a last look at the foundry. The boss stood inside the yard, his arms crossed. He stared at her for a moment, then turned and went inside.

11

"Father in heaven, grant Mary solace in her suffering. Provide her the strength to continue her life despite her heavy burdens, the fortitude to expunge her fear of evil deeds done against her in the past, the hope for a better future, and the faith to be accepted by You and your angels. I ask this through Christ our Lord. Amen."

This, Alex's first prayer since Christian Brothers school, he said in the morning on his knees. He slept little that night. He spent it tossing and turning, getting up and arming himself to go on tour in front of the Bakers' house. Immediately after Madeline's revelation about Mary's hunger for him, he thought he had fallen like an angel expelled from paradise, joining with those devils who had attacked him and laughed at him at Christian Brothers. He had misunderstood Mary's gaze. It was not a spiritual longing. He had no desire for her body. His mission was over. He might as well pack his bags and go, but where? His demons would follow. The gun could end it all. He ran along the river until he was far enough away from anyone who might hear. He took out that cold weapon, cocked it, took aim at a stump, and fired. The weapon's retort startled him. Undeterred, he cocked the pistol again. The next bullet would go into his brain, of no more value than the stump.

Why was it he thought then of that Protestant book that Christian Brothers regarded as contraband but that the boys circulated secretly? Christian's trials before he reached the Celestial City were infinitely greater than Alex's. If he pulled the trigger, hell would be his destination. He would join in on the torture visited upon suicides down there. Never would he see his mother again. His mission was to save Mary's body and spirit. And there was another responsibility he had neglected—he must do more to convince Eliza to come to Ottawa.

He went to the Baker house. Madeline looked at him. "You've thought more about what we discussed last night?" Her voice was smooth, as if discussing the weather.

"Not overly," he lied. "Is Mary up?"

"No, the invalid will likely spend the day in bed. She is no better and no worse. You may go up to visit her, if you wish."

Without another word, he ascended the stairs. Mary's bedroom door was open, her head and shoulders propped up on pillows, looking as wan as ever and brightening like a child when she saw him. "Is it late?" she asked. "It seems late."

He assured her that it was early, his usual time for coming, and that she might think it late only because the skies were darkened by clouds. When he offered to help her over to the window to see the wagons and pedestrians going by on Concession Street, she shook her head and held her hand above the bedcovers for him to hold. Cold, weak, so thin. She tried to draw his hand under the bedclothes, but he drew it away. Not for him, that forbidden touch.

"Mary, do you pray?"

"Why do you ask?" she said, startled.

"I could say a prayer with you, if you want."

"We were never taught to pray in this house. I thought you told me you were not a believer. Am I wrong?" Now she was the one who seemed worried about him.

She was right; he had told her that. The tray on the bedside table held her breakfast. She had not touched it. "I guess this is not the time to discuss faith. Breakfast is here. The fruit looks fresh and juicy. May I help you to a piece?"

"I'm not hungry, but I'll have some fruit for you, if you insist."

She nibbled. It was so often the same answer, as if she had overeaten the night before. He reached for her hand, which lay again outside the bedcovers and was about to ask her about the painting. Why the lustful expression on her face? What did he have to do to meet her needs, so she could climb out of the pit she had dug for herself? Questions trampled around him like a team of horses.

"Something bad has happened. Tell me," she demanded, her eyes wide.

He could not say. The answer might kill her; she was that delicate. "I was just worried about your health on our wedding day, which is less than two weeks from now."

"I love you, Alex. You worry too much. The dressmaker is coming tomorrow to fit me up."

"Will you be able to get out of bed for that?"

"Of course, I will, silly lad. Now help me to a drink of water, and then I'll have more of the breakfast, just to show you." She struggled to sit. He helped her up and held the water glass while she drank like a baby. She giggled. He gave her a napkin and a piece of toast. She took small bites of it.

He heard a scraping sound next door. It seemed to come from the direction of the photograph of her father. He was a big man with a beard and a penetrating look on his face, not the kind of person one would wish to confront.

"Should I go see what that was?" Alex asked.

"No, that will be Victoria cleaning Maddie's room. She'll be coming in here next to clean up me and my room."

"Oh, I must make my exit then," he said, trying to make her laugh.

She gave him a girlish pout. Was it merely because she did not like parting with him under any circumstances or because she had to wait to expose her body to him?

⁜

A few days later, Mary finished the carrots on her plate. Admittedly, the serving she allowed Victoria to give her was minuscule, and the beef and potatoes lay untouched. He caught Mary and Victoria smiling at each other.

"I'm saving room for dessert," Mary said to Alex, her eyes twinkling. She had some colour back and had been well enough to try on her wedding dress and sit up for a few hours in the afternoon.

"What a good girl you are! May I offer you some wine?"

Mary shook her head, smiling, and looked over at Madeline, who had been gloomy all week. "Mary is not a little girl," she said, putting her fork and knife down.

"Sorry," Alex said. "I'm just happy she's eating again."

"You've been a good influence," Madeline admitted begrudgingly.

"What's the matter with you, Maddy? Is it the bleeding that women have? I know—"

"How do you know about that? What an improper topic to bring up at the table. If you must know, that dastardly George has been causing me no end of trouble. In front of my lawyer, he makes threats about breaking in here to punish us. He's a monster. I hear noises at night that keep me awake, worrying he will invade."

"Can't our lawyer lock him in jail?" Mary asked, putting her hands on the table as if to keep it from moving.

"No, Mr. Ditchling says that would jeopardize our case against him. You don't understand such things, Mary." Madeline stared at Alex while saying this. He knew he did not meet her expectations. He was not worthy in her eyes. He had not gotten rid of George.

Mary pulled on Alex's coat sleeve, and he turned to her. "Alex, we would feel so much safer if you stayed here. Please, don't be prudish. We need a man in the house, so Maddy can sleep at night. It's not just for her but for me and Victoria too."

He looked around. Victoria bowed slightly. He thought it interesting that Mary should mention her.

"As I said before, it's not proper—"

"No, but with George like a mad bull ready to gore us, it is proper and right. Maddy, please."

Where did Mary learn about bulls and goring? From books? The image of it frightened him.

"I agree with Alexander that it is not proper. He can guard the house from outside," Madeline said.

Mary stifled a sob. "Maddy, you know best," she said, as if the line were rehearsed. "You always do."

After the meal, Madeline left them alone. Now Alex had to be serious. "Mary," he said, trying to be calm and understanding, "I must tell you that Madeline has shown me the drawing."

Mary breathed in deeply, looked as if she would collapse. "She had no right to do that. Now you will spurn me like a woman on the street."

He held her up, taking her in his arms to steady her. "I'm not the heroic man in the drawing. Are you the woman? Have I mistaken what you want from me?"

"Alex, run away from here. I'm not the woman in the drawing, not inside, and I love you . . . but our marriage never can be. It will destroy you." She sobbed. In his arms, she was as soft as a kitten. He worried that Madeline would overhear.

"Be calm, my darling, I'm devoted to you. I'm comforted to hear what you say about that drawing. Sometime you can tell me more. Only on one thing do I need assurance: you must move away with me from this terrible house."

"I can't. This house is where I stay," Mary said, shaking with grief. He continued holding her and thought he could be patient and convince her after the marriage. His life's goal would be to protect her.

12

"Miss Malkins, are you determined to leave Kingston? This has always been your home. I could rent out the house rather than sell it," Taylor said, the law journals on his shelves surrounding him like sentinels. He was an elderly and gentle lawyer who charged her family low rates for the rare services they required.

"Mr. Taylor, the passing of my mother, following the deaths of my father and brother, makes me determined to leave and start a new life elsewhere. Thank you very much for agreeing to handle my affairs. For the next while, I'll be in Ottawa looking for employment." Eliza took a spare key out of her reticule and placed it on his desk. She did not lower her head toward him, worried he might see through her mourning veil that she had sheared her hair.

"Very well. I'll follow your instructions and mail you the revenue when I sell the house. Before you go, I can provide you an advance payment, which you may need as means for travel."

"I did not expect that. It's a godsend. Thank you so very much Mr. Taylor." She watched him make an entry in a dog-eared ledger and then bend over awkwardly to turn the combination on a safe behind his desk. He counted out the banknotes and handed them to her.

"No need to thank me, Miss Malkins. Your father was a gentleman and a schoolmate friend back in the day."

Eliza did thank him. Then she backed out of the office, reaching behind her to open the door. Taylor looked puzzled, but she thought she succeeded in departing without giving him much cause for suspicion.

She was not in the mood to enjoy the glorious afternoon. Her shoes clicked along the road at a great rate. The uneven brick forced her off balance a few times. Oh, how she preferred men's boots! Luckily, the neighbour woman was not in sight when she reached her own house. She wanted to put her fingers in her ears to block out the sound of the foundry. Her house was spruced up better than most of the dwellings on the street because of her labours, but it would not likely fetch a good price, a small house in the poor part of town.

Once inside, she threw off the veil and got down to work on the remainder of the packing. She had instructed Taylor to sell all the furniture with the house and to donate the clothing to the Anglican Church. She had picked out two stacks of clothing—Pater and Paul's. She packed them into two valises. What about her own clothes? What, in Ottawa, should she be? Alex would likely scoff and send her packing if she became a man. However, what felt right? As a woman, she would never have a lover or a child. As a man, she would be a fraud. She took out a penny—a toss would decide. If Queen Victoria came up, she would be a woman. She tossed. Victoria, that exalted, grief-stricken widow, did come up.

She decided to ignore the coin and become a man. Time to leave the name Malkins behind too. The sun streamed in. She would be Mr. Light . . . no, Mr. Fairlight. Timothy Fairlight, esquire.

⁂

Arriving in Ottawa the following evening, Tim Fairlight checked into Russell House, where he hoped Alex continued to stay. Why had he, Tim, come to Ottawa? Why not Eliza? Even if there was one chance in a million of regaining Alex, he or she wanted to take it, find out about those weird sisters, and determine how they had put a spell on him.

Out on Elgin Street, Tim spotted more stuffed shirts than he expected—no doubt the result of the national capital being established there the year before. Pater, if still alive, would have smashed a jar against the wall. Kingston, according to him, was the rightful choice. Dressed in Pater's Sunday suit, men who had never seen Tim before tipped their hats as he proceeded along Wellington Street. He examined every face, hoping to recognize Alex. He wanted to encounter him by accident instead of arranging a meeting. Would Alex recognize him and be disgusted, or would he think it a grand joke?

Although hungry after the journey, Tim went for a walk to Concession Street and had no difficulty recognizing the Baker residence. Alex was right about mystery hanging about the house like a shroud. The shrubs in the front garden were sparse and poorly tended. Vines strangled the place. Shutters upstairs were open and left to bang against the house in the breeze that had come up. Blinds were closed. Once he caught the silhouette of someone passing by. He went back to Russell House and had a beer and a wretched serving of mutton pretending to be lamb. He spent a restless night in his room.

The next morning, he got up early, dressed in his brother's clothing, and went down to the lobby. He pretended to read a book but kept his eye out. Alex almost eluded him as he darted through the lobby and onto the street. Tim followed, not wanting to startle him, then came up behind him.

"Mr. O'Shea?"

Alex stopped, took a step away and then, staring at his face, said, "Pardon me, but you resemble Eliza Malkins' brother."

Tim nodded.

"You weren't lost at sea after all?"

"I have looked in the glass, and yes, I do look like him. It never occurred to me to dress up like Paul to give Mater a thrill. I could have fooled her into thinking Eliza had gone away, and he would be living with her from then on. I suppose I'll go with to hell for that. You've told me many times that is where you will go. I'll keep you company." Tim would say anything to get Alex out of the mood he was in, which Tim interpreted as desperation.

The ghost of a smile appeared on Alex's lips. "So now you're . . .?"

"Tim Fairlight, and Fairlight I shall stay."

"How? You said nothing of this when you last wrote to me." He brought his hand up to his forehead.

"I have a long tale to tell you, and I would like to hear about your plans. First, do you hate me for going around like this?"

One of the passersby slowed, no doubt curious about Alex, who looked like lightning had just struck him. Tim glared at the nosey person and indicated with his head that he had better move on.

"Eliza—"

"Please, call me Tim Fairlight, at least in public."

"You're here just for today?"

"I'm moving on from Kingston. I don't know if I'll stay here. It depends on whether I can find a job." In fact, it depended on Alex.

Alex bowed his head. "I would hug you," he whispered, "but in this place, it would be scandalous, even dangerous. Eliza Malkins was my best friend, and Tim Fairlight shall become my best friend. God bless you." He looked up and smiled.

They laughed and shook hands like brothers.

"Unfortunately, I have to go now, or Mary will be worried. She goes to bed by seven, and I'll fly back to Russell House right after that. Can we meet in the lobby?"

Tim agreed, although disappointed at having to wait so long. However, he had to scout for job opportunities anyway.

✥

Alex was true to his word and arrived a few minutes after seven. He suggested they take a walk into Lower Town and find a public house, where they could talk.

"Do you truly plan to stay here in this frontier town and make a go of it as a man?" Alex asked as they walked over Sappers Bridge. Clouds threatened to rip open any time. There were no sounds of boats on the canal, only the nightly incantations of the drunken day labourers on the Lower Ottawa side.

"Yes, Tim Fairlight is easier for me. I asked the hotel clerk about foundries, because I worked for one in Kingston. There's one near Shoddy-air—"

"You mean the Chaudière Falls?"

"Didn't I just say that? As for being a man, I don't know what I am, and I could care less. For years I was teased about looking like a man, and I had to swallow my resentment. How could a woman be treated like that? But then, women are treated badly all the time. Do you know that I now feel I truly am a man?" Had Alex given him much thought, or was he wholly taken up with those sisters? Had he changed his mind from what he had expressed in Kingston and in letters?

"I have always thought of you as an ideal woman, brave and honest. How can you abandon that? You've stood up for yourself, and I have tried and failed to help you when you needed it most." What did he mean? That business with Hughes?

Their voices were getting elevated, and passersby were watching. Tim pressed his finger to his lips. They should speak of this later, but he saw that Alex would keep it up.

"I'm a miserable cuss to have as a friend. Bad luck follows me like a shadow. My demons have killed my family and now threaten Mary . . . I have put a gun to my head."

"Alex! You're my best friend. It breaks my heart to hear you talking this way. I see nothing whatsoever fiendish about you. Look at me." Tim stopped, and Alex looked at him in the eyes, deadpan. Did he see Eliza or Tim?

"You gonna start fightin'?" a burly man said, teetering and almost falling under the hooves of a passing horse. "Bring out yer knives. Go to it boys!" he continued after he righted himself.

Tim did not know why Alex started laughing, but he joined in. Not a chuckle but a series of ripping, shaking, choking laughs. "Tim," Alex said, "you got to pull out your pig sticker first."

Tim felt his pockets, shrugged, and pulled out a red handkerchief. "Alas, this constitutes my sole weaponry. I shall have to choke you with it," he said, attempting to be fierce but with a voice quavering with laughter.

"Ahh . . . yer both bloody stuck-up C of E farts," the spectator muttered and moved on. They resumed their laughter, and Alex put his arm around Tim's shoulder.

"Well done, Tim, I need to get work as well. The newspaper won't take us after what happened in Kingston. I'm willing to do manual labor if I can't get a writing job—there's a lot of that here."

Tim felt more relaxed than he had in a long time. "The same for me."

On Rideau Street, they saw the working men, French and Irish, swilling back beer, shouting, and singing.

"Where are you leading me? It looks like a den of iniquity," Tim said.

"I am taking you to a den of iniquity. It's called Grant's Hotel, and there we will find many other gentlemen like the one we met on the bridge. Nevertheless, the drink is good, and there are tasty bits to eat. I'll have to protect you from the alluring ladies, like the one over there making eyes at you." A plump, skimpily dressed tart looked pointedly at Tim and massaged her large bosom.

"Well, this is a first for me," Tim said.

"You better get used to it."

They turned onto York Street. Right then Alex stopped and whispered, although no one was within earshot. "Tim, tonight I'll pour out my soul to you. I hope it won't destroy our friendship. God may not forgive me, and I have no faith in the Fathers of my family religion. Will you, my brave friend, hear me out?"

"Yes, willingly. Alex, I've been waiting a long time for this." Tim took out his handkerchief to wipe away his tears before they went into the tavern. Alex told the waiter that he would pay extra for a private room, where they could talk.

Inside the room, the goings-on of the rest of the tavern were reduced to a dull roar. Both of them picked at their food. Alex asked Tim to tell him first what he had been doing back in Kingston. Tim told him about how, at first through a whim, he tried on male clothing and then, exasperated by the maid's job and hired by the foundry, he had gotten by until he was exposed.

"You're such a brave soul and, I must say, a handsome man."

"Don't think I'll cruise the waters for a mermaid."

"No. But seriously, will the foundry be right for you? The same unfortunate discovery might happen again."

"I doubt it, if I'm careful, although I don't speak French."

"I have an idea . . . ."

"Save that until after you tell me what's been happening here. You're still going to marry that girl?"

"She's not a girl, although sometimes she seems like she's fourteen years old. Eliza—Tim, I'm not in love with her." An astonishing statement!

"Then don't marry her. Come away, and we can make a life together as friends."

"Just listen to me." Alex stared at him. Was it rudeness or a threat? "I need to marry her to protect her. My mother commands me to do it."

He told of how Mary was the reincarnation of his mother, whose death lay on his conscience like the heaviest object in the world. She was weak, sickly, and would surely die if he did not protect her. It was the only way to escape from the devils that had hunted him ever since he caused his mother to drown.

"My friend, you need to see a doctor and escape from the clutch of these witches," Tim said when Alex was finished. Alex folded his arms and looked away from him. Tim had wounded him.

"That's easy for someone like you to say," Alex replied through tight lips. "Someone who is not sensitive to the promptings of the spirit. You had better be quiet and listen to the rest of my story. You may change your mind."

Where did this anger come from? What about their normal, easygoing friendship?

"I'm sorry, Alex. Please continue, if you have more to say. I promise I'll listen and be quiet."

"There's more. At this stage, more whiskey will help." He had already downed two whiskies. Alex went out to the bar and came back, followed by the server. They had eaten little, and they explained that the food was excellent, but they were not hungry.

Alex took a large swallow of whiskey. "I told you about those devils who attacked me in Christian Brothers. God did not save me. I never believed in Him again."

He paused for another drink. Tim wanted to hold him, tell him that all would be well, as if he were Alex's parent.

"I didn't tell you what those devils did. They raped me. Repeatedly. I was bleeding. I'm left with no desire for the act of procreation in marriage."

"Oh, Alex, you've told me so much that my heart is breaking for you. I kept something back from my story that, until now, only my mother knew, and that is so shameful she wanted to keep me closeted. In that part of me where the pee comes, I'm neither a woman nor a man. I'm a freak. My mother examined that part of me when I was four. She tried to remove it, but I wouldn't let her. She kept reminding me about it later. One time I wanted to run away to the circus." Tim's blood froze as he spoke.

Alex nodded slowly. "You're brave and deserve a good life as a woman or a man, your choice. I had no idea, my friend, that you carried a burden heavier than mine." He reached out his hand. Their stories were told.

"Do you want more whiskey?" Tim asked. Of course he did.

Tim went over to the bar. A short brown-haired girl, face painted, came to his side as he waited for the drink. "You're such a handsome man, and you're new here. Do you want company tonight?"

"No, thank you. I'm about to go home," Tim said, feeling quite secure in his new identity and determination. The drink came, and Tim started off with it.

"Are you sure? I can do anything you want," the girl said, following him. Tim ignored her, but at the table, the girl made a motion to sit with the two of them.

"Go away." Tim said. "This is private."

"See? I told you Eliz—Tim. They will come to you like fruit flies," Alex said after another gulp of whiskey.

"So, we're still best friends?"

"You bet . . . till the end," Alex said, slurring his words.

Tim thought he should get Alex back to Russell House and his bed. He downed the rest of his drink. "Right, let's be off," he said.

Alex looked disappointed, but he got up to settle the bill and visit the urinal. Tim was glad he had drunk very little, as peeing with men present would be more than a challenge. They started off silently, swollen with each other's secrets.

As they neared the hotel, Alex stopped. "Oh, I forgot! There's that thing I want to ask you." His voice was loud, and there were pedestrians nearby.

"Can it wait until we get to the hotel?" Tim asked. "I'll come to your room, and you can tell me there."

"Okay, gotta remember, gotta remember," Alex mumbled.

In Alex's room, Tim helped him to the bed. "You can sleep in your clothes tonight, alright?"

"Sure. Do it sometimes. Once in a while on the floor."

Tim made sure Alex was covered by a blanket. As he got close, Alex grasped him by the lapels of his suit. "That other thing, 'portant."

"Are you sure it can't wait until morning?"

"No, I go early in morning . . . should be on guard tonight but may slip on 't. You wanna job?"

"I do, Alex. It's a necessity, and I'll go around tomorrow, starting with the foundry."

"You wanna help me? Mys'try hauntin' me, Baker house." His eyes were bright. He tightened his grip.

"What are you asking, Alex?"

"I talk to Mad'lin in morning. Tell 'er she need butler and you, Furlit, fill the bill."

Alex released him. Was he serious? He looked up at Tim like a little boy.

"I'll help you if I can. Let's talk more tomorrow, my friend," Tim said.

Alex closed his eyes, and Tim extinguished the lamp.

13

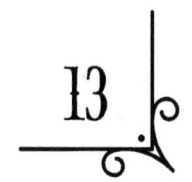

A week later, it was Tim who ushered Alex into the Baker house. This, in itself, was not a surprise, but his appearance in new livery was stunning—a double-breasted, long-tailed coat with gold buttons, white cravat, new shoes shined brightly, hair slicked back. She—he must stop thinking of her as Eliza and as Tim Fairlight instead, or the trick would be undone. Tim must be aware that Madeline had extraordinary hearing. No words could be exchanged between the new butler and the visitor without risk.

Tim took him to Madeline, who rose from her desk, offered her hand, and called him "Alex." Dressed in what looked like a new burgundy gown, she was as elegant as always, and her warm smile led him to think she had good news for him. Or was she smiling like an overfed cat at a bird?

"Alex, you will join me for dinner. Fairlight, please bring us the brandy bottle and glasses." Tim bowed and strode off to carry out his mission.

"Where's Mary?" Alex asked.

"Asleep. I'm afraid our Mary did not sleep at all last night, even with the aid of the laudanum drops. Today she is having spells of crying and cursing. She refuses food and drink."

"Have you called a doctor? She can't go on this way." He got to his feet, ready to run out in search of a physician.

Madeline remained the soul of tranquility. "I know her better than you do. You had better sit down to hear me out if you still want to marry her." Tim carried in the tray with the bottle and glasses. He set it down and poured each of them a drink, made Madeline's fuller than Alex's, received an acknowledgement from his mistress, bowed, and returned to the kitchen, from which odours of roast pork permeated. Alex had not eaten all day, and the first hunger pang came to him. He sat and complied when Madeline offered to clink glasses with him.

"By the way, I'm pleased with Fairlight and am grateful you recommended him. He is not an experienced butler, but he is anxious to please. There's something about him . . . what can I say . . . that fits in with a house that I own."

Strange. She became somewhat like Scheherazade telling one of the tales of the Arabian nights while she spoke of Tim. But there was a twist to the story: it was as if she wanted to establish a male harem somewhere in this cold, musty house.

"I'm pleased that Mr. Fairlight is filling the bill," Alex said. "I think I can safely give over your pistol to him, and he can guard the house. By always having an armed man in the house, you will be safer."

"Let me manage my own household. A servant like Fairlight has no idea how to use a gun. And besides, he has his own duties to keep him occupied. I'll forget what you just said. Let's go on with what we were talking about before." If there was a queen bee in this house, he had most certainly found her. Bees—he should not have thought of them—their honey is sweet, but they swarm like a wake of vultures. He avoided hives.

"Getting back to my future wife, there is no doubt in my mind that she needs to see a doctor." If she could command that he stay on guard then so could he on this one matter.

She raised an eye like a dragon would toward someone walking into her cave, where her treasure lay. "For your information, I have offered, ever since George attacked Mary, to call in a doctor when she is this way. She insists that no man touch her body. 'Kill me first, Maddy,' she screams, and I have real fears. In her state, a doctor might insist on taking her away to an asylum. But just you see, in a few days or a week, she will return to her old self."

Could all of this be Madeline play-acting to get him to attack George? Perhaps. Her moods were as changeable as the dresses she wore.

"Alex," Madeline said, laying her hand on his forearm, "you're the best and only man who has come into Mary's life since Father died. She loves you and will be a good, faithful wife. Knowing that she has been terribly wounded by Uncle George and will likely continue to have these attacks of hysteria, are you still willing to marry her? You must go in with your eyes open and promise to protect her. She is the dearest person in my life, and that is why I need your word."

If he hesitated, it was only because Madeline had given him such mixed messages about Mary. Did she love him spiritually or did she have carnal desires or neither?

"Yes . . . I give you my word," he said at last.

"And now, can you do Mary a favour? She cries and asks that you stay in the house. I appreciate your opinions on propriety, but this is an unusual situation. She will feel so much safer if you stay here, as will I."

How could he refuse? He said he would be pleased to come and stay.

"Good. Your room will be ready in three days. It will be Father's room, on the same floor as Mary's and mine."

Victoria came in looking puzzled at their intimacy. He had seen Victoria and Mary shooting friendly looks at each other, but the maid was intimidated around Madeline.

"Dinner is served," she said.

In the dining room, there were only two place settings. Before he asked, Madeline said, "A tray has been taken up to Mary, even though she refuses to eat."

"Perhaps if I visit her, I can persuade her?" Alex said.

"Oh, I don't know. Even if you turn the food into foolish playthings, she will not open her mouth to let them in." Madeline laughed and took a great swallow of wine.

"Maybe some oinks and snorts from Mr. Piggy will do the trick tonight."

She nearly choked on her wine, and her face reddened. Alex realized he had insulted her. It was too late to recover by telling her that, despite her weight, she was an attractive woman.

"Alex, have dinner with me, and then, by all means, play food games with my little sister," she said grudgingly.

In truth, he felt starved. As they ate, she once again told him of her vision of female captains of industry. She acted out the parts she would play down at the mill. "Quit your squawking, and get those logs through the saw! We're going to beat the record of all our competitors, and you men need to imagine you're parts of a machine, like steam engines pulling trains down the tracks." She stood to issue this oratory, quite filled with brandy. Alex applauded at the end.

"I'm sorry I couldn't convince my editor to print your piece before I left Kingston," he lied.

"Oh, there will be other opportunities," she said, "especially when I charge out into the world. Just you wait."

When they finished the main course, he said he could wait no longer to see Mary. Madeline called Victoria to show him up to Mary's room. At the top of the stairway, Victoria paused. "I have tried so hard to get Miss Mary to eat. I sang her little songs I remember from my childhood. Sometimes I creep upstairs in the night to see if she's sleeping and stay with her if she's not. I'm sorry, Mr. O'Shea, but I can't help her today."

"It's a comfort having you nearby," Alex said, thinking it must be hard for this little maid to carry out covert activities. But he still had doubts about her. Was she not Madeline's secret agent?

Mary lay in bed, her head turned away. She might be sleeping, so he moved a chair next to the bed and a night table, where lay an untouched dinner and a full glass of water. She turned to look at him, and a faint smile came to her face. "Alex, I was afraid you left me," she said in a low, croaking voice. She blinked, and there would have been tears if there had been water left in the well.

"I'm sorry darling. Now I'm here, and here I shall stay."

"Are you still angry with Maddy?"

"No, don't worry your lovely head about that. Madeline and I are friends, and she invited me to stay in the house, starting in a few days."

Her smile became pronounced. "Where will you stay, in the servants' quarters?"

"No, just down the hall from you, in your father's room."

She looked alarmed and shook her head and began to choke. He convinced her to drink. What was it about her father that frightened her so? Alex said he could stay in the hotel if she preferred, but she bowed her head as if in prayer. "Please come, Alex," she said.

"Very well. Now, let's see what we can do with Mr. Beet here."

"No. Not now. I'm not hungry or thirsty. Alex . . .."

"Yes?" he said reaching to hold her hand when it emerged from the bedsheets.

"Last night I talked about things with Maddy, and she said I should tell you before we get married."

"Can you tell me later when you're feeling better?" Alex asked

"No! Now. I lie awake all the night waiting to tell you . . . I don't know if I'm still a virgin. When Uncle George grabbed me, tore off my clothes, and beat me, he . . .."

Rage ripped through him once again. He squeezed Mary's hand so tight she pulled it away and put both hands over her eyes and sobbed. He leaned over, petting her arm. "It doesn't matter," he said repeatedly. But now he would take his revenge on George even if he should hang for it.

"Alex, what I mean to say is that George did not put his stick in the place where women make babies but in the hole behind. It hurt so much that I bled. I was too ashamed to tell anyone for a while, but Maddy suspected, and I told her the truth. She comforted me. No one has a better sister than I do." All this rolled out quickly, as if rehearsed—she had, of course, been thinking of what to say, and he was proud of her for telling him.

Now he could see her harrowing nightmare in his mind's eye. Rage and fear drove all rational thought away.

He did not think he was sickened by the green monster of jealousy. His passion for Mary was not romantic in the sense of taking her innocence away in the wedding bed. He wanted to protect her, and this mission remained. He could protect her from George by getting himself hanged. How happy would that make her? But there was no question that his father would do only one thing if someone had dared to violate his mother that way—reach for his rifle.

He tried once more to get her to drink, and she did have one sip. He had no humour left to tease her into taking a bite of food.

⁜

It fell upon Alex to avenge George's savage assault on Mary's body. If he shot him with witnesses around, he would be hung. If he shot him in private, he would be the first person suspected, as he had already threatened him with a gun. Mary would suffer, starve herself to death. Why wouldn't she let him take her away from Ottawa and that mournful house? Mary wanted to remain bound together with Madeline, as if manacles held them bound to the house their father built.

These familiar thoughts kept roiling in Alex's head during a broken sleep and again in the early morning as he wandered aimlessly along the banks of the Ottawa River down toward the harnessed Chaudière Falls, the heart of Canada's lumber industry. He walked with a ragtag group of workers down an industrial road running east and north and came upon a sign in front of one of the mills, not the largest by any means, "Baker Lumber Company." So, he had come to beard the lion in his den. He checked for the gun. But what could he do?

He saw a door with a sign, "Management Office," and went straight in. His entrance barely interrupted the talk among a small group of men who stood drinking coffee and talking to George Baker. George pointed his finger at Alex. "Is that who I think it is?" he growled, straining his one eye.

Another man in the group turned to look. It was Benson. "I'll show you out, Mr. O'Shea. You have no right to be here."

Before Benson reached him, George spoke up. "No, Hal, let him take a chair and wait until we finish our business." Benson glared at Alex, who found it interesting that George had called him by his given name.

He did not pay much attention to the talk of shanties, the American market, and timber purchased from another mill that went broke. He thought only of what was coming. What lever did he have?

Before long, the men filed out. George took out a pen to sign a document and make notes on others that lay on his desk. Benson came over to stand next to where Alex sat, keeping a close watch on him.

"Now, O'Shea, why have you come?" George asked.

"I—"

"Come closer to where I can see you."

When Alex walked forward, Benson marched in step, keeping just enough distance that he could watch Alex's hands and grab him should he draw a concealed weapon. Did Benson know? Had he collaborated in Mary's despoliation?

Alex went straight to the point. "You, sir, are a villain who brutalized your young niece and made her so sick that she takes neither food nor drink. She is the woman I love and will marry. You'll not get away with your crime. I'll see to that!"

George glared at him with his one eye. Alex saw that Benson was ready to launch himself on him, stopped only by George holding up his hand. The silence was so terrible that he recalled a childhood memory when he had killed a perfectly innocent robin with his slingshot. When he brought it inside, his father was disgusted and, after trying unsuccessfully to revive it, made Alex wait in a chair until he came back and spanked him. It was an omen! He ought to have thought of it before.

George broke the silence. "Mr. O'Shea, you're a liar. I did not hurt one hair on Mary's head. Madeline Baker has deceived you, and you're foolish for believing her."

"I did not hear what you did from Madeline. I heard it directly from Mary, and I believe every word she says."

"Did you? I'm surprised, as I had such a favourable impression of her in the short time I got to know her. Most young women jump aside when they see my blasted face, but she did not. I tell you, she is being forced to tell you lies. I would not put it past that hellcat Madeline to do that." No matter what he said, the evidence against him was overwhelming. The devil peering out of the one eye laughed at Alex.

"Madeline is the one who keeps her alive. I accuse you, the lumber magnate who wants to strip your brother's rightful heirs of all their property and turn them out as paupers!" Alex shouted, wishing he had brought the gun. He held out his fists.

"Think over what I have said," George said. "Despite your anger, it is the truth. Benson, show Mr. O'Shea out."

Alex wouldn't go without stating the plan he had conceived while waiting. Benson took his coat sleeve, but he yanked it away. "You underestimate me. I'm a newspaper man. What the courts have not yet said, the newspapers will, and you will be ruined."

George roared with laughter, sticking out his chin and showing Alex the mangled, blind side of his face.

Alex started to rush forward, but Benson grasped his arm and squeezed tight, forcing him off balance and away from George. Where did Benson get such a grip? "You cannot tangle with me, Mr. O'Shea," Benson said, as if reading his mind. "Before I joined the late Mr. Baker's staff, I was with her majesty's forces in the Crimea."

When they were out in the yard, stared at by workers, Alex turned to Benson. "You once warned me there was evil in that house. What did you mean?"

"I can tell you no more now than I did then, and I give you the same advice—run away from that evil before it destroys you." Benson escorted him to the road and then returned to the management room.

Alex stomped away, stopping once to pick up pebbles and to throw them with all his strength into the Ottawa River until his shoulder and arm ached. His brilliant idea now seemed nothing more than an idle threat. He could not expose the harm done to Mary; it would be the death of her. He had no evidence unless a doctor examined her. Madeline was probably right; Mary would become hysterical. And what credibility did he have after being fired from his last job?

When he was a block away from the Baker house, he saw someone coming toward him. Could it be? Yes, it was Tim. He stopped, looked around to check on the presence of other pedestrians, and watched Tim approach wearing what must be a new coat and a top hat. "What are you doing?" he asked when Tim was within earshot.

"I'm out to procure spirits for the mistress. We need to talk. I have only a few minutes." Tim seemed stiff and formal.

"Good. I know just the place." Alex led him to the same forsaken lot where Benson had taken him a few months before. A man escorting a lady came their way. They passed by, bowing politely.

In the lot, Tim dropped the formality. "Alex, have you ever noticed anything odd about Miss Baker?"

"Many things. She is changeable and dominates others, especially Mary."

"True, but there is another—"

Tim paused as Alex's attention turned to a crow that flew overhead, cawing. He held his breath until the crow passed out of sight.

"What was that?" Tim put his hand on Alex's shoulder.

"Nothing . . . as you were saying?" This was no time to be weak.

"I was saying that Miss Baker is strict toward everyone but me. No matter what I do—and I'm learning the job as I go—she is all smiles and blushes toward me. Sometimes she touches me."

"Where does she touch you?" Yes, once or twice Madeline had been flirtatious toward him as well, but he had never taken it seriously—more often she was angry with him. But with a servant?

"Only on my arms and shoulders so far."

"Does she suspect us?"

"No, I doubt that. There are two other things I have to tell you, and I don't have much time. First, she has been cleaning up her father's room. She told us not to interrupt her while she works on it, a personal task she claims to be overdue. The fire's going all the time, and I suspect she's burning all manner of things."

"It's hard to picture Madeline as a scullery maid," Alex said, musing over an image of her in evening clothes, scrubbing floors and keeping the fire burning.

"Once when she was closeted with Mary, she left the door open, and I went in. It's a haunted kind of room. The strangest sight was a drawing of a naked girl—I think it's Mary when she was younger."

Alex fumed. Did one of the drawing masters do that? If so, why was it in her father's room? Did it excite him? Was he a pervert, or did he see it as art?

"Did the drawing look like an exercise in classical art?"

"No, it was pretty crude. I'd rather not talk about it. I suspect that Madeline destroyed it."

"How about that other drawing I mentioned to you, of Mary and me?"

"No. It could be in Miss Baker's chamber. Only Victoria is allowed to go in there, and she's very tight-lipped about her mistress. I truly must go, but there's something I want to leave with you."

Tim surveyed the lot in each direction and then drew out a handkerchief that contained several pieces of ashy leather. Alex held them up to the light. The pieces were stained with something.

"That, I would suggest, is blood. If I'm not mistaken, these were parts of a riding crop. The leather is cut just like one Pater showed me that had been in our family. He told me that I could use it on bad boys who bother me too much." Tim smiled.

"What do you think it means? If it's human blood, does it belong to anyone we know—wait a minute, George might have used it on poor Mary. But why would he leave it there, and why would Madeline want to dispose of it?" He felt another impulse to run out and kill George. Still, he was confused.

"You put yourself at risk going into that room," Alex said, putting the handkerchief back into his pocket.

"I only wish to be of service, sir," Tim said, bowing, withdrawing, indicating he had to be on his way. Eliza had become a manly man.

Alex got an idea. The detective in his novel was shallow. He would rewrite it and use his friend as the model for his leading character.

14

Tim was learning the role of butler—supervising the work of Victoria, who slept in the room next to his in the servants' quarters, and of Cook, a gruff woman who bustled in and out, producing average meals in the overheated kitchen. Beyond this he had to manage the ordering and delivery of food and beverages, keep the house accounts, order cabs, and take care of any repairs needed in the house or work in the garden.

He rarely had a chance to talk with Alex, as his time was circumscribed, including changing shifts with Victoria in watching over Mary, who was like a child in every way except her age. Madeline had ordered that Mary be guarded every minute of the day. When Mary was ill or having daytime naps, Tim contemplated her diminutive face, her pert, little nose and mouth, in every way like a doll he once had until Mater threw it out, dismissing her child's tears by saying she was too old for such things. What a complete contrast Mary was to herself when she was a girl and a woman! Alex told her that his desire was to protect Mary, and that was understandable but to marry her and couple with her on the wedding bed? It would be like breaking china apart, shattering the doll into pieces and destroying Alex as well. Besides, he still had fantasies about being with Alex himself. This little doll was in the way.

Another difficult part of his day was standing by while Madeline went about her paperwork. She liked to read excerpts from letters she had received or was writing. Out of context, they meant little, but she wanted Tim to agree with her opinions. He had learned to bow and say, "Yes, Miss Baker." Sometimes, after a period of silence, he would glance and see her eyes were on him with what appeared to be a look of desire. He always turned away, and she would hum a little tune that he did not recognize before she returned to her work.

The secrets of the house were not coming to light quickly. A week had gone by. Victoria was a quiet, nervous young woman who suppressed things and did not converse with him in anything other than work topics, no matter how hard he tried to be jovial and encourage her. Perhaps the previous butler, Benson, had made advances on her, and she was determined not to get into the same situation. Or could she have sensed his feelings about Mary?

One night before Alex moved in, Tim prowled around the main floor, waiting to see Alex come out to his guard position on the opposite side of the street. Victoria came rushing down the stairs, bearing a lamp. She was sobbing, her clothes in disarray, very unlike her usual prim appearance.

Tim stood near the entry to the servant's quarters and apologized for making Victoria start. "Whatever is the matter? Has Miss Mary taken a turn for the worse?"

"She is asleep . . . I don't want to talk."

"Talk would be good for you. I see you're distressed," Tim said.

"No, I don't know you well enough. Hal would have known what to do about it."

"You mean Mr. Benson, my predecessor?"

"Please, just let me go to bed," she said. She pushed past him and went directly to her chamber.

What could it mean? What would Benson have done? He went to the salon, still in the dark, pushed aside one edge of the curtain, and saw that Alex had taken up his position on the street. He heard Madeline walking upstairs. It would be too dangerous to go out and converse with Alex about this curious incident. His friend looked cold out there. Why didn't he put on extra layers of clothing? He watched Alex dig around in his pocket, remove a flask, and take a long swallow. The liquor would warm him, but hopefully this would not be another night of excess.

15

Evening came, and Alex was now installed in the father's bedroom. It was sparse, with no art on the wall and no clothing in the wardrobe or in the chest of drawers. He writhed in the late William Baker's dressing gown, which Madeline had bestowed on him and insisted he wear in the evenings. "This gown cost Father a fancy sum, but now it is destined for you—or the rag man," she had said. He fancied that, wearing the gown, he might finally understand more about the house's secrets, especially in this chamber, the scene of so many sighs and memories.

Alex went down the stairs and checked the de Sade collection in the library. Madeline had taken down another volume and placed the one from the desk back on the shelf. Now that he was residing in the house, he had a chance to play detective along with Tim. Once he had checked out de Sade, he searched the Dickens collection on a lower shelf. *Sketches by Boz* might amuse Mary when it was his turn to come into her bedroom after Victoria prepared her for sleep. They talked and, lately, even in her weak state, she became excited about the wedding, which was only three days away.

Alex suggested she needed to hear him read, or she would never fall asleep. Light humour brightened her thoughts.

Returning to the drawing room, he found Madeline working furiously at her desk, crumpling a page and throwing it over her shoulder. She glanced up. "The law is an ass," she muttered.

He picked up the paper and returned it to her. She directed him to throw it into a wastepaper basket. "I see you've been reading Mr. Dickens's Oliver Twist, Madeline."

"I read that book years ago, and that is the only good line I remember from it."

"Let me not disturb you," he said and went to sit in the salon, waiting his turn to go up to Mary. Madeline soon came along. "Goodnight, Madeline. I hope you have a pleasant sleep," he said.

"The same to you," she replied as she clomped up the stairs. He would see Madeline again when she came into Mary's bedroom to administer the laudanum.

After Victoria slipped down the stairs like a timid rabbit he ascended, listening to the creaking sounds as he went. The house was not all that old, compared with the ancient buildings in England he had visited while studying there. Still, it pretended to be in the grand old-fashioned style. He wondered if the builder spared extra expenses. Doors needed an extra push to close, most windows could not be opened, and breezes found chinks to creep through.

Mary lay propped up, as usual, looking like a beautiful doll, her blue eyes and little chin pointed at him. However, there was a line on her forehead.

"My darling, what's happening?" he asked.

"I wish our wedding was tomorrow. Another three days is too long."

"The days will fly by. Don't worry. Now, let me read you more from Mr. Dickens. Remember how much you liked A Christmas Carol? You will have pleasant dreams."

"Wait, I have something for you." She struggled to move to the edge of the bed, opened the drawer of her night table, and drew out two tarnished objects, which had been hidden under a handkerchief.

He saw spots of red on the bedsheet where she was lying and on her nightdress. "Mary, you've been bleeding. It looks fresh. What happened to your back?" She frowned and covered up with the top sheet.

"I was picking at my old wound, that's all. Victoria will clean it up in the morning." She was terrified and looked at the drawing of her father across from her bed. He knew he could not get her to say more.

He examined the objects she had handed him. "These are cufflinks."

"Yes, they were precious to Father. See? They have his initials on them, W.B. I took them from Father's room when Madeline wasn't looking. Will you wear them on our wedding day?"

"You little sneak. You must be proud of yourself. Yes, of course, I'll be proud to wear them." A lie. Why should he be branded with Baker's initials? And why was he wearing this dressing gown? It had revealed no secrets.

He pretended to be delighted with the cufflinks, and it brought a little smile to Mary's lips. The blood had looked fresh to him and more than would come from scratching a scab. How could he investigate? He put the cufflinks in his pocket. Perhaps in the morning Tim could enlighten him about the blood from Mary's back.

He started reading from the beginning, "Our Parish." Every so often he glanced at Mary, who again had the worry mark on her forehead and whose eyes wandered about the room. She paid no attention to him. He heard the creaking of the house, and there was that sound again on the wall from Madeline's room. Could Victoria be cleaning again? About halfway through the second chapter, Mary tugged his arm and asked him to come close. Whatever could it be?

"Alex, promise me. As soon as we're married, take me away from this . . .." She could not find the word. He saw this was not pain or childishness but fear of something imminent.

"Of course, I'll take you away. It's what I've always wanted. Oh, I'm so relieved you have finally come to your senses. Madeline—"

"You mustn't say a word to her, and please keep your voice down. We need to leave soon. Soon! And can we go far away?"

He was shocked. The questions about the house circled in his head and demanded to come out. "Why? Are you afraid of Madeline?"

"She would make me obey her and stay. It must be a secret."

"But you're a woman in your own right. It's your decision who you marry and where and when you go." He had raised his voice without thinking about it.

"Shhhh . . . we mustn't say more. She will be here soon with my sleeping potion. Please, start reading that book from the beginning." Her eyes were wide with fear, her jaws clenched.

He returned to the opening pages. Mary closed her eyes. When he finished the first chapter, he stopped. She reached over to him. "Go on. I like it now."

He was a few pages into the second chapter when Madeline came to the door, glass in hand. "Why does Victoria not prepare and serve the sleeping medication?" Alex asked. "It would spare you the bother."

Madeline looked as calm as a bishop, making him feel like a little boy. "This is a strong medicine, and I have been reducing the drops. Only three of them now. In the wrong hands, something terrible might happen. And with you lurking here, this is the only time I have for privacy with Mary."

She looked like she expected an apology, but he wasn't about to offer one. "Goodnight, Mary. I'll see you in the morning," he said, looking at her starved, worried face and avoiding Madeline's. He felt her anger in the air, and it nearly caused his reservoir of rage to boil over.

In the father's dreary bedroom, he thought about Eliza—Tim. They had no opportunity that day to talk together, as Madeline tracked their movements. What new discoveries had Tim made? For once, Alex limited his nightly whiskey to two glasses, with the intention of getting up early in the morning and arranging a rendezvous with his friend. While drinking, he heard voices in the hall, and he went out to investigate. Madeline and Tim were out there.

"I'm sorry, Miss Baker; I thought I heard you calling me," Tim said as he descended the stairs.

"I have a pretty loud voice. Don't mistake it again," Madeline said.

And she has sharp ears, Alex thought. He must talk tomorrow with his spy.

⁘

At dawn, the sky was red, and Alex thought of the sailor's warning as he donned his suit. He slipped down the stairs and startled Victoria, who was dusting.

"Cook will be here in an hour, sir," the timid creature said, looking as if she had been spanked.

"I'll be going out for a walk before the rain comes," Alex said.

Victoria bowed her head. She was nervous in his presence and soon went into the drawing room.

Mary habitually woke late in the morning after a restless night, so this was Alex's opportunity. He went directly to the servants' quarters and found Tim polishing a pair of Madeline's shoes. Other pairs were lined up.

"She has quite a collection," Alex said.

Tim looked amused as he set down the brush. "Have you noticed she changes them frequently, and every time her foot slides into a shoe, it needs polishing?"

"Let's slip out for a half hour," Alex said. "We won't be missed."

They went out through the servants' entrance and walked until the house was out of sight. No one was around that they could see.

"Is something bothering Victoria? I met her when I came down—" Alex stopped as he spotted a grey cat cleaning itself up the street. Black ones were to be avoided entirely, but other dark shades could also be evil.

"Oh, she's dreading the thought of going up to her ladyship's room to help her dress," Tim said. "It's interesting; you should observe her nervousness. When she came down to the servants' quarters one night, she was crying and refused to let me console her, just went to her room and did not want to have the tea the servants customarily drink together. It must have been quite the reprimand."

"I can't picture her making a mistake," Alex said. "She is such a meticulous, caring little woman. Actually, I was hoping she told you if she had seen blood on Mary's sheets or night dresses. There was some last night." Alex told him how Mary had dismissed it as blood from scabs.

Tim's eyes widened. "Poor Mary. She's a captive in the house. Now, it could be as Mary says. I have tried to get Victoria to confide in me, but no luck so far. I'll try again."

"Our big challenge is coming. Mary wants me to take her away from the house soon and to keep it a secret from Madeline. I'll need you to help, my friend."

He was surprised that Tim's immediate reaction was to frown, though he agreed to help. "You can count on me. I'll be glad to get away too."

Alex looked for the cat. It was still cleaning itself, and someone was coming their way, a man. "Yes, I would venture to say a storm will come before evening," Alex said, looking up at the sky.

"I hope not," the man said as he passed. Neither of them recognized him.

Alex saw the cat coming their way. He told Tim it was time they returned.

Close to the house, Tim leaned in close. "Alex, I know you love Miss Mary, but do you truly know her? Only Madeline has the power to delve into Mary's thoughts."

"I will get to know her in the course of time." Alex watched the cat, deciding it was not an omen. He felt secure and lucky at last.

⁂

Alex checked his pocket watch—eleven-fifteen in the morning. This was late, even for Mary, to sleep in. He sat in the salon, keeping an eye out for her coming down the stairs. He listened to Madeline's curses as she went through papers at her desk in the drawing room, and he thumbed through a recent *British Whig* that Tim brought him, reading about a civil war in Japan.

Victoria came rushing down the stairs so fast she almost fell. Alex jumped up and went to her, but she pushed him aside and went into the drawing room. He followed.

"Miss Baker, I looked in on Miss Mary. She is sound asleep, but there are smells of her being ill. Her pillow and face are covered with sick."

Madeline gathered her skirts and raced up the stairs, with Alex following. She shouted at him to stay back and went to the bed, approaching it reverently. Mary's vomit-covered face was turned toward the door. Her eyes were closed. Madeline felt her hand. "Victoria! Get Fairlight to run to Dr. Brown's. He's on Sparks Street. Keep knocking if the door is locked, and demand of whoever answers that the doctor come immediately. It's an emergency."

"Surely, I can help," Alex said. He felt like his blood had gone down to his feet and filled his boots. He had missed the portent—unless it was the grey cat—but perhaps this was only a minor malady. He stepped toward the bedside.

"This is a family matter," Madelaine said, pointing to the door. "Wait out there, and close the door when you go! It may be infectious."

"I'm her fiancé. She needs comforting. I don't care about the risk." He took another step toward the bed.

"You're not yet her husband and supreme commander. When I say 'no,' I mean it!"

"When Mary wakes, she will want me. Let's try to wake her."

"She is not conscious," Madeline said.

Alex felt himself reddening, mouth slavering, eyes glaring. Madeline gave him a shove with all her weight. He nearly tumbled. When he was out in the hall, she slammed the door.

Alex paced the floor. Victoria came back from her errand and cowered, waiting to hear if her mistress would ask her in. Alex heard Madeline opening and closing Mary's drawers. What was she looking for? Before long, he heard Tim's breathless voice. Following him up the stairs was a tall, dour, balding man, who carried a large rectangular bag. Madeline opened the door. The doctor looked at Mary, felt for a pulse.

"I'll need a few minutes alone to examine the patient," he said to Madeline.

In the hallway, Alex kept well away from Madeline. Victoria bent over, taking out a handkerchief to hold over her eyes. Madeline stayed near the door, as if she could peer through the wood to see what was going on inside. Tim stood next to Alex. It was not long before the doctor opened the door with a somber expression and closed it behind him.

"Who is the patient's next of kin?"

"I'm Mary's sister," Madeline said.

"Tell me about Mary's condition—I'm her fiancé and I should be included," Alex said.

"I want to talk in private. Do you have a room?" the doctor asked, looking confused because of the rift between the two of them.

"My room is here. We can talk privately. Alexander, you will be informed," Madeline said.

"How dare you?" Alex said. He felt like hitting her.

"This is no time for squabbles," the doctor said, frowning at Alex and then turning to Tim. "Please ensure no one enters the patient's room while I'm absent."

"Christ!" Alex shouted. He went to smash his fist against the wall, but Tim deftly caught his arm, pulled it back, struggled with him, and then draped his own arm around Alex.

"You ought not smash the plaster, Mr. O'Shea."

"I've lost her. Innocence cannot strive in this world of devils!"

Victoria looked at Alex as if he were a monster. She seemed desperate to run away.

"Let's wait until the doctor comes out. If you don't mind, sir, I'll keep you company," Tim said, giving him a hug and then remaining with his arm around Alex.

It was not a man who hugged him but his friend Eliza. Under that decent livery was the body of a woman—he would never regard her as a freak, even if she said that of herself.

Madeline and the doctor were a long time conferring, their voices lowered. When they emerged, Madeline looked askance at Tim, so close to Alex. She asked Tim to see the doctor out and then dismissed Victoria. When they were alone, Alex stood like a statue looking at the wall. Madeline placed her hand on his shoulder. With her weeping and shaking, he could not refuse her placing her body against his, wrapping her arms around him. "I'm so sorry, dear Alex, but Mary has passed away. I have been rude to you because of worry about dear Mary."

"You want me to leave now?" Alex said.

"No, no. Please stay here while Mary is above ground. That would have comforted her. Victoria and I will clean and prepare her, and then you may sit and watch over her. Please."

"Very well," he said. He refused to console her with any other words.

16

Tim woke in the dark. Where was he? Oh yes, on the divan in the salon, where he had been cleaning up spills from Alex and Madeline's late-night brandy spree. Two days until Mary's funeral.

What was that sound? The clinking of something metal. It came from upstairs—was there an intruder? George? Hearing footsteps in the upstairs hall, he felt his way to the door of the servants' stairs, still watching the foot of the stairway as a dark lantern shone on the stairs and someone came down. The figure carried a long bag. Quite a large figure. Not Alex and not likely Madeline, unless she had dressed in something entirely different from her usual habit. He heard the person cautiously opening the locks. He went back to the window and saw the figure moving down the street.

He threw on a coat, went outside, and used his own key to lock the door behind him. Concession Street was deserted except for, down about a block and in toward the river, the dark figure. He ran after it. There it was again, now turning west. He followed, not too closely, and walking quickly rather than running, so as not to stand out if the person looked back. Some gentlemen who had taken much to drink were talking outside a tavern on Sparks Street, but the figure went past them, and so did Tim, even though someone hailed him as "Spratt, my ol' pal." He ignored the comment and kept his eye on the dark figure.

When the person reached Sapper's Bridge, he or she stopped and swung around. Surely, the person could see Tim, but he still could not make out who it was. Tim wobbled and bent over, muttering, pretending to be a guzzler who had lost a coin on the ground. When he looked up again, the person was going over the bridge into Lower Town.

Now Tim was worried. He knew about the lowlife Irish and French who inhabited parts of Lower Town. What if Madeline or Alex had been attacked in the house and lay injured or worse? He had deserted his post.

He ran back to the Baker house, removed his shoes, and crept up the stairs and along the hall. All was quiet. He had oiled the hinges and handles recently, so he could open doors without a sound.

He opened Alex's door and heard him snoring. He lay almost sideways on the bed. Best to let him sleep.

He suspected Madeline to be a light sleeper. She had already caught him once sneaking upstairs, and a second time would be a firing offence. All he could say this time was that he had heard strange noises and needed to ensure himself she was safe. Inside the room, a lamp was on, and the air was heavily perfumed. Clothing was strewn on the floor. The bed was still made, and no one was lying in it.

So, the figure had been Madeline. Why all this secrecy, and where had she gone?

A mirror was askew, and he spotted a crack in the plaster behind it. He went over, thinking perhaps temperamental Madeline had thrown something and damaged it. He would be called upon to either arrange for it to be fixed or to do the job himself. When he moved the mirror aside, he discovered it was not a crack. It was a fist-sized hole that went right through the thick wall between Madeline's and Mary's bedroom. The hole was not recent, as the plaster had yellowed. It must have gone back to when Madeline and Mary were girls. Did they communicate with each other through this secret portal? He squeezed his hand through and felt something move on the other side. If he remembered correctly, a portrait of the father was hanging in Mary's chamber at that location. If the mirror was moved, Madeline could hear everything going on in Mary's bedroom.

He must keep the secret to himself. If Alex knew that Madeline had overheard his last, confidential conversation with Mary, he might kill himself.

❖

On the eve of Mary's funeral, night fell on the Baker house. Tim was the only person moving about, ferrying large bottles of liquor and caddies of food to the inmates, who had little more than one word to say to him. Brandy bottle and a selection of chocolates to Madeline. Whiskey bottle and biscuits to Alex. Water and dinner remains to Victoria, who lay abed and had not taken food or drink all day. Cook cleaned the kitchen before leaving, so Tim decided to do Victoria's job and tidy the salon and drawing room.

In the drawing room, he cleaned the top of Madeline's desk. She had been working at the desk frequently since her foray into Lower Town. When Tim had approached, she turned over the paper she had been working on. He had checked the desk drawers before. Now nothing seemed to have changed. He took out the de Sade book. It was the same volume, but as he flipped through it, a piece of paper slipped to the floor, landing face down. It must have been the bookmark. He picked it up to put it back in place. When he turned it over, to his surprise, he saw a lewd drawing of a young woman, not Mary, who lay on what looked like grass, naked and with legs open wide and a look of sexual craving on her face. Impulsively, Tim closed the book and put the drawing in the inside pocket of his coat. Something to show Alex, who might recognize the girl. It was time to visit the mistress one last time before turning off the lamps and going to bed.

His knock on the door was answered by a slurred voice. "Please, come in . . . dear Fair . . lit." He opened the door slowly and saw her primping before her mirror with a glass of brandy in hand. She wore only a night dress with the buttons half done up. She started toward him, staggering.

He hurried over and took her arm, helped her to the bed. She spilled some of the brandy on the covers. He offered to take her glass, saying perhaps she had drunk enough.

"Nonsense. I deserve to be tipsy. Fetch the bottle, and a bring a glass for yourself."

What should he do? The wise thing for a butler would be to convince her to lie on the bed and make his retreat. But he was also a spy. Madeline might reveal something he could tell Alex. With Mary's passing, Alex had said nothing to him about his detective job being over. So, he did exactly as she asked. She gulped her brandy while he sipped.

"I have not had the opportunity to extend my sympathies on the loss of your sister," he said.

Madeline leaned over to rest her head on his shoulder. "I'm alone in the world. I was Mary's guiding star. The light has gone out. Men have made overtures to me, but I turned all of them away because of my mission to save Mary . . . and . . . can I tell you?"

"Yes," he said, putting his arm around her, expecting she would throw it off and say it was improper, but she snuggled closer to him. That was fine so long as she did not search his suit pockets. "Ottawa is a rough place. Men from Toronto or New York will be more to your liking," he continued.

"I need to explain something to you. All men are so gross that I like women more. I even go across the River . . . but leave that. There are some exceptions. Some men are different—like you." She kissed him.

"Mistress," he protested, "I think you have had too much to drink. I'm your servant, and I bid you goodnight."

He attempted to rise, but she held him back, weeping. "You're a servant whose role is to obey," she said in a weak voice. "Now go into my closet and take out an easel covered by a cloth. Don't take the cloth off until you set it in front of me."

Tim suspected what it was. Mary's drawing still existed! Now, here was something. The closet was in shambles, underclothes lying around, half-filled liquor bottles. He carried the easel out, as she requested, setting it up close to the bed.

"Now, shut your eyes tight, pull off the cloth, and come toward me. I'll guide you to your seat." Again, the good servant followed orders. She helped him to sit directly beside her, so close he felt her body warmth.

"Keep your eyes closed until I say 'three.' One, two, three!" she sang out like a child.

"What?" Tim said, trying to move away from her. She clasped her arms around him.

"You have some spongy places under your coat. What kind of shirt do you wear?"

"The ordinary kind. I assume that drawing is Mr. O'Shea and your sister? It's shameful."

Madeline softened and began to sob. "Yes, I was even more shocked than you when my sister showed it to me. This was supposed to be his gift to her. He brought in a villainous man—I don't remember his name, French I think—to draw a portrait of the two of them together. O'Shea said I should not come into the room during the work, as it would disturb the artist. When I asked to see it later, he refused. But Mary told me O'Shea planned to hang it over the fireplace when he opened up our house as a bordello, and she showed me where the painting was."

"He is represented like a god here while Mary—"

"Is a lustful whore. You know she was never that way. I have so few images of her that I sometimes come here and look at it, outraged, and I blush to admit . . .."

"Go on."

"I let it do what he intended by it. I feel lustful," she said, running her hand down his body. He tried to hold her off, but she was like a wildcat. She reached his groin and groped his genitals before he decided to get rough and push her away. She fell back on the bed, bumped her head on the frame.

"You're a freak! Get out of my house before I shoot you!" she shouted so loudly that everyone in the house must have heard.

"I'll take my leave now. Please, don't attempt to rise," he said and went out her door, where he saw Alex standing in an old-fashioned nightgown, wavering in his drunken state.

"What the hell, Eliza?"

"I'm Fairlight. You must have had too much to drink, Mr. O'Shea," Tim said, equally loud, and then stepped toward him. "Go to bed. Mary's funeral is tomorrow." He wanted to say more, but Madeline could overhear everything.

Tim went downstairs, fetched his few possessions from the servants' quarters and said goodbye to Victoria, who was out of her room, shivering, a blanket clutched around her, probably wondering whether or not Armageddon had arrived.

He went out on the street and looked up at the house before heading downtown. There were more secrets to be ferreted out of that mournful place, but now he was at a significant disadvantage.

17

Upon waking, Alex had a terrible headache. He felt like he was in limbo. It was the day when Mary would go under the ground. What was that disturbance during the night, when Eliza seemed like a stranger to him?

He searched for his pocket watch. It lay under a chair. He must have thrown it there. Ten in the morning. Four hours from now, the funeral would take place.

After a hasty wash, he put on a suit that was not as dirty as the one he wore the day before and went downstairs. Madeline came to him. Her breath was sour.

"You look as bad as I feel. Why don't we go into the drawing room for brandy before we eat?" she said.

Because of that room's associations with Mary, he would not go there. He remained standing in the hall, his hands in his pockets. He reached under his coat, withdrew the gun from its holster and, grasping it by the barrel, held it out to Madeline.

"What's this? I need you to guard me, especially now. Mary would have demanded it. Besides, something new and frightening has come up. We need to talk. You just sit here in the salon, and I'll pour you a brandy."

"No. Please, just tell me now," Alex said.

"Very well, have it your way. I have been frightened out of my wits every moment of the night and day in this house. George has continued to threaten me. Thank you for guarding me during the most vulnerable hours. I have two things to tell you. First, I have hired a guard who will be here full time and accompany me wherever I go."

"That will be a relief for you. I'm glad to hear it. Has he started already?"

"No, he cannot leave his current position until the end of next week. And, there is a second thing. Mr. Ditchling told me that George has issued an ultimatum on reaching a settlement. He demands that I meet him at eight o'clock on Monday night at Ditchling's office."

"That's only three days from Mary's funeral. Is he not aware you're grieving?"

"Ditchling said I must come. He will send a clerk from his office to protect me. I know what this could mean though. One of George's henchman will come to this house and break down a set of shutters and a window to come inside. He will shoot me when I come home, and George will have an alibi. Alex, I know this house makes you sad, but could you stay here and protect me, just from seven until nine on Monday? Please?" Madeline went down on her knees and looked up at him, tears streaming down her face.

"Poor Madeline. I'll be moving back to the hotel today after the funeral, but I'll be at your door by seven on Monday and prevent anyone from breaking in," he said, placing his hand on her shoulder. She rose and wrapped herself around him. He let himself go as limp as a slug.

"And until the guard is here, you will carry the gun and keep watch from the street?"

"Yes." What was she up to? But this way, he could keep an eye on nightly comings and goings for a few more days.

"Mary lost a true treasure in you," she said.

18

They were finishing the funeral when Tim approached the cemetery. The first snow of the fall was coming down in clusters, which melted shortly after they landed. The trees were coated white. Tim wore a navy uniform that had belonged to his brother. He saw the snow-covered dresses and suits of the mourners who, by turn, scooped up scant handfuls of pebbly clay and threw them down into the earth. Immobile Alex teetered at the edge of the grave, head bowed and hat removed, his hair white with snow. Tim stood well away, by another cluster of graves, the Sanderson family. A man was nearby who he thought at first was visiting these other graves but, noticing his missing eye, he realized it was the dastardly George. With what Alex had told him, Tim ought to go and find a spade to hit the man on the back of his head. But what was this? Tears streaming down his face from his good eye and falling onto his suit. Tim offered him a handkerchief, which he accepted.

"Did you know the deceased?" Tim asked, perhaps too directly. George must have been curious about him the same way.

"Mary, my dear niece, was taken away before her time," he said.

"I'm sorry to hear about your loss," Tim replied. "How did she die, if I may ask?"

"Some say she just stopped eating and became one of those fasting girls you read about in the newspaper. I think she was plain unhappy. Her father was mean to her, and her sister took over his evil ways."

"Could you not help?" Tim felt like he was going too fast and too far. George looked wary. "I'm sorry. It's none of my business," Tim added.

"Why are you here?" George asked.

Tim thought about telling him that he had come to visit the grave of his great uncle, William Sanderson, but that would cut short the discussion. Why not tell him the truth?

"I was briefly the butler in the Baker household until Miss Baker dismissed me, for no reason that I could determine."

"You don't say! Well, I'm not surprised at that madwoman's behaviour. My brother drummed it into her."

Now that Tim had George's full attention, perhaps he could uncover a secret.

"How did you get the butler job?"

"In Kingston I had a slight acquaintance with Alexander O'Shea. Recently, I was discharged from the navy, arrived in this town, and went looking for work. He put forward my name to Miss Baker."

"That man!" George said, pointing at Alex. "He confronted me twice, the first time with a gun in his hand. What do you say to that?" For the first time, he looked fierce, American Civil War ferocious.

"That surprises me. When I was at the house, he was always peaceful, but I can't naysay your word, sir. He is, as I said, an acquaintance."

George softened. "If you're out of work and not averse to getting yourself dirty, you can come and see me about a job. I'm George Baker, and my mill is down by the falls." He held out his hand. His grip was firm, and Tim also tightened his hand. The few seconds of pain seemed to be a ritual for men.

"Timothy Fairlight," Tim replied.

"When you come around, you might strike up a parlay with Benson, your predecessor at my brother's crazy house," George said as he turned to go. "No going public with it though." With that, he made his way to Coburg Street.

Mary's ceremony was over. Two husky workers hovered with shovels, ready to cover her up. Alex was on his knees at the edge of the grave. A little push, and he would fall in. Madeline walked over like the queen of the ball and reached down to lift Alex's arm and take him away. Tim hoped that Alex would throw her into the grave, but he shook off her hand, stayed where he was, and Madeline glided ceremoniously to a waiting coach. The gravediggers stepped up to the pit and began shovelling. Alex shouted at them to stop.

Weaving around other graves, Tim came up to Alex and stood by his side. Alex glanced at his trousers. "Leave me in peace, whoever you are. Can't you see I'm mourning?" he growled, not shifting his gaze from the partially-covered coffin.

"It would be better if you came away and talked, my friend."

Alex started and tilted forward. Tim stopped him from going over the edge.

"Tim . . .."

"Tim Fairlight, your friend, who you have difficulty recognizing."

"Where were you today? I looked for you?"

"There's a reason. I'll tell you when we're away from here."

When Alex was on his feet, he panicked, his eyes crazy, his limbs shaky. Tim pointed to a bench not far from the grave.

As soon as they were a few steps away, the gravediggers recommenced their work. "You ever see the like of that before?" one of them muttered,

"You're a stripling in this here business," the other replied. "By the time your beard is down to your knees, you'll see enough shades of grief that nuthin' will surprise you."

Tim brushed the snow off the bench before they sat down.

"I ought to be down there with her," Alex said. "That's another wonderful soul lost to this world, because I didn't act when there were . . .. You better leave me Tim or Eliza or whoever you are, for I'm an albatross that sinks every good vessel. I have a gun. Hell is calling out my name, summoning me."

Tim put his arm around him. "I'm here and will advise you. You know I'm your friend."

Alex pointed at the uniform, "You're your brother again."

"Yes, I thought this was a day to stop being the butler and to become a navy man. I believe the butler position is open. Do you want to apply?" He had to say something to get Alex out of his desperate mood. The ghost of a smile appeared on Alex's lips.

Tim continued, "There is detective work yet to be done. I'm no longer employed by Madeline. Later, I'll tell you why and also about what a man I met said to me. Do you promise to do one thing for me? Keep an eye on what's going on in that house. If not, I'll parade naked in front of the parliament buildings and the newspaper office, so everyone will know I'm a freak."

Tim felt like he had a child in his arms. Better to get him curious than to leave him in the slough of despond.

"What did you find out?"

"Later, in good time. I don't want to hear any more talk about you being the cause of Mary's death."

"Money will run out before long."

"Oh, that's the least of our worries. I have a lead on a job, and we'll rent a shack. Later, we'll move on if you want."

19

At seven on Monday evening, Alex arrived at the Baker House, eager to get this gremlin of a place off his shoulders, resolved that this would be the last time, and cheered somewhat by the day he had with Tim and their plan to become, to the world, two odd bachelors living together.

Madeline let him in. "I have set out some cold cuts, bread, and whiskey for you in the kitchen," she said, putting on her boots.

"Where's Victoria?"

"Away. She's been requesting to visit her family in Sussex, and I permitted her to go today."

"It must be lonely for you."

"Why, yes, it is, my lovely boy." She grasped him and kissed him on the lips. "Now go into the kitchen while I straighten my corset. I can't be in company with naughty parts of my body hanging out."

Standing by the kitchen door, he heard her shuffling around, followed shortly by the firm closure of the outside door. She was off without using her keys to lock the door. He rushed to the front window and caught a glimpse of her walking stiffly down Concession Street. Why alone? She had said a clerk from the lawyer's office would accompany her.

He ran up the stairs and tried the door to Madeline's room. It was locked. In all the time he had spent in the house, he had never heard Madeline turning the key. He looked at the floor. Sawdust not fully cleaned up. The lock was shiny new. A locksmith must have come that day.

He went through other rooms, looked in drawers, closets, under beds, and behind curtains. He went down to the drawing room. The de Sade book was no longer in the desk drawer. It was back up with the other volumes in the library.

Mary's room was last. He opened the door. It looked just as it had excepting for Mary in the bed. He couldn't go in, never again. Her privacy had been invaded too many times. He closed the door and went sorrowfully down to the kitchen and started in on the whiskey. Madeline was supposed to return within two hours.

Nine o'clock came and went. Alex looked at his pocket watch at least every five minutes. Five minutes after ten, when the hour and minute hands on the watch looked foggy, he heard the latches turning. He staggered out of the kitchen.

"How's . . . was it?" he asked.

"Nothing was achieved at the meeting, just as I suspected. It went on and on and on. George threatened and had a lawyer, who was another villain. It was a waste of my time. But how about you? Did you have any intruders?" She removed her coat, revealing her low-cut dress.

"No . . . I heard none. How come Mr. What's His Name didn't send a man?"

"Mr. O'Shea, you're drunk. You better get to bed and sleep it off."

Alex wandered toward the stairs.

"No! You're no longer a guest here. Go to wherever you're staying, and leave me in peace. I need to sleep without being disturbed. Here, take your coat." She opened the closet door and reached into his coat pocket. She pulled out the cufflinks, staring at them in surprise.

"What gives you the right to take Father's cufflinks? They're precious. I suppose you were going to take them to a pawn shop."

"Mary gave 'em to me."

"Mary? They weren't hers to give. Besides, I don't believe you."

She rifled through his pockets again, removing something he could not see and then handed his coat to him and opened the door.

He kept his eye on her as he wove his way out of the house. "Yer a pretty . . . witch," he said. He heard the door slam and the bolts being thrown. *Did no good,* he thought. *I have the keys.* However, when he searched his pockets, the keyring was missing. The gun was still in the holster though. He meant to give that back to her. Now what to do? Throw it in the river? Good idea, but the best he could do was weave his way through the burgeoning fog toward his hotel.

20

The next morning, Alex did not respond to the soft knock on his hotel door. Tim opened it and breathed in Alex's foul air. It had been another spree. Only his head stuck out of the sheets. His clothing was strewn on the floor around the bed. He was so embryonic that Tim wanted to curl up next to him, look after him like Eliza had Mater. Oh, terrible thought, Mater and Alex. Over the past few days, there were moments when Alex had been absorbed in the future life, writing and working, living independently. The next moment he would climb into a pit of self-hate and bitter memories. Tim could do little for him in such dark times other than encourage him to work on an article he wanted to submit to *All the Year Round* or to write at least one page of his novel.

He was in no shape to accompany Tim to look at a house for rent in Lebreton Flats. Tim closed the door gently and descended the stairs, nodding as one gentleman to another in the lobby before going out the hotel door. A bitter north wind blew up straw and dust. He was glad to be wearing Pater's overcoat. He strolled down to the river, briefly observing the construction of the new parliament building.

He might find a job there, though it would last for only a few weeks until the snow came.

He headed toward Chaudière Falls and the patch of land that LeBreton bought for a song and then tried to sell to the British for many times more than he paid. Odd that they should name the area after such a man. It was also strange that this rough town should have been picked over beautiful Kingston for the national capital. Nevertheless, he was glad to get away from Kingston. He needed to have Alex in his life. Not since Pater died had he cared for anyone as much as him. He had been tempted to steal Alex's gun in fear that he would harm himself. Alex had been madly in love with Mary but could do nothing to save her. He kept saying he could have taken her away from the clutches of her domineering sister. Then why, Tim asked, was Alex spending so much time guarding Madeline?

Tim did not believe that George was a despoiler of young women, especially not his niece, who he cared for deeply. Alex was sceptical when Tim told him about the encounter with George at the funeral. There was no point in mentioning George's offer to employ him at his mill.

He encountered a woman out walking with her four young children. A little boy stepped in horse muck, and she wiped off his shoe but did not chastise him. Nice.

Did Madeline want Alex for herself? Perhaps she had wanted him all along. He did not say this in words, but he dropped some hints in his "confession." Was he jealous? Alex was his best friend, and if the metal maiden claimed him, there would be little of him left for Tim.

He had these thoughts while listening to the roar of the Chaudière Falls. A lot of construction was happening at the Flats—some large buildings and, behind them, small houses for the workers. He arrived at Oregon Street and, waiting in front of a house, was Mr. Macintosh, who Tim and Alex had met the previous day at his nearby office. They shook hands. Tim now made sure his grip matched that of any man he met. He explained that his friend was feeling indisposed that morning, but Tim could act for him.

They went inside. Slops, empty bottles, and dirt everywhere, and the stink of rot and urine. "They were supposed to clean up when they left, those bloody Irish! They're off to the west, so I don't suppose I can catch them," Macintosh said, his face red.

"Nothing that water and soap can't fix. Can I look around?"

"Sure. Feel free. The privy's out back, but it's probably worse than this."

The place had two small bedrooms, a common area, and a small kitchen, nothing more. Tim could picture them there. Alex could have a desk in the common area and finish writing his detective novel. The privy was indeed a miasma, but with lye soap and vinegar, it would be usable. Tim took note of the cleaning solutions they needed to purchase.

Macintosh was out front again, not wishing to inhale the malodorous fumes of the house he owned. "I thought you two gentlemen were above living in a sty like this. I'll not take offence if you want to keep looking," he said, expecting Tim to hold up his nose.

"No, sir. This will do fine. We will both be taking up work in the area. May we move in tomorrow?"

Macintosh smiled and shook Tim's hand again, squeezing more tightly this time, so Tim put in greater effort to reciprocate. He paid Macintosh for the first month. After he tucked the money away, Macintosh asked if Tim was going back toward the parliament buildings. On impulse, Tim said he was going the opposite direction.

⁕

Alex's eyes had bulged with rage when describing the road to the Baker sawmill. He ranted every hour about George, the villain who had brutalized his Mary. But ever since Tim met George on the day of Mary's funeral, he could not fit together his perception of a grieving, gentle man with Alex's portrayal of him. He would anger his best friend by getting into the middle of it, but he must not let Alex's rage burn him up without trying to solve this mystery, even if it meant working for George for a while to get to know him. He also needed to talk privately with Benson, who might hold the key to unlock the mystery.

When Tim arrived at the site, he saw police horses hitched to a fence and two policemen in uniform out in the yard talking with workers. Had there been an accident? Tim understood they occurred quite frequently in the timber and lumber industry. In the yard, he walked around looking for George. One man who looked more senior to the others stood with his hands on his hips, his head down, staring at the ground. He looked up when Tim approached.

"Your name is Benson, is it not?" Tim said, guessing.

"The police already questioned me. I told them—that man over there—everything I know."

"Why are the police here?"

"You're not with them?"

"No, I met Mr. Baker at his niece's funeral. He said I could come here to apply for work."

"I see. Well, your timing is bloody awful. Mr. Baker was murdered last night, not far from here. If you want to know, I suspect his other niece, Madeline, put her friend, Alexander O'Shea, up to it."

"No, that couldn't be true. I know where Alex was last night, and he had nothing to do with it."

"Well, you better tell the police where he is. And if you still want work here, you need to apply to Miss Madeline. I wouldn't advise it though. This place will become a hellhole under her."

"From what I know of her, I think you're right." Tim tried to keep the disgruntled man talking. Could Alex really be suspected in this murder? What about Benson? He was an odd man.

"Now, I must go. I'm quit of this place. George Baker was a grand boss, far better than his brother. Apply somewhere else," Benson said. Might he be lying?

"Mr. Benson, wait—"

"No. I'm gone."

Benson walked out the gate and down the road, an agonized man. Tim watched him go. He tried to listen in on the questioning for a while. The workers were denying any knowledge. A policeman approached him and asked if he had been at the mill the previous night. Tim told him he had just arrived to look for a job. The policeman took down his name and said he could go. He shook his head angrily when Tim asked him for an account of what happened.

21

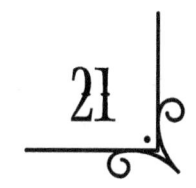

"You look refreshed, a shiny new O'Shea," Tim said, not without irony.

Alex had just gotten into his stained shirt and rumpled trousers. Now he recalled Tim's urgency the previous night to clear out of the hotel as soon as possible.

"Not so fast, Eliza. I'm tossed at sea. Does my face look green?" Oh, he must start calling her Tim instead of Eliza.

"You're still as green as the Irish, but we need to hoist anchor and be off to our new terra firma." Despite his enthusiasm, Tim appeared anxious.

"When we get to Lebreton Flats, I shall have to rise with the birds to keep up with you. I must say I'm happy to be relieved from guard duty." His relief began the day before, when Tim told him that George was dead. Now he was done with Madeline. That set him off on another celebratory spree. He had not realized how guard duty on the street made him feel desperate, especially after Mary had passed, as he would find himself imagining how George violated her. He cared little about who killed the man, as George seemed to be the kind of cranky, crazy man who made many enemies and had few friends. Tim expressed a different opinion of George, but he hardly knew the man. Now he could get on with his new life: finishing his novel, finding a job, and living with Tim.

They collected Alex's books and put them in boxes. When they were packing his clothes, Alex found the gun in its holster. He put it in a box with some of the clothes.

"I wondered if you still had that," Tim said. "Give it to me. I'll take it out now and dispose of it in the river."

"It belongs to Madeline. I'll take it back to her when I have the strength."

"No, I don't think—"

Alex took out his pocket watch. "There is only a half hour left before the wagon will come for our worldly goods. Forget the gun. Shall we trust to our new hideaway to provide us coffee and breakfast?"

"By all means, Alex. We must rub shoulders with our new neighbours, no matter how rough they are," Tim said as he picked up a heavy box.

"The wagon man can carry down our goods," Alex said.

"What, you mean to pay extra? We must live within our means. I have already taken down my boxes."

"Well, look at you . . . ."

There was a knock on the door. "He's here early," Alex said. When he opened the door, two police officers pushed him back into the room. Before they closed the door, he saw the hotel clerk standing in the hall looking like someone had just pinched his behind.

"What's going on? You have no call to do this," Tim said, looking at them and the pile of boxes.

"Be quiet, you! Which one is Alexander O'Shea?" The fierce-mannered policeman had a tight grip on Alex's arm as he kept his eye on Tim.

"I am," Alex said. "Why do you want to know?"

"Constable, the cuffs." The other policeman pulled out handcuffs from a bag he carried. They bent Alex's arms behind his back. He felt the bite of cold metal and heard the clicks of the locks.

"I say, you have no right to treat my friend this way without revealing the charge against him," Tim said, stepping forward. "You're disrupting us from making our departure."

The policeman pushed him back and took out his baton. "Any more of that, and I'll knock you down and take you in too."

They searched Alex's pockets and then rooted through his goods. The constable came across the pistol. He opened the chamber and sniffed the cylinder and the barrel. "One bullet missing, sir."

"Alexander O'Shea, you are under arrest. You'll regret it if you resist," the policeman said, lifting his handcuffed wrists behind his back. "As for you," he said to Tim, "give your information to Constable Whipple here, and grant him access to all your goods. He will search your goods. You'll not leave town during the proceedings against O'Shea."

Alex's immediate worry was that Tim might have brought some women's clothing from Kingston. He gave Tim's woeful face a smile just before the rough policeman whipped him around and out into the hallway. The policeman walked behind Alex, holding his arms up by the cuffs and steering him as if he were a horse pulling a buggy.

"Where are you taking me?" Alex asked as they went down the stairs, a tricky proposition, as he was off balance. A hotel guest, with whom he had held a brief conversation on the weather, was ascending and stopped, leaning against the railing as they passed.

"Gaol. I'd advise you to keep your mouth shut," the policeman replied.

Going through the hotel lobby and then turning down the streets leading to Sappers Bridge, Alex did not want to see the faces of the people they passed. It had warmed up after the cold snap on the day of Mary's funeral. Keeping an eye out for animal droppings, he looked at the trees, buildings, and the river as if he was taking them in for the last time. He had never studied the windows on the upper floors of buildings as he did now. What went on behind them? Did people live there, or were they used to store goods for the commerce that took place below? He also thought about the charge against him—it must have to do with George's murder. Who would have led the police to him? Surely not Madeline. Benson must have been the one. Finding the pistol in his room was bad luck, but Madeline would be able to get him out of this.

On Sappers Bridge, a drunken man gave way. "Oh, that's a trussed-up turkey, eh? What'd he do?"

"Shut up, or we'll arrest you for drunkenness," the policeman said.

When they arrived at the gaol, the policeman had a discussion with the guards. "I'm innocent!" Alex shouted. "Why on earth are you arresting me?"

One of the guards, a grim-looking, muscled lad who was perhaps eighteen, came up to him. "You'll find out, but not now. The rules here are that you keep your trap shut, or we will punish you."

The police handcuffs were taken off and new, heavier ones put on him. Three guards took him up some stairs and down a short hallway with tiny windows barred with iron. Before he was thrown in his cell, he caught a glimpse of the eyes of the man in the neighbouring cell. "So, my neighbour comes," the man said.

"You be quiet, Whelan, or we'll beat you. You know the rules here."

While two of the guards stood at his cell door, the young one removed Alex's handcuffs and asked if he had a lawyer. Alex said he did not, and he would not get one. "A lawyer will be assigned to you," the guard said before he bolted the door.

There was hardly any light in the cell, only the feeble glow of a gas lamp through the barred window. His wrists were sore. If he reached out his arms, he could almost touch each side of the cell, and it was not much longer than it was wide. Through whispered conversation, he learned that Whelan had been found guilty of murder on September 15, and Alex expected to follow him to the gallows. Perhaps it was fitting that the hangman would be the last man he met in this life. He was guilty of four deaths—his dear family's and Mary's, his intended. Eliza was well rid of him.

⁂

Two days later, guards came into Alex's cell and chained his arms behind his back.

"That's swift justice!" Whelan said as they passed his cell.

"Clam up!" a guard snapped, rapping his baton against the cell door.

"Good luck, Patrick," Alex said. The guard hit him on the shoulder, making him angry.

They steered him out of the cellblock and down a set of stairs. He went deliberately slow, as if he had a game leg. "Where are you taking me?"

"On a little holiday from death row. Don't worry, you'll be back. Now shut up. Prisoners are not allowed to talk."

They took him down one floor into another cellblock, where the stench was overpowering. A door was unlocked, and he was thrown into a slightly-larger space than his habitation upstairs, but three other men were already in it. They watched him like cats awaiting the arrival of a mouse as his chains were removed. They were all so close he could smell their sour breath.

When the door was locked, one of the inmates, a tall, slim man with a scraggly beard, ambled forward and grabbed him by the arm, tugging him to the back of the cell, while the other two staggered past and stood in front of the small grate on the door. The man who gripped Alex leaned over, his beard touching Alex's skin. "You hurt any children or women?" he whispered.

"No, I'm innocent. I didn't hurt anyone," he said. The man looked around warily and then put his finger to his lips, admonishing him to be quieter.

"We all say that," he whispered, grinning widely. "We have rules here."

More rules, Alex thought. Did he want to survive this?

"The first is you save some of your food—we 'specially like apple cores, any fruit part, bits of potatoes, we're not fussy."

"Why?" Alex imagined this was a scheme for giving larger rations to the stronger men.

"Because we got a jolly bag going. Each of us takes turns being the keeper, hiding it under our blanket or in our clothes, even putting it in one of the pails we use to empty ourselves." He opened his mouth gleefully, and Alex smelled the stink of a foul alcoholic brew.

"We had our totties this morning, and there won't be more for a while. You'll get your reward the next time. Keepin' with our tradition, you get to guard it now. Don't be thinkin' of sneakin' a drop. We keep watch, we do," he whispered with a stern, investigative regard of Alex's face.

Paying no attention to the human waste he got on his hand and arm, he reached down into one of the pails and fished out a quart-sized leather bag and held it out to Alex. It was an initiation, and Alex dared not refuse it without starting a fight. He took it and followed the instruction to place it under a blanket at the foot of a narrow upper bunk, which he assumed was his. The man nodded at him, then tapped the other two prisoners on the shoulder and nodded at them. Alex did not nod back to anyone. He was exhausted and had no choice but to lie down and sleep, although he would have preferred death. He climbed into his bunk but kept his legs crooked, so his feet were out of the way of the filthy bag. He felt like vomiting.

Sometime later he became vaguely aware of the three men snorting and laughing, pushing each other around, and banging into the bunk, where he pretended to be asleep. He heard the rattle of a key and the squeak of the door being opened.

"O'Shea!" a voice commanded.

He climbed down from his bunk, aware that the other men were watching him suspiciously, because he was the jolly bag guardian. They were the same guards who had taken him to this cell. One spun him around and handcuffed him again. "Phoof, you stink like the rest of this lot here," he said. Alex knew he would be punished if he responded.

They took him down more stairs and along a hall until they came to a room with large glass windows, where a little man in a suit sat twiddling his thumbs. They shoved him into the room after they removed his cuffs. "Don't try anything," a guard said. "We'll be watching."

The little man invited him to sit at the table. A piece of paper was in front of him. He took out a pad of paper from a leather satchel, along with ink and a quill pen. He stared at Alex before he began to talk. "You may speak here. My name is Potvin, your lawyer, as ordered by the court. I have been told that grave charges will be made against you at a committal hearing scheduled for October twentieth, three days from now. Before we proceed to give you the little detail that I know, I need your consent to have me represent you." He slid the paper across the table. It not only demanded his consent but also said Alex agreed to pay legal costs up to the value of all money and property that he had. Vultures! Potvin held out the quill for Alex to sign at the bottom of the page.

"Mr. Potvin, I did not ask for you or any other lawyer. I intend to defend myself."

Potvin looked like he had heard this a hundred times. "Truly, truly. You're not aware of the law, which says you cannot represent yourself. Even if it was legal, you wouldn't stand a chance. As I understand it, you don't have training in our profession." He looked around, as if he had a herd of lawyers with him.

"Why would that make a difference? I know that any charges against me are a heap of lies and I'll say so."

"You're not allowed to speak in your own defence. That also is the law. Unless our profession cross-examines Crown witnesses and presents evidence on your side you, sir, are doomed."

He backed away a little. So, Potvin suspected Alex to be a murderer, and he just wanted to scavenge a fee from him. "How will they show I'm guilty?"

Potvin breathed heavily. "That is yet to be seen at the committal hearing and, if necessary, a court trial. All I know is that the allegation arose at the coroner's inquest into the death of Mr. George Baker. I did not attend that proceeding. I have been informed that there may also be another allegation against you. Police are concluding their investigation into that matter."

Alex became a fire-breathing dragon, getting up to his feet, shouting, slamming the table with his fist. "It's not fair! This is all made up. I want to kill whoever is behind it. It has to be Benson. He's always making up lies. I want to kill him!"

"Quiet, quiet!" Potvin said, but it was too late. The guards came in and soon had Alex in a stranglehold. The little man looked as if he saw his fee slipping away as the guards cuffed Alex and dragged him out, still yelling. They knocked him down with a truncheon. "Down to the hole with you," one of them said.

✥

He was a rat, curled up, filthy, and ready to spread pestilence. Alex would never grow accustomed to living in that dark hole. He would die there. He waited for death to come.

He saw a dim light in the stairway. That's where his keeper came to drop off the dry, cold excuse for nutrition that he would never be able to eat. But more than one person was coming this time. Most likely the keeper was bringing him the Grim Reaper. The light grew brighter.

Even once they were by his cell, he could not see their faces. One of them spoke, not his keeper. "Mr. O'Shea, I have come to talk with you and to convince you to change your mind about being represented by a lawyer."

"A lawyer? I can lie as well as the best of them," Alex said, the words pouring out of him.

"I told you, sir; he's mad," the keeper said. Was his name Max? Alex seemed to remember him mentioning it.

"I can only spend a few minutes with you, Mr. O'Shea. My name is McPhee, and I'm the police magistrate, along with two other justices of the peace who will be adjudicating your committal hearing tomorrow. Mr. Potvin has written to my office to say he will not be representing you. Do you have another lawyer in mind? You and your counsel have a right to attend the hearing, and he has the right to cross-examine the witnesses."

Alex approached the bars, so he could see the man. He had a sharp beard and piercing eyes, and he wore a black suit and a grey vest. He carried a cane. "I'll come and ask questions myself. I have reported on trials, and I know my way around a courtroom."

"This is not a trial, sir. This proceeding is to decide whether or not the evidence presented against you is sufficient to put you on trial."

"You said I had a right to attend." Alex would catch up this slick character somehow.

"You do, but the law does not allow you to speak. I urge you to engage Mr. Potvin or some other eligible counsel. I can refer you to an alternative lawyer, if you wish."

This was the time for Alex to stand up straight, throw off the rat, and speak for himself. "I'll exercise my right to be present, and you will see that I'll not be stifled when I speak out to destroy this trumped-up evidence against me. I will not have a lawyer."

McPhee was silent for a moment. "In that case, Mr. O'Shea, you will do yourself harm and disrupt my proceedings. You still have a day to change your mind, but if not, you will be detained here, and the proceedings will go on without you. In the event that you're committed for trial, your counsel may purchase the signed depositions of the witnesses. You'll not be able to read about the hearing in the newspapers. I have decided that the public and the press will not be present."

"Too much gossip over the D'Arcy McGee murder I suppose?" The newspaperman in Alex was back.

"I'll not comment on that. I came here in your interest, and now I'll leave."

"See, don't you think he's mad?" the keeper said on the way back up the stairs.

Alex devolved back into a rat and crawled into his grimy corner.

22

"It's all right, your master will be back with you soon," Tim said to Alex's unfinished manuscript, yearning for his friend's return.

What a pleasure it was to throw off the wig and women's garments! He stuffed the used articles away. His first thought was to tie them in a bundle with a rock and throw them in the river, but they might be useful again. He was relieved he had not brought along any women's garb when the police searched his possessions at the hotel. The street sellers at the By Ward market were puzzled when Tim sifted through their clothing and held them up to himself before making an offer. But they did the trick. Whereas Tim Fairlight had been turned away from the police station and the courthouse when he asked about Alex, a sobbing Miss O'Shea, Alex's sister, poor wretch, so unnaturally tall and unwomanly, was informed that morning of the name and whereabouts of his lawyer.

He put on Pater's Sunday suit, something he had not sported since coming to the Flats, where everyone wore rough work clothing. However, no one paid much attention to their neighbours, even though the dwellings were squeezed together. And at this time of day, only the women would be out and about.

Today, he resembled one of the owners. On other days, he had looked like a rough worker. He earned a few dollars moving sand and stones at the parliament building construction site. He helped an elderly man paint his house. Then, to his delight, Taylor sent him the payment for the sale of his house in Kingston. He had to write a letter in Eliza's writing that authorized Tim Fairlight to collect the payment from the post office. Now he was able to spend all his time finding out why Alex had been arrested. It had to be for killing George. He remembered the evening when the murder happened. Alex told him he needed to go to Madeline's house. He believed Alex had told him the truth.

As he emerged from the hut and kept his eyes on the road to avoid the many animal leavings, he thought about the headline on the front page of the *Citizen*, which came out two days after George's death: "Three Ottawa Murders in the Same Night." According to the article, George Baker was shot in the back on his way home from the mill he owned. The police had a suspect in custody. That same night, in what was believed to be an unrelated incident, two people from Lower Town were killed near the Ottawa River.

Ever since Alex's arrest, Tim had been watching outside the Baker house. The windows were draped in black, and there had been no suspicious movement in or out. He felt like breaking in and choking a confession out of that witch, for surely she had something to do with George's murder. Could she have seduced Alex into carrying it out for her? Perish the thought.

He approached the address on Sparks Street for Murray, Danbridge, and Potvin. It was one of those buildings thrown up in a rush and as likely to come tumbling down with the slightest earthquake. The firm was on the second floor.

"Sir, do you have an appointment?" The clerk's spectacles made his eyes look like fried eggs, sunny side up.

"No, but I must see Mr. Potvin on an urgent matter concerning the O'Shea case." He looked around and saw no one waiting for any of the lawyers in the firm. Were they all in court?

"As it happens, Mr. Potvin is in, but he may be occupied with other priorities. Please, have a seat while I consult him."

Tim was tempted to ask what could be more important than a murder case. Potvin's door was open a crack, and Tim heard him making whiney sounds, though he could not distinguish the words. The clerk emerged a moment later. "Mr. Potvin is able to spare five minutes for you. Come with me."

He opened the door as if leading him into a palace, but it was a mere closet, with great stacks of paper on cabinets and the floor, hardly leaving room for the little man to sit behind an old desk, which had a chair in front of it.

"I must say before you sit down that I'm not officially representing Mr. O'Shea and have no expectations of doing so. Do you understand the judiciary, young man?" Potvin addressed him like a teacher would a student.

Tim sat to get a good look at the man. "A clerk at the courthouse told me you're Alex's lawyer."

"Who are you to question me on this matter?"

In his rush to get news about Alex, Tim had not thought about who he should be. Alex's brother from out of town?

Too weak a lie and one likely to be discovered. His business partner? Too strong a lie—it might lead to Kingston. Then it came to him.

"Mr. O'Shea is a writer of detective novels. I'm a detective from Toronto. He wanted to know about my work and, in that way, we became acquainted and struck up a friendship. What is more, I have his authority to provide money for his defence."

This may not have been wise, as his first instinct was to rid Alex of this weak legal creature. But a sharper lawyer would see through his lies and keep him from getting involved in the case. Moreover, Tim could maneuver the man. Potvin looked at him quizzically. Tim took a roll of banknotes out of his pocket and counted them. Potvin's eyes watered at the sight.

"I was appointed by the justice department after O'Shea was not forthcoming with the name of a lawyer. I have attempted to discuss the case with him, but all he did was throw a fit. He seemed quite mad and has an illusion he can represent himself—"

"He needs a lawyer, because he can do little while incarcerated."

"That is correct sir." So now he was calling Tim "sir." Money did that.

"I can add that Mr. O'Shea has harmed his own defence by refusing to be represented by counsel at his committal hearing. A clerk from the police magistrate's office has kept me informed."

"What evidence led to the charges against him?"

"I don't know. The clerk said that Mr. O'Shea was hysterical when the magistrate made a special effort to convince him to engage representation."

"I can tell you that Mr. O'Shea is definitely not mad. When you met him, did you do anything to make him angry?"

"No. He raged about someone named Bentham or Ben-something—"

"Benson."

"Yes, Benson."

"Go on. What else did he say?"

"There's nothing more to tell. The guards hauled him away after he became hysterical." Potvin's face was red.

"As I told you, Mr. O'Shea permits me to be his agent. If it will make you feel better, I'll write a letter to him that you can deliver. Once he reads it, I'm sure he will receive you differently and will confirm you as his lawyer and me as his representative outside the court." He held his breath. Potvin gave him the impression that Alex was a dead man.

Tim continued as Potvin mumbled to himself. "And would it not be good for your law firm if you were able to prove a man innocent who all the police and powerful citizens think is guilty?" Tim held out two of the notes, and Potvin took them cautiously, as if they were on fire.

"My clerk will provide you the means to write your letter, and I'll go again to see Mr. O'Shea. If he agrees to have me, I'll purchase a copy of the witness depositions from the committal hearing," Potvin said, shoving the money into his desk drawer and then rising.

Tim held out his hand and gave Potvin a hard squeeze. The lawyer winced. "We'll meet again tomorrow afternoon," Tim said on his way out.

"Well, yes, I suppose . . . sir," Potvin replied weakly.

✥

The next day, Potvin told Tim that Alex had agreed to have him as his lawyer. They sat together and discussed the depositions. "I'm sorry to say, but it looks like an open-and-shut case," Potvin said.

The horror of it was that Alex was charged not only with George's murder but also with Mary's. On George's murder, a coroner, the arresting officer, Benson, and Madeline provided evidence. Concerning Mary's murder, which did not come to light until George was killed, the coroner who examined her exhumed body, Dr. Brown, Madeline, a druggist, and a police officer who searched the Baker house, provided evidence.

After he left Potvin's office, Tim felt like he would be swamped by the muddy streets. The trial date was not yet set, but Potvin said it would not be far off. He had heard that the Justice Department wanted to clear away its business before Christmas break. It was ludicrous. Surely some witnesses would come forward on Alex's behalf. Why had not the police found them?

The wind was cold. Most of the passersby outside the Concession Street house wore heavy woollen scarves and mittens. Tim saw a man in a suit carrying a satchel—surely Madeline's lawyer—arrive at the house around one o'clock and then depart an hour later. Shortly after that, Victoria came out and turned the opposite way on the street from where Tim stood. He rushed to catch up with her, but she turned into a public house before he reached her. He waited outside. In a few minutes, she emerged holding a bottle.

"Victoria, you remember I always treated you kindly. Now I'm working with Mr. O'Shea's lawyer and have a few questions for you. We can keep this secret from your mistress."

She stared at Tim as if he was about to charge her with murder.

"You know that Mr. O'Shea would never hurt Mary. He has been charged with murdering her. That is so wrong."

"It is wrong, but I must take this bottle to my mistress. She is waiting for it and told me to hurry," she said in her soft voice.

"I can come along to Miss Baker's house and question you there."

She looked like she was about to be eaten by a lion. "No, no, please. Ask me your questions out here and then let me go. Please."

Tim suggested a spot sheltered from the wind. No one was in sight. She moved there with small steps.

"Concerning the death of Miss Mary, did you ever see Mr. O'Shea hitting her or giving her sleeping medication?"

"My mistress says she did."

"That's not what I asked. Did *you* personally see these things?"

"No, but I did see horrible marks on Miss Mary's back when I got her ready for bed."

"Apart from Miss Baker, could anyone else have seen something?"

"Benson may have. He left to work with Mr. George Baker."

Tim planned to seek out Benson. He wondered if Benson might have had a falling out with George and was the one who killed him.

"When you helped Miss Mary to bed shortly before she died, were there fresh bleeding marks on her back?"

"Sometimes."

"Was the fresh bleeding only on nights when Mr. O'Shea had been up in Mary's room late at night?"

"My mistress says they were. I can't tell you more. Now please, let me go; I'm late." She looked down the street, terrified that Madeline might come out to find her.

"I have one more question and then you can go. Did you ever see angry disputes between Mr. O'Shea and Mr. George Baker?"

"No, but my mistress says Alexander threatened many times to shoot him . . . I must run." And this she did, speedily for someone with such short legs impeded by skirts and petticoats.

She knew more than she let on, but if she remained under Madeline's thumb, she would not be a good witness for Alex's defence. Nevertheless, Tim thought, Potvin could cast doubt on her evidence if Madeline pushed her forward for the prosecution.

❖

Tim retrieved the drawing of the naked girl. In their search at the hotel, the policemen did not bother to open the rag-eared novel where he had hidden it. He had a hunch that nagged him. He tucked the drawing into his coat pocket and went across the canal to Rideau Street, where rowdiness and seduction were in full bloom, despite two policemen in uniform who patrolled the street, occasionally poking inebriated folks with their truncheons and saying, "If you don't move on, we'll lock you up!"

A policeman approached Tim as he took in the scene. "Are you sure you want to be out here, sir? It's not safe this time of night."

"Officer, I'm looking for my nephew, who was seen going this way. He's tall and has curly red hair, never wears a cap, eighteen years old. Have you seen anyone meeting this description?"

"No. You should put in a report to the police station. Over here he's sure to turn to evil, or something bad will happen to him."

"He may have gone over to a friend's. He's a good chap. I'll just look about here, and if he doesn't appear within the next few hours, I'll make the report. Thank you."

The policeman turned his attention to a tussle that broke out nearby. The impromptu discussion gave Tim an idea. He walked a block farther and came to where women of various ages stood in front of a public house. He approached one of them, a young woman who was perhaps twenty years old, her long hair tousled.

"Good evening, sir, are you in need of company?" she asked, smiling lasciviously.

Tim moved his head, indicating they should stand apart from the others to talk. "I have a strange request. If you can help, there's money in it for you."

"Nothing's too strange for Sadie, depending on how much you pay."

"What I'll pay for is not what you expect. I'm trying to find out what happened to my cousin. She came over from Ireland while I was away on a long business trip. I arranged for her to stay in my house, but when I returned, she was missing. I have looked and looked and am afraid she was the girl who was murdered along with a man near here. She matches the description in the newspaper. Can you help me?"

"You're a policeman, aren't you?" she said, backing away a step. The other two women she had been with looked over. So, the police were still investigating. The *Citizen* reported the police as saying there was no connection between the shootings on each side of the river on the same night.

"I'm not. I bet the police have already talked with you. I'm only looking for my cousin, and I'll pay you five dollars if you can help."

She stepped closer again. "Even if I send you to someone else who knows something?"

"Yes, you will get the five dollars and the other person ten, as long as I'm told the truth."

"Well, hand over."

"Not until you take me to the one who knows."

"Take out the money then, and you shall have your wish." She looked over at her two companions. It had to be a slow night for them. He took out the banknotes. This was dangerous.

"Ahoy, Delight!" she said, waving her arm. Both women started over, but Sadie clarified she wanted only the one.

Delight was older. Sadie's mother? Would a mother and daughter be out selling themselves together?

"What is it, darling? Is this man being mean to you?" she asked, even though her eyes lit up at the money in his hand. That amount must have been much more than they were paid for their usual work.

"He says he's Totsie's cousin, and he wants to know about her. He'll pay."

"About her on the night she was murdered, and I want to make sure that Totsie was my cousin, Rose O'Leary," Tim clarified.

"How?" both asked. Tim asked them to accompany him to the nearest streetlamp. He took out the drawing and showed it to them. They were alarmed and looked as if they would run off.

"That's Totsie all right. But if you're her cousin, how did you get it? You proper folks don't make this type of naked stuff of your cousins, or do you?" Now it was Delight who lectured him on propriety.

He lowered his head and rubbed his eyes. No tears, but they would not be able to tell. He wiped his face with his sleeve. "This piece of filth was in her room when I came back from my travels. It led me to think she might be coming over to a place like this to sell her body." Now he spoke like a genteel man of affairs, offended that his dignity had been doubted.

He retrieved the drawing from Delight and took the two of them to a darker, more isolated, spot. "Totsie had just come over to work with us. Or for our boss, Max, the man who was killed. He probably convinced her to come. He had a way of doing that. She was a quiet one, she was, not laughing at our little jokes. How she took up our trade I don't know, and we could tell she didn't much like it. But some of the gents like such girls. She . . .." Delight stopped when a swaggering man came over.

"My turn, mister, this gal's my regular," he said, grabbing Sadie's arm. She looked torn and reached out to get the money from Tim.

"You can ask Delight for your money, if she answers a few more questions."

"You a policeman? Why, I'll . . .." the man said, preparing for a fight.

"You'll do no such thing," Sadie, said, dragging him away.

"You were saying . . . my main interest is in the day she died," Tim said.

"That day! She was so excited, almost jumping up and down like a little tot. I tried to dig it out of her, but all she said was, 'There's lots of money in it.' At least two gents approached her but she turned them down till I see her going off with the boss."

"Which way did they go?"

"Down street, away from Sappers."

"And then?"

"The last I see of them. Give me our money now. I earnt it," she said, upset he had put the banknotes in his pocket, not wanting anyone else to see the transaction.

"First, tell me anything else you saw that night. Anything out of the ordinary."

"No, 'twas just as always, except our boss didn't come back. We didn't mind at all, preferred it that way, as he was rough with us . . . except there was one thing now I think on it. I was just coming back from doing business behind a house on other side of this here street, and I sees an old widder coming along there keeping out of the lamplight and folks' way. I could see she was a poor old 'un. Her clothes, they was ragged. She bends over, but methinks 'tis odd, sometimes the way she moves she seems like a young'un.' I keep me eye on her, and she goes right up to Sappers. 'Now, why would a poor old 'un go there?' I says to meself."

"And that was all? Nothing more?" Tim asked, reaching into his pocket.

"No more. I earn the cash now. Losing business by keeping in the dark with you."

"Well, here's the money for you and for Sadie. Thank you."

"Now you don't go tellin' the policeman, or I be mad," Delight said, moving away.

"That is not my intention," he replied, although he might in fact do just that. Suddenly feeling exhausted, he slumped away toward Lebreton Flats.

❖

A young woman holding a screaming infant answered Tim's knock next door to where Madeline lived. She could not hear what he said and asked him to return in the evening when the master was home.

"Is the mistress of the house in?" he said loudly, so anyone else inside could hear. "I just want to talk with her for a minute. I'm a police detective." The infant swung its arm and hit the woman in the eye. She started crying, and a dog barked loudly. She retreated indoors.

Tim spied on Madeline and knew when she went to the mill. He had already questioned another neighbour, who said the Bakers kept pretty much to themselves and, no, she did not remember seeing anything unusual on the night of George Baker's murder, either on the street or at the house. The neighbour did not remember a man arriving at the Baker House around seven in the evening and leaving a few hours later and did not see an old woman coming to the Baker House in the early hours of the next day.

He waited, quite sure there would be no hope at this house. The dog kept barking until a woman's harsh voice said, "Pip, sit, stay!" The dog's name was coincidental—Tim had been reading Alex's copy of *Great Expectations* just before all this havoc.

A stern-looking woman came to the door. She resembled Pip's mean older sister, except she wore fashionable clothes. After Tim went through his routine, she told him her name, Higgins, and asked him to come inside. He waited patiently in an anteroom chair while she disciplined the dog once more and closed the door.

"My husband and I have lived here all our married life, and the whole time, there's been strange goings-on at the Bakers. Mr. Baker was never friendly. He hardly acknowledged our greetings when he went by. Now his poor, wounded brother was different. We felt sorry for him, and

I would talk to him sometimes, and he was friendly. It's too bad somebody murdered him."

"What about the daughters?"

"That Madeline is proud. We're not good enough for her. Is there another girl?"

"Yes. She was sick and kept indoors all her life. Now, going back to George Baker, did you see anything out of the usual on the night of his murder?"

"That was a while back. Hmmmm . . . oh yes, we went out for dinner at my husband's partner's house and came home late. We didn't see anything unusual on the street or toward the Baker house. The servants had stayed up, and we sent them to bed and then went to bed ourselves. Then . . . it was already the next day . . . I remember looking at the clock, and it was nearly one in the morning when Pip began barking. He's barely more than a pup, so I rushed out of bed, not wanting him to wake the servants or the children. He was on his hind feet barking at someone out the window. As I shushed him, I saw an old woman, all in black, shuffling along. Sometimes she sped up. She looked like someone from Lower Town, and I asked myself, 'What's this poor creature doing out at this time?' She might have seen me at the window, but she didn't raise her head, and she kept on going."

"In which direction?"

"Away from the river."

"So, she might have gone to the Baker house?"

"Maybe. I couldn't see that from the window, and Pip had calmed down by then, so I went back to bed and didn't think about it until you asked."

"Did you tell this to the police?"

"No. I didn't see what it had to do with anything."

He thanked her for the information and asked if she would agree to testify in court. She looked nervous but finally said she would. He left her in a state of puzzlement. As he walked away, he thought, yes, now he had some evidence, although it was as thin as ice in springtime.

⁕

The court case was only a week away, and Tim was desperate to track down Benson. He made forays into Baker Lumber yard, aware one of the men could inform Madeline of a stranger sniffing around or that she might come out and happen to see him. In fact, he had just found a friendly worker who told him he knew Benson by going for beers together at the Golden Hotel, where Benson was staying when the door flew open, and Madeline charged out, collecting two husky men to come with her. "What are you doing on my property? You're a thief!"

"Just asking questions, Miss Baker." Tim gazed at her familiarly, as if he was ready to resume where they left off at her house.

"This has nothing to do with you. The police have already concluded their investigation. You're up to no good and will be sorry if you ever show your face here again." There was only scorn on her face.

Two men seized his arms, escorted him off the property, and gave him a boot down the road. But now he had a lead.

He went to the Golden Hotel on Sparks Street. The clerk was an officious man with thick spectacles who kept picking at his nose as if a fly had just flown up it. When Tim said he was a police detective the man brightened. "Oh yes, Mr. Benson was a very upright man who never caused us any trouble. We were sorry to lose him."

"Do you know where he went after he left? It's important," Tim said, leaning forward on the counter and glaring at the man's frightened eyes.

"Now I think on it, there may be something in the register. I think he wanted . . . ." He opened the register as if it were a prayer book and ran his forefinger along the lines. "Yes, he left behind a trunk and asked me to send it to him at this address in Kingston."

Tim recognized the address on Earl Street, not far from the cricket grounds office, a boarding house run by a Mrs. Stephenson. And so, back to Kingston Tim went.

⁕

"Mr. Benson, it's good to see you again," Tim said as Benson came out of Mrs. Stephenson's lodging house, dressed in a suit. He seemed not to recognize Tim.

"I didn't tell you that I'm a detective when we met at the Baker mill on that unfortunate day."

"You lied to me." Benson looked bullish.

"I'm sorry about that. Yes, I was on the scene incognito. We detectives do that."

Benson scrutinized him. "Why are you here? The lawyer said I should talk to no one."

What lawyer? Obviously not Potvin.

"A new line of investigation has opened, and I need to question you here. If you prefer, I can take you into custody, and we can go to Ottawa." Tim was going on the line here, knowing that he could be accused of tampering with a crown witness.

Benson looked anxiously at passersby. "I need to leave for work in ten minutes. I won't say a word until we go somewhere private."

"What line of work are you in now?"

Benson did not answer, only walked solemnly toward the cricket grounds. Tim was familiar with the place, because he, then she, used to go there with Pater to watch matches. They entered the grounds, dead leaves crunching beneath their feet, and then stopped. Benson turned suddenly. "What are you investigating? I already said I would come to Ottawa to testify."

Tim knew what his testimony would be—Alex had prepared him for that. "You'll testify that you saw Alexander O'Shea threaten to shoot George Baker."

"Yes, I pulled Mr. Baker back, or O'Shea would have shot him that day at the house."

"You were a servant in the Baker household long before Mr. O'Shea arrived. Did you see anything unusual or improper back then?"

Benson scowled and took time to think. "What does that have to do with George's murder?"

"On his second visit to the house, you warned Mr. O'Shea to stay away, that there was evil in the house."

"Supposing I did, and he got swept up in that evil and became a murderer. What does that have to do with anything?"

"Miss Baker will allege that Mr. O'Shea violated Mary, flayed her back, and poisoned her to keep her quiet. Does that seem likely to you?" Benson became red in the face, gnashed his teeth, and looked like he was about to choke. He looked away.

"Mr. Benson?"

"That damned bitch! She doesn't deserve to live," he said, addressing the cricket fence.

"When you come to the trial, could you please give testimony on what you know about Miss Baker and her late sister?"

Benson waved him away, but Tim stood his ground, though he could not get any more words out of him. Benson walked away with a handkerchief to his eyes.

23

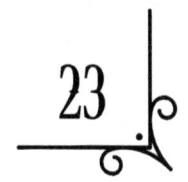

Alex felt like he was a cockroach filched out of a drain when the guards escorted him up into the prisoner's box. On his wrists he wore tight steel cuffs that the guards called "nippers." The courtroom was half full of men and women, none of whom Alex recognized. The judge was seated at the front of the courtroom, and next to him was Police Magistrate McPhee, who had visited him in prison.

After the prison, the air in the courtroom was refreshing. He looked out the window, saw snowflakes glancing against it, and wished he could be outside breathing the cold, fresh air, even if it would be the last inhalation in his life.

The court sergeant asked the prisoner to rise and to face the judge. The mumble of the onlookers stopped. The clerk rose, paper in hand. "Alexander O'Shea, you're indicted on two offences of murder. On Sunday, October the fourth of this year, you did with malice and aforethought murder Mary Baker. On Monday, October the twelfth of this year, you did with malice and aforethought murder George Baker. What say you to these charges?"

Alex looked around the courtroom. Everyone had their eyes on him, the accused, bloodthirsty murderer of a beautiful young woman and her loving uncle.

The sergeant got to his feet. "Prisoner, direct your plea directly to the judge, and be quick about it."

He would have said that his neglect had led to Mary's death, and he was not guilty on the second charge. However, Potvin's visits and the messages he related from Tim made him look directly into the judge's eyes and say, "Not guilty."

The judge called for the Crown and the defence counsels to select the jury from the panel. They were all men, most of them with beards and suits, although some were more fashionable than others. They sat in the front rows of the courtroom. When the indictment was read, these men were the ones who looked most scornfully at Alex. One by one, they came up to the jury box and were questioned. Alex knew that each lawyer had the right to excuse, peremptorily, up to twenty jurors. They would return to their seats until all the dismissals were used up, and then they would have the chance of being selected again. Two jurors were rejected with cause. One by the crown attorney, because he said he was a pacifist, and the second by Potvin, because he said it would be a short trial, seeing that it was obvious the prisoner was guilty.

This went on and on. Alex put his head on the railing, imagined his mother's face looking down and telling him not to worry, and then Mary's dead face. He fell asleep, only to be startled awake by the judge slamming down his gavel.

Potvin approached the prisoner's box. "What happened?" Alex asked. "I fell asleep."

"That amazes me. The twelve members of the jury have been selected. We get down to business at two this afternoon."

◈

When the case reconvened in the afternoon, the judge asked Moore, the prosecuting lawyer, to call up the first witness. Moore was a stern-looking man approaching middle age who had an air of confidence about him, as if he was a professor about to carry out an experiment he had performed dozens of times before in his laboratory.

"The Crown calls upon Coroner Milton."

The coroner wore a black suit and had a grizzled, pointed beard. He testified that he had examined the bodies of Mr. Baker in the locale where he had been shot and Miss Mary Baker, whose body had been exhumed eight days after her death.

"Mr. Baker was killed by a single bullet that entered his back and exited his front after passing through his heart. The bullet was found lodged in a tree where the path turned some twenty feet away. On further examination, it was found to be a thirty-eight-caliber bullet. Miss Mary Baker's stomach had traces of a high dosage of laudanum. In our inquest, we determined that it was a sufficient amount of poison to cause her death."

Moore had a few more questions for the coroner that Alex could not comprehend. He imagined poor Mary's body being pulled out of her coffin and a knife cutting open her stomach.

When the coroner stepped down, Moore called Officer Gleason to take the stand. A poker-faced policeman came out of the clerk's room, approached the stand, and took the oath.

Alex became alert. He saw Tim among the spectators. *Brave Eliza—Tim. You're the most faithful person I have ever met.*

"Officer Gleason, what can you tell us about the murder of George Baker?"

"The evidence points to the killer hiding in some bushes while waiting for the deceased to come by. There is a spot in the bushes where the grass was flattened and small branches broken. We were unable to make any clear impressions of footprints. As the coroner has testified, we found the bullet that killed Mr. Baker at the site."

"Do you recognize the accused as the man you arrested on October fourteenth?" Moore asked.

Gleason pointed at Alex. "That is the man."

"Did he surrender this weapon to you? You may examine it if you wish." Moore held up a pistol. The policeman expressed no desire to look at it. He said it was a Colt thirty-eight caliber and that all but one of its chambers were filled with bullets. At the scene of the arrest, the officers thought it had been fired recently, an assertion that was subsequently confirmed by the expert at the police station.

"The accused did not surrender the weapon. We searched and found it hidden in one of the boxes in his room at the Russell House."

"Why were there boxes? Had not the accused been resident in the hotel for some time?"

"According to the hotel clerk, he had been resident. The morning we arrested him, he and another man, who identified himself as Timothy Fairlight, were in the act of moving out."

"I see," Moore said, "he was about to escape?"

"Well, yes, I would say that. He was angry when we arrived to question him."

"Thank you, Officer Gleason. I would like to place this weapon in evidence." Moore approached the clerk and handed him the gun.

"There is a second matter, concerning the murder of Mary Baker."

"Yes. Just after the death of Mr. George Baker, we searched the Baker house on Concession Street. The prisoner had been staying there until several days prior to the murder. We did not find any evidence concerning Mr. Baker, but in searching through a dressing gown that the prisoner had been wearing, we found a small, partially filled bottle of medicine. Miss Baker had no idea why the prisoner possessed it. We took it to a chemist, who said it was laudanum. As you will see, that bears directly on the poisoning of Mary—"

"That accusation will be made in due time. Do you have the bottle with you? Yes? Then please put it into evidence. Your witness." Moore gestured to Potvin, who looked like he needed some wine to pep himself up.

"No questions, your honour," Potvin said in his high, scratchy voice.

"The Crown calls Harold Benson." Benson was swearing to tell the truth, the whole truth, and nothing but the truth when Tim got out of his chair near the back of the court, walked to the front, and whispered in Potvin's ear. The judge frowned and lifted his gavel. Tim walked soundlessly away and resumed sitting at the back of the courtroom. Tim smiled at Alex. What could this mean?

"Mr. Benson, were you employed by the late Mr. Baker?"

"I worked for both Mr. Bakers. First, the late William Baker and then the late George Baker."

"What led you to leave the Baker household and work with George Baker?"

"There was dissension in the household, and I liked Mr. George. He was a respectable human being."

"Did the 'dissension' you speak of coincide with the defendant's arrival?"

"Yes, pretty much."

"Did you ever witness the defendant threatening the late George Baker?"

"Yes, on two occasions. A few weeks before the murder, Mr. George Baker arrived at the house to attend a meeting with Miss Madelaine Baker. O'Shea pulled out a handgun and threatened to shoot Mr. Baker if he did not leave immediately."

"Did you think this a serious threat or just a bluff?"

"It was no bluff. I have seen men in the Crimea hold a gun as tightly as he did, and had I not pulled Mr. Baker away, I'm sure he would have been dead the next minute."

"You mention a second time when a threat was made."

"Yes, just before the murder, Mr. O'Shea came to our office at the mill. He accused George Baker of having forced himself on Mary Baker for immoral purposes and beating her upon her back and shoulders until she bled. Mr. Baker was shocked that someone would accuse him of such dastardly deeds. It was not in his character."

"Did the accused pull out a gun on this occasion?"

"No, but I worried that he would, so I kept a close watch on him and escorted him out."

"One last question, Mr. Benson. How certain are you of this evidence you have presented?"

"I write in a diary every night, starting when I was in the Crimea. Never know when you're going to be struck down."

Moore had no further questions.

Potvin rose to his feet. "Mr. Benson, are you aware that a bitter legal dispute was going on between Miss Madeline Baker and Mr. George Baker before he moved out of the house?"

Benson nodded. "Yes, I'm aware of there being some kind of disagreement. I don't know the details, as neither Miss Baker nor Mr. Baker confided in me on that topic."

"If the dispute was over control of the mill, could that not have been a motive for Miss Baker arranging to have George Baker killed?"

Moore shot to his feet, "Your honour, that is a hypothetical question beyond the expertise of Mr. Benson to answer. The defence is trying to plant suspicions that have no basis."

"Mr. Potvin, I agree that you have stepped beyond the line here. Either you ask your question in a different way or withdraw it. Gentlemen of the jury, I order you to ignore the insinuation in Mr. Potvin's question."

"I withdraw the question, your honour. No more questions."

Alex looked at Tim, whose eyes were only on his. Tim shook his head, not in frustration but in a just-you-wait kind of way.

"I call Miss Madeline Baker as our next witness," Moore said.

She emerged in delicate tears, wearing the most revealing mourning dress that Alex had ever seen. Moore exchanged looks with her, smiled sympathetically, and she calmed down. Were they in league? Alex stared at her. For a second, she rested her eyes on him, and her face became hateful before returning to the visage of the poor, eligible maiden. She went through the swearing-in with a sweet, little girl voice. Then she appeared to take in the face of every juror and everyone in the courtroom, bestowing her virginal warmth upon them. She started and frowned once when looking at the back of the courtroom. It must be Tim, Alex thought. She paid no attention to the question counsel posed to her.

"Miss Baker? Are you with us?" the judge demanded.

"Your honour," Moore interposed, "this lady has been through unbelievable distress, and she deserves time to compose herself."

"I'm sorry," Madeline said, sounding contrite and starting to look sparky.

"Miss Baker, I'll ask you again: do you believe the defendant carried out the murders of your uncle and your sister?"

"I know he did," she said without hesitancy. Madeline had become Alex's enemy and accuser. Why had Mary loved her?

Moore asked her a long series of questions. Alex tried to pay close attention, even though Mary's words of that last night, her wish that he take her away, came back and overlaid the proceedings. He was guilty, because he did not act immediately and whisk her out of the house right there and then.

He heard Madeline attest that, yes, her sister always had a nervous disorder, which worsened after the death of their beloved father, and she had attached herself to O'Shea as if it was her father come back from the grave. Madeline claimed she didn't like O'Shea, but he flattered Mary and, for a time, the two of them allied against her, even though her father, on his deathbed, made Madeline Mary's guardian. O'Shea threatened her with his gun, and even though she told him it was inappropriate, he spent long periods of time with Mary in her room. Then Mary became withdrawn, and she stopped eating. O'Shea was angry with both of them. Madeline found the opportunity to talk to Mary alone one night, and she confessed it all, that O'Shea was punishing her by stripping off her clothes and doing an indecent act with her as well as whipping her until she bled. She showed Madeline her back. It was bleeding terribly. Here, Madeline gulped water and sobbed so much that Moore raced up to the witness stand to give her his handkerchief.

"Did you confront the accused over his abuse of your sister?"

"I did. He was outraged. He went to look at Mary's back and came back saying I was wrong, that Uncle George had come in and done the deed. He showed me his gun and said it was loaded, and the next bullet from it would end

George's life. I said I would go to the police. He pushed me down—I still have the bruise on my leg, if you want to see it."

The gentlemen of the jury leaned forward, but the judge said it would not be necessary. Alex looked around the courtroom. Every person savoured Madeline's words as if they were exotic wines.

"Miss Baker," Moore said, "what, in your opinion, was the prisoner's motive in insinuating himself into your household and murdering two of your family members?"

"Money. Once Mary was wed to him, he could control one third of our valuable business. With Uncle George out of the way, he would have even more. I have no doubt from the way he threatened me to keep away from his doings with Mary that I would be the next victim of his greed, leaving him fully in charge and rich. But Mary confronted him first, and he killed her to keep her quiet."

Potvin rose and raised an objection that this was pure speculation. The judge overruled him.

"Miss Baker, much of your testimony portrays the accused as carrying out violent, immoral acts against your sister and coercive acts against yourself," Mr. Moore said. "Do you have any evidence for this?"

"Yes. It's in the drawing."

Potvin rose and said a drawing was not mentioned in Miss Baker's deposition.

"Your honour, it's new evidence," Moore said. "Miss Baker found it after the committal hearing. She was suffering from too much grief to search her house and find things the defendant had hidden away." He gave Madeline a loving look.

The judge nodded. "Very well, proceed."

"With your permission, I would like to provide, for your eyes and those of the jury, a lewd drawing that my client has found in her house. Miss Baker, can you elaborate?" Moore asked. A collective gasp filled the courtroom when Moore said the word "lewd."

Two policemen brought forward the drawing, covered by a sheet.

"This will not be for the eyes of the courtroom," the judge said.

"No, your honour. First, Miss Baker, how did you come across this drawing?" The policemen skillfully unwrapped the drawing and held it so only Madeline could see it.

"Mary told me where to find it on the night she died, but O'Shea must have hidden it again the next day. He was the last to see her before she died." Madeline once again became overcome with grief, and the drawing was covered up.

"Before the drawing is shown to his honour and the gentlemen of the jury, do you know anything about how it was created?"

"Yes. O'Shea brought in a man to do it. He had a French name that I didn't understand, something like Renard. All the work was done behind closed doors. I was told it would be a wedding picture, and he wanted to keep it a secret, until the day they married. The artist was there for about a week. Mary came out of these sessions in a deep depression, and she refused to speak to me about it until the day O'Shea killed her."

The judge demanded to be the first to be shown the drawing. His eyes grew round as he looked at it. "Take great care in showing this to members of the jury."

Potvin shot to his feet. "Will the defence be permitted to view the evidence as well?"

"Yes," the judge said, "though let's not see you taking any pleasure in it."

After the drawing was shown around, as if the jurors were given the opportunity to witness a freak show, Moore said he had one last question for Miss Baker. "Where you on the evening of October twelfth when George Baker was murdered?"

"I was at home. My maid, Victoria, can attest to that."

Moore sat down. Potvin said he had no questions for the witness. The judge called for a recess until the next day. Then he darted off, as if he had urgent business to attend to in his chambers.

Alex's keepers took him away with scorn, pinching him as they reattached his shackles and digging in their nails. Potvin ran up to them. "My client needs to be put in a single cell. You know how it can be with prisoners on trial. The other prisoners might tear him to pieces."

"He deserves it, as long as they do it slowly," one of the guards said.

"I could have you chastised by the warden," Potvin said, seeming to have grown taller by a foot since the first time Alex spoke to him.

"Take it up with the warden. We can't decide where he goes," another guard said.

"I will. You take care of yourself, Mr. O'Shea. Your defence has not yet presented its case." With that, Potvin dashed away.

Before they took him out, Alex heard angry voices in the courtroom and saw Tim and Madeline shouting at each other. Rough men pushed Tim down.

⁜

Alex woke up the next day in a single cell. "For your own safety," a more humane guard said. Apparently, secrets flew around like bats in prison, and he was likely to be killed by his cellmates for being such a coward as to shoot a man in the back and poison his sweetheart. He would have cared little before yesterday, but Madeline's words made him so angry that, if he had that gun back, he would not have hesitated in murdering her right in the courtroom. But then he had looked at Eliza, whose eyes were locked on his, and she smiled. No, Tim, even here he must think of her as a man. Tim whispered to Potvin. He knew they were in league. On reflection, Alex thought there was a sliver of hope, brought about by his only friend in the world.

His gaolers came in the morning to chain him and haul him into the tunnel leading to the courthouse. He complied with their rough handling like a wooden-headed puppet on strings. Oh, how good it was to get away from the stink, including his own. Once again, he was pushed down onto a chair in the dock, and the guards stood at attention beside him. When the judge entered, Alex stood, along with everyone else in the courtroom. They all took their seats in harmony with the judge, who asked Moore if he had any more witnesses.

"Yes, your honour. I call upon Doctor Wilbur Brown to come forward."

The doctor, who had attended Mary at the time of her death, took the stand and swore the oath.

"Doctor Brown, you examined the late Mary Baker at the time of her death?"

"Yes. She was deceased by the time I arrived at the house."

"And did you form any opinion at the time regarding the reason for her death?"

"Yes. It was quite evident to me that the young woman had died of an overdose of poison."

Alex remembered Madeline entering Mary's room that night with the laudanum. Only three drops she had said. So that was how!

"What were those indications?" Moore asked.

"The smell and volume of vomit. The colour of her skin. There was a glass in the room with a small amount of liquid at the bottom. I took a sample, as I suspected that her ingestion of it may have caused her death, and poured out the remainder. Subsequently, a chemist confirmed that the liquid was an extremely high dosage of laudanum."

Moore ended his questions. Potvin stood up. "Doctor Brown, immediately after you examined Mary Baker, did you keep your suspicions about the reason for her death to yourself?"

"No, I informed her sister of my suspicion and asked if she could throw any light on the circumstances. I asked if it could it have been suicide. After her shock subsided, she assured me that the younger Miss Baker could not have taken her own life, because she had been housebound due to illness and could not have procured such a poison. She said she knew someone who might have forced it on her: the defendant."

"Did you believe her?

"I did, but I'm not a lawyer like you, sir, who can tell truth from deceit." Some chuckles broke out in the courtroom and among the jury members.

"Silence!" the sergeant shouted.

"Did you confront the defendant about it?"

The doctor looked at Potvin as if he was an idiot. "No, of course not. By then it had become a police matter."

Potvin sat down.

Beaming, Moore said he had one more witness. "I ask Edward Daniel to come forward." A bearded man in a suit emerged from the clerk's room carrying a book under his arm. He looked familiar to Alex. Yes, he was the chemist from whom Alex bought the laudanum for Madeline.

"Mr. Daniel, are you familiar with the accused?" Moore asked, pointing his large forefinger at Alex.

"Yes. I met him on one occasion, when he came into our shop to purchase laudanum. I have his name in here." Daniel tapped his book. There were some gasps and curses from the courtroom, and the sergeant rose to his feet again. "Silence!"

"Mr. Daniel, don't many people purchase laudanum from you without you writing down their names?"

"Yes, but this was such a large amount of this strong medicine that I was concerned that someone might take an overdose, so I asked the gentleman for his name and address

". . . Alexander O'Shea, residence Russell House, six ounce bottles of laudanum, September twentieth, eighteen sixty-eight," he read. More grumblings from the audience, but the sergeant only needed to motion, and there was silence.

"In your opinion, how much laudanum would be fatal?"

"It would depend on the constitution of the person taking it, but I would say a third of an ounce would be enough to poison the healthiest person."

Moore took his seat.

Tim sat behind Potvin. Alex signalled with his eyes at the bench on the opposite side of the courtroom, where Madeline sat with a handkerchief pressed to her face. Tim tapped Potvin on the shoulder and whispered to him. He rose. "Mr. Daniel, did the defendant tell you why he wanted such a large supply of laudanum?"

"I don't remember. We have so many customers coming in. I recall that he knew very little about the medication and that he wanted it for someone else."

"Did he say it was for Miss Baker?"

"He may have. Yes, it's coming back. I think he mentioned a name like Baker, although I didn't write it down in my book."

Daniel looked at Alex somewhat sympathetically. He was a decent person, but his evidence was damning. How could Alex have been so ignorant as to buy the very poison that Madeline would use to kill Mary? His own stupidity was on trial here, and he had killed Mary by it. Alex wanted to stand and confess that he was guilty of neglect. He had disregarded omens, was ignorant in every way.

Alex became alert when he heard Potvin call Timothy Fairlight to the stand.

No, Alex thought. *Please, don't put yourself in harm's way. Our friendship will become a miasma that will pull you down with me in this sick, deep place.* Why had Potvin gone behind his back? Alex would have refused this adamantly. He was afraid he would be responsible for the downfall of everyone close to him, Mary and Eliza.

Eliza—Tim—stood with square shoulders, his words firm and manly as he took the oath.

"Mr. Fairlight, what is your relationship with the accused?"

"We have been friends for about eight years." Tim looked at Alex and smiled.

Careful! Just say you think me to be a good character and get off the stand.

"How did you come to know the accused?"

"We both lived in Kingston and had common interests: the city's heritage, books, and writing."

Eliza, she was still Eliza.

"You're aware that Mr. O'Shea stands accused of two murders. In your opinion, is he capable of carrying out such actions?"

"Definitely not. He is an ethical, honest man who would never commit murder, let alone such cowardly murders as those of Mary and George Baker."

That's enough. Go now.

However, Potvin looked like he was just warming up. "You said the accused lived in Kingston. Did he tell you why he came to Ottawa and took up residence in the Baker house?"

"He came to Ottawa, because he met Mary Baker and fell in love with her. They were to be married. He resided at Russell House until just a few days before the young lady passed away. The register at the Russell will prove this. Madeline Baker asked him to patrol the street at night to keep guard. He only considered moving into the house because of his betrothed's health and because he felt she was at risk."

"Risk? Could you explain that to the jury?"

"He believed her being cooped up in the house, like a prisoner, was bad for her health. Also, Madeline Baker led him to believe that George Baker had been abusive toward his niece and might break into their house. He was there to protect her."

Alex could not see Madeline's face, but from the look Tim gave her, Alex believed a staring match was going on. *Please, Eliza—Tim—don't go near that flame.*

"Were you in Ottawa at the time of Miss Mary's death?"

"Yes."

"Had you ever met Mary or George Baker?"

"Yes. I worked for a time as butler at the Baker household, so I was familiar with Miss Baker and her late sister. I met George once, just after the funeral service for his niece."

What? Tim never told Alex that. Was he making up a story to help him?

"What was George Baker doing?"

"He was watching the service from a distance, under the cover of trees, and he was weeping. He said he would not be welcome at the funeral, and it was obvious to me that he was grieving deeply. We talked for a time, and he asked me to come by the Baker sawmill if I wanted a job."

"Did you go to the mill?"

"Yes, but the police were there. It was the morning when Mr. Baker's body was found."

"Where were you and Mr. O'Shea on the night George Baker was murdered?"

"We were staying at the same hotel, Russell House. We had an early dinner, because Miss Baker had asked Mr. O'Shea to come over to her house from seven until nine, because some source had told her that George planned to send an assassin into her house to attack her that night, after she returned from a meeting with her lawyer. He said she was going to hire another guard, who would relieve him from the duty of watching over her house. He returned after ten, and we had tea together."

"Did you believe he was at Miss Baker's?"

"Absolutely. He was getting up every night to keep watch outside, and he was exhausted, unable to carry out his daily writing."

"Was he armed?"

"Yes, with a revolver that Miss Baker gave him and insisted he carry, because, as she said, her uncle was a crack shot. He felt very uncomfortable about having it and planned to return it once she hired another guard."

Oh, brave Tim. You're looking straight at Madeline and telling the truth.

"Do you have anything further to add to your testimony about either of these murders?"

"Yes. Shortly before Miss Baker fired me, I found another indecent drawing in the drawer of her desk."

Moore rose to his feet. "Your honour! This witness is biased and telling lies to the court to place further injury on Miss Baker, who has already lost her beloved sister and uncle. This man is obviously a collaborator with the accused. Please, inform the jury to ignore the testimony of this witness and whatever foolish piece of malicious evidence he has invented!"

Tim, you should have stopped. Now you may be sent to prison as well.

"Mr. Potvin, do you claim that the piece of paper you have in your hand is evidence the police did not recover?"

"I do, your honour."

"Then show it to me."

Potvin brought it to the judge. His eyebrows shot up, and he was struck dumb for a moment. "Show it to Mr. Moore," he said.

Potvin went over to Moore, who reached out his hand to take it. Potvin shook his head and asked Moore to turn toward the court as Potvin held out the drawing for his opponent to see.

"Your honour, this is meaningless, immoral sewer waste," Moore said. "Has my learned colleague lost his mind?"

"This is no time to issue insults," the judge said. "I'll see both of you in my chambers."

Tim gave him an optimistic look. If only Alex could go down and talk with him, go for a walk outside, he would gladly put his head in the hangman's noose after that. But he feared this was the last time they would see each other before he was condemned. What was going on in Tim's mind? Did he have other tricks up his sleeve? He knew Tim was telling the truth, but would the jury believe it?

The judge and the two lawyers returned. Everyone awaited the judge's words. "Gentlemen of the jury, adjudicating this case is becoming like negotiating a peace treaty. Mr. Moore has presented me with persuasive arguments that Mr. Fairlight's testimony is biased. I ask you to ignore his evidence in making your decision. Mr. Potvin says he will introduce further evidence to validate the page that he wants the court to accept as evidence. I have agreed to accept it provisionally. You'll step down, Mr. Fairlight."

Tim came out of the witness box, hands clenched into fists. *Please don't go near Moore.* He did not.

The next witness's name was Noam Sidowski, originally from Poland. He said he was an expert in art, having studied for three years at the Lenski Institute in Warsaw and becoming a teacher and mentor, especially of drawing, in the seven years he had been in Canada. He was a studious-looking man dressed in an old-fashioned suit. He had a salt-and-pepper goatee and spoke with an accent.

"Mr. Sidowski, I would like you to examine a drawing already introduced into evidence, and then I'll ask you a question."

The judge directed the clerk to bring out the drawing of Mary, Alex, and the tree. The jury looked up at Alex with disgust and anger on their faces. What good would this do to remind them of his shame now?

Sidowski took a loupe out of his coat pocket and scrutinized the drawing, held up by the clerk and the record keeper. Unlike others before him, he betrayed no emotion. His enlarged eye traveled slowly up and down and then left and right and back again. At long last, he put the loupe away.

"Mr. Sidowski, have you observed anything peculiar about the drawing?"

"Yes, two artists created it. The tree and the naked man on the left were created meticulously, with short strokes of the pencil and with shading done carefully. The woman and the dead snake on the right were done by a more aggressive artist who used long strokes and shaded carelessly."

"Now, Mr. Sidowski, I would like you to examine the tentative evidence introduced by Mr. Fairlight, and I'll have a similar question for you," Potvin said, sounding more confident.

"Mr. Potvin, I hope you will steer us back to the case in hand. So far, I don't see the connection," the judge said.

"You will, your honour," Potvin assured him.

Sidowski took out the loupe and polished it with a red handkerchief. He examined the piece of paper that the clerk handed to him and then turned back to Potvin.

"Have you noticed something similar to the other evidence?" Potvin asked.

"Yes, the sketch was done by the same artist who drew the woman in the first drawing. The style is exactly the same, although the subject depicted is a different person."

"Your honour, I have no more questions for the witness and request this drawing be formally admitted as evidence," Potvin said.

The judge asked the clerk to show the evidence to the jury and to shield it from the eyes of others in the courtroom. Again, eyes popped as it was shown to them.

Moore rose. "Mr. Sidowski, you claim to be an expert on drawings. Were your studies in Warsaw exclusively on drawing?"

"No. My studies were in art generally: its history, techniques, painting, sculpture, and drawing."

"Therefore, you're not a specialist in drawing?"

"Perhaps not in my studies, but I have been exclusively drawing and teaching drawing since my arrival in Canada."

"Returning to the drawing with the man, the woman, and the tree, could not the part on the right-hand side have been the same artist as the one on the left, working in a hurry, drawing bold lines and paying less attention to fine details?"

"In my opinion, that is highly unlikely. The pencil was held at different angles in the left-hand side of the drawing. The style is decidedly different."

"What if someone switched from using the right hand to the left or the other way around?"

"I have never heard of anyone doing that, but the style would be different."

"No more questions."

No matter how many straws Moore grasped, the jury, given the way some of them smiled and nodded, regarded him as their champion. Alex knew who finished the drawing—she was sitting right behind Moore. If only he could testify. But someone else might know: Victoria. If she was called, would she back up Madeline's testimony?

"The defence calls upon Detective Cullen as the next witness."

A tall, somber man ascended to the witness box and took the oath. He said he was from Montreal but had been called in for the investigation.

"Detective Cullen, can you identify the young woman in the drawing I'm about to show you?" Potvin fetched the drawing from the clerk and handed it to Cullen. He looked at it closely, his expression steady, then nodded slowly before he handed it back.

"Yes," he said. "It is the unidentified woman whose murder took place in Lower Town on the same night that Mr. Baker was shot near his lumber mill."

"Is this a drawing of her as she lay as a corpse?"

"No. This is a . . . suggestive drawing of her as she was in life."

Potvin turned the witness over to Moore, who rose majestically. "Detective Cullen, after the time of the murder of this woman and another man in Lower Town, you indicated to the newspaper that there was no apparent link among the three murders."

"Correct."

"Do you think that now?"

"This drawing requires us to re-examine the evidence."

"But do you not think that a lewd drawing brought forward by Timothy Fairlight, a witness this court has determined to be a liar, and who was no doubt brought in by the accused to finish the horrid drawing of Miss Mary Baker, points to him as the Lower Town murderer?" Moore's voice boomed at the end of this utterance as Potvin jumped to his feet to plead with the judge.

"Silence!" the sergeant shouted. "Silence!"

"Mr. Moore, I caution you on ignoring the protocol of this court. Jury, please disregard the prosecution's last question. Do you have any other, this time appropriate, questions to ask the detective?"

"None, your honour."

Oh Eliza—Tim—how could you knowingly risk putting a noose around your own neck, so we would swing together? You did not look up at me, because you knew I might go out of control and speak out. But what can I say? This is madness.

"The defence calls upon Delight to come to the witness box."

A woman with straggly hair and a ragged red dress entered the courtroom, swinging her hips. Moore jumped to his feet and pointed his finger at her. "Your honour, have we not already had enough masquerades to disgrace this institution? Potvin has obviously paid a woman of the night to come forward to tell us lies."

Delight proceeded as if she hadn't heard him. "You're jumping to conclusions, Mr. Moore," the judge said. "Please, sit until it is your turn to cross-examine."

The clerk came forward to administer the oath. "Madam," the judge said, "give your surname as well as your Christian name."

"Christian, sir? I'm no Christian, not since . . . well, leave that be. I have one name, Delight."

"Very well." The judge glanced at Moore to keep him from raising another objection.

Potvin got the small drawing from the clerk and took it to Delight. "Miss Delight, do you recognize the person in this drawing?"

"Yes, 'tis Totsie. She were our friend who got herself kilt."

"Where were you on the night that Totsie was murdered?"

"I were out on Rideau Street with my friends."

"Do you know where Totsie went that night?"

"She went off with Max, the man who was kilt too, to I dunno where. I only find out after."

"Are you aware of why Max and Totsie went away together?"

"Yes, 'twas secret then but suppose now it dunna matter. That day Totsie told me that a lady was goin' to pay 'em a whole lot of cash to do stuff. I dunno what."

"Was this Max there the whole evening before he took Totsie away?"

"No, he was off somewhere until nearly ten. Back for little while, then off with poor Tot."

So that's how Madeline killed George! Alex thought. *She paid a man in Lower Town to do it!* And she had requested Alex to stay at her house without anyone knowing and then denied it later. He dug his nails into his palms.

"Did you notice anything unusual that night?"

"Well, much later, I was just coming out of an alley, and I sees hobblin' along, leanin' on a stick, an old biddy bent over, dressed all in black. She look odd, 'cause sometimes she don't move like an old 'un, and she go directly on Sappers. Never seed that before."

"No more questions," Potvin said.

Now it was Moore's turn. "Miss or Mrs. Delight, what kind of work do you do on Rideau Street?"

"Me and others help people."

"Very good. And do all the men pay you for the help you give?"

"They does, out of the kindness of their souls."

"Was this Max the pimp for all of you prostitutes?" Moore glanced archly at the jury while Delight looked like a hen who was about to cluck.

"He were our boss."

"Did my learned colleague, Mr. Potvin, pay you to come here today to tell lies?"

Potvin jumped to his feet. "Your honour—"

The judge waved his hands, and the sergeant jumped to his feet. "Silence!"

"Mr. Moore, rephrase your question, and keep insinuations out of it."

Moore bowed to the judge. "Very well. Delight, did you get any money for coming here today?"

"Yes, a bit, for a plate of food and a drink waiting for the cart to get me. I tells the truth tho."

Moore tried again to get the judge to dismiss the evidence, but he refused. "Even a cat can look at a king, Mr. Moore. I'm sure the jury has had enough for today. I know I have. Counsels, plan to be more gentlemanly in your conduct tomorrow." He banged his gavel.

As Alex was taken out, he felt like he was under the ocean with miles of water pressing down on his head, preventing him from responding in kind to Eliza's cheerful smile.

24

At court the next morning, Tim was among the first to arrive. Only a few spectators were there to get the good seats. Madeline lounged in the chair next to Moore's. Tim came up to his spot behind Potvin's chair. He heard a hissing sound from Madeline. Then she jumped up and strode over to him.

"You're a freak, a collaborator, a thief, the slimiest worm that ever crawled out of hell. You'll be hanging with O'Shea, mark my words," she said, her face contorting viciously.

Tim looked at her casually. "Remember where you are, Miss Baker. This is a courtroom, and there are witnesses here. You're prejudicing your case."

"No, I'm just making my mark!" She swung her large hand toward his face. He saw it coming, caught her wrist in mid-air, held it tightly, and hoped his grip pinched.

"Stop this immediately! Miss Baker, come over here" said Moore, who had just come in. Tim gave Madeline a defiant look as he released her arm. She marched over to Moore.

"Dear Mr. Moore, I hope we get the guilty verdict today, and I want you to make sure that his accomplice sitting over there gets hung as well," she said, like a child whining to her parent.

"The proceedings may well conclude today, Miss Baker, and I'm confident justice will be done. Now, if you don't mind, I'm busy preparing for the day with this gentleman here." Moore turned to his assistant. She poked his arm, and he turned to have a whispered discussion with her, his face red.

Instead of taking her seat behind Moore, Madeline strode to the back of the courtroom. Potvin arrived, his bravado increased remarkably. He nodded affably to Tim as the spectators poured in. The courtroom was more than packed. Some people stood, and there was a lineup of folks outside who complained they were not allowed in. Tim turned to see Madeline sitting along the aisle in the back row.

The judge brought everyone to their feet and then asked Potvin if he had any more witnesses or if summary arguments could begin. Potvin called upon Detective Cullen. Moore protested that the policeman had already testified.

"Your honour," Potvin said, "more evidence has come forward that is important to this case." Looking like a sneaking cat rather than the mouse he was before, Potvin began his questions. "Detective, what new evidence has come to light?"

"Following yesterday's proceedings in this courtroom, I and another officer investigated once again the crime scene in Lower Town, where two murders took place on the same night as Mr. Baker was killed." Tim watched Madeline squirm as if a fire had broken out in her under linen.

Moore stood. "Your honour, this trial is about murders committed by the defendant. It has already been established that there is no connection between the murders in this case and those two others in Lower Town."

Potvin looked like he wanted to run over to Moore and scratch his face.

"The evidence you provide, Detective Cullen, must be relevant to the case in hand," the judge said, "as Mr. Moore points out. Are you saying there is a connection?"

"The evidence will point to a connection, if not fully proving it."

The judge nodded. "Very well. You may proceed, Mr. Potvin."

Potvin arched his back, again like a cat. "Detective, what is the new evidence you discovered?"

"Constable, please bring forward the evidence," the detective said.

A uniformed policeman brought him a parcel, some objects wrapped in a blanket. Cullen unwrapped it. Tim heard an intake of collective breath from the spectators. Inside were two weapons: a handgun and a rifle.

"Where were these found, and what are they?" Potvin asked.

"In the canal, by the scene of the Lower Town murders. After yesterday's proceedings in this court, I returned to the scene with this constable. I asked him to disrobe and dive into the canal. He found this thirty-eight-caliber revolver, a Remington Model eighteen fifty-eight, with five bullets in its chamber, near where the unidentified man was shot. Upon further exploration, and I thank him for his hard work, he recovered this forty-four-caliber Henry repeater rifle, not far from where the young woman, named yesterday as Totsie, was found bludgeoned to death. The evidence points to the butt of this rifle as her murder weapon. A forty-four-caliber bullet killed the unidentified man at the scene."

"You said you now think the murder cases may be connected," the judge interposed. "How?"

"The revolver we reclaimed from the defendant was the same model as the one in the canal. They are somewhat rare. It is highly unlikely that this is a coincidence."

"Do you now have a suspect in custody for these murders?"

"We do not."

Potvin ended his questioning there. Moore came on like a bulldog. "Detective, given that the accused was arrested while trying to hide the twin weapon, surely that makes him the prime suspect for these other murders as well."

"We have not finished our investigation, so I can't speculate."

"Well, I'm sure it's clear to members of the jury who the perpetrator of these murders is. I thank you, Detective." Moore sat down like a magistrate.

"I call Harold Benson to the stand," Potvin said. When Benson entered, Madeline shouted out that he was a big liar. Benson paid no attention to her. After the judge ordered Madelaine to remain silent or be ejected from the courtroom, he reminded Benson that he was still under oath, and then Potvin began his questioning. "Mr. Benson, have you ever seen firearms like those just put into evidence?"

"Yes, I remember when the late Mr. William Baker had those ones or others identical to them, the rifle and twin pistols. He had me polish them. I went out with him when he shot at targets near the river. He had holsters for the pistols and a sling for the rifle. I carried the rifle and a picnic basket."

"So, it was just the two of you going for this target practice?"

"No, often Miss Madeline came along. She became quite an accomplished shooter, especially with the rifle. He was proud of her."

"Why did Miss Mary not accompany you?"

"She was too young then and was not well."

"What was her malady? Some form of epidemic?"

"I think not. She kept to her room except when the tutor came, and . . . ."

Madeline looked like she could fly across the room and strangle Benson.

"And what, Mr. Benson? Did you witness anything that may have caused her to keep to her room?"

Benson reddened. Tim worried he would have a heart attack. "Mr. Potvin, may I whisper it to the judge? It is not proper to say with ladies present."

The judge interceded. "If it bears on this case, you must say it aloud for all to hear."

Benson cleared his throat. "One night, I heard cries—Mary's cries for sure—coming out of the master's room. I was not usually in the upper quarters of the house at that time, but the cries were so loud, I heard them from the bottom of the stairs. I thought maybe the master was out at his club, and Miss Mary had gotten up and taken a tumble. I crept up the stairs and opened the door. There . . . I saw that Miss Mary, still only a child, was without clothing and on her stomach on the bed, and the master had her legs spread and was doing something improper to her. And . . . Miss Madeline had a whip or a riding crop and was hitting Miss Mary on the back. It was only a glimpse. I closed the door and crept back down the stairs."

There was such chatter and so many exclamations in the court that the sergeant stood and shouted "Silence!" four times. Members of the jury turned to each other with round, open mouths. Heads turned around, looking at Madeline.

"Liar!" she shouted. "You did that to Mary with O'Shea!"

"Be quiet, Miss Baker, or I'll have you taken away from the court," the judge warned.

Potvin waited for the court to quiet down before resuming. "Did anyone discover you had looked in?"

"Yes, the master. He chased me down the stairs and gave me such a warning with his mouth and his fists that I bear the marks to this day." He touched a scar under his eye. "He said he should fire me for invading his family's privacy, and he warned me that if ever I told anyone, he would shoot me."

Potvin sat down, and then it was Moore's turn. "Mr. Benson, do you have any proof of what you have testified?" Moore asked calmly.

"I know what I know and say what I saw, and I have my diary."

"Has someone paid you to say this today?" Moore asked.

"No. I resent anyone who suggests such nonsense."

"Temper, sir, that has no place in the courtroom."

"Mr. Moore, that is my call to make," the judge said.

"I'm sorry, your honour. Mr. Benson, did you not have a grudge against Miss Madeline Baker? After all, you left her employ to decamp with her uncle George."

"I didn't like her, sir. I'll make no argument with that, but I tried not to show it. After Mr. Baker died, I stayed to try and help Miss Mary, if I could."

"You're aware that the accused lived in the house for a time, and, according to Miss Baker's testimony, he asserted his control over the sisters. He was arrested while trying to conceal one of the pistols. Where were the weapons kept?"

"In a locked cabinet in the master's room."

"Well then, Mr. Benson, if the accused had found the key and stolen one weapon, might not he have taken them all?"

"I suppose."

"Now, turning to what you apparently saw in a blurry half-second in your master's room, could you have imagined it?"

"No, sir. It has been burned into my brain."

"Burned into your brain? Could it not have been something else very wrong that you did that caused the late Mr. Baker to hit and chastise you? Maybe you fell and were knocked out and woke up with an impression of what you thought you saw that wasn't true at all?"

"No, sir, burned into my brain, as I said. I warned Mr. O'Shea that there was evil in the house, but he didn't keep away."

"Oh, so you collaborated with the accused?"

The judge pounded his gavel. "Mr. Moore, I have had enough of you asking insinuating questions. Unless you have any more reasonable questions to ask the witness, I'll excuse him, and we can proceed with the trial."

Moore bowed respectfully, and Benson left the stand, coming down the aisle with fire in his eyes. Madeline sat like a statue, exuding outrage.

"The defence calls Jane Higgins to the stand."

This was another piece of the puzzle that Tim had unearthed. The woman came forward and took the oath with no hesitation.

"Mrs. Higgins, where do you live?" Potvin asked.

"Our house is on Concession Street."

"Miss Baker's house is next door?"

"Yes, she's one house farther away from downtown."

"On the night of George Baker's murder, did you happen to notice anything unusual."

"Around midnight or a few minutes after that, my new dog, Pip, woke me up. He was looking out the window at someone going by, so I looked too. It seemed to be an old woman."

"Mrs. Higgins, yesterday a witness testified that, the same night, she saw an old woman with a cane, her back bent, wearing a shabby black dress, going as fast as she could across Sappers Bridge toward Upper Town. Did the person you saw meet this description?"

"Yes, in every detail. And I did think to myself, poor thing, what's she running from, moving so fast?"

"Did you see where she went?"

"I saw her continuing toward the Baker house but couldn't see more."

Now it was Moore's turn. "Mrs. Higgins, you and your husband must be good friends with the Bakers, living next door to them for how many years?"

"Sixteen. No, they kept to themselves, and hardly a word has passed between us in all that time. The last time I talked to Miss Baker, she threatened my Pip."

"Your child? I'm aghast to hear it."

"No, my puppy. He hasn't been trained yet, but he's a very good dog."

"Oh, I see, your puppy. I suppose he was merely doing his business on her flowers. But, leave that. The next question I want to ask is why the old woman didn't see you watching her when your dog made so much noise at the front window."

"She had her head down and hurried along. She may have heard Pip barking, but it was dark in the house, and I doubt she could have seen anything at our window."

"One last question: were you in court yesterday?"

"Yes."

"So, you would have heard that false confession by the lady of the night who was paid to make up a story about this woman. Did you decide to corroborate her story to take revenge on the neighbour you hate?"

The judge pounded his gavel. "Witness, you don't need to answer that question. Mr. Moore, I have warned you before about keeping your insinuations for your final address to the jury. Gentlemen of the jury, I ask you to ignore what Mr. Moore has said. Mr. Potvin, I'm thinking of calling it a day. Do you have any more witnesses to bring forward?"

"Your honour, there is only one more."

"Very well, you may call this witness, and then we will have closing arguments tomorrow morning and turn this case over to the jury."

"The defence calls Victoria Lawson to take the stand."

Oh, hallelujah, Tim thought. Victoria has come to the court! She could clinch the case for the defence. She had to have seen evidence of Madeline's abuse of her sister. The spectators watched the clerk's door, as did Potvin.

"Is Victoria Lawson here?" the judge asked.

"Yes, she is, your Honour," Benson said, smirking at Madeline, whose expression suggested that Benson would be a dead man, joining the others. Benson went out the clerk's door and came back, escorting Victoria. They looked like a pair of newlyweds.

Everyone's eyes were glued to Victoria, except for Tim's. He heard the maid being sworn in and then testifying that she had found bloody nightdresses belonging to Mary going back to the time when Mr. William Baker was still alive and much before Mr. O'Shea came to the house. Then he saw Madeline slide out of her chair, open the courtroom door, and slip out.

He got out of his chair, walked past spectators who complained that their view was being blocked, and approached Detective Cullen. After a few hurried words, Cullen called the constable, and they ran out of the courtroom just in time to see a cab speeding away from the courthouse.

Cullen turned to Tim. "What's happening here?"

"She's going to her house to fetch something and then to flee."

Cullen hailed another cab. "You can come along. Are you a detective on holiday?"

Tim said he was not, but Cullen looked unconvinced. They headed for Concession Street, Tim giving instructions to the cabby en route. It had rained that morning, and the streets were mucky.

The journey was a short one. They were rewarded by seeing the cab in which Madeline had fled in front of the house. Cullen got out and talked with her cabby, then returned. "The driver said she has gone in for something, and then he's to take her directly to the train station. Mr. Fairlight, can she escape from a back entrance?"

"Yes, one of us should go around and watch there."

Cullen directed the constable to go. Then he instructed their cabbie to move down the street in case Madeline had not yet spied what was going on.

Tim and Cullen went to the front door. It was locked. They waited. Before long they heard the latches being thrown open. Madeline came out, only to be blocked by the two men.

"You!" she shouted at Tim. "Mr. Cullen, do you not know this man is a murderer and a freak? He tried to rape me. I had to throw him off."

"I have heard enough of your conspiracies. Come along with me peacefully to the courthouse, or I'll be obliged to take you into custody."

"Me? I'm the victim here. The evil servant who was testifying at the courthouse is a liar, forced to lie by this freak, and she has stolen my money! It's a lot, over five thousand dollars that, by working my fingers to the bone, I have put by. I knew she had done it by the look on her face and her alliance with that other villain, Benson."

"Come along. I have had enough of this. If the judge allows it, you can have your say in court." Cullen forced her toward the cab. The other policeman came from around the side of the house. He held out handcuffs, but Cullen shook his head and then turned to Tim. "Mr. Fairlight, do you wish to accompany us?"

Tim shook his head, his eyes on Madelaine. "I'll take the other cab."

As Tim walked away, he heard Madeline shouting. "First, it was me that Father took to his bed. I went down to the kitchen at night to eat fatty scraps, so I would get ugly, and he would stop. He never wanted a chubby girl. I'm the victim! I'm the victim!"

As Tim returned to the courthouse, he felt a strange sympathy for the raving woman.

25

Alex felt like he had travelled to another planet when he was set free from the gaol.

During his last two days there, he attended another trial, not a continuation of the last one but a trial in his head. The prosecution lawyer kept saying, "You could have saved her from her evil sister. Why didn't you act?"

The defence lawyer was, to his astonishment, his mother. "Alex, my dear boy, you did what you could and acted in good faith."

The judge, also a shock to him, was Eliza. "I must hear out the arguments on both sides and not be swayed by my friendship with you," she said. "The most important question is whether you acted with intent. Did you?"

"No, I swear."

She pounded her gavel. "Case dismissed!"

He felt far from glorious when he walked out of jail to the sunny, snow-covered streets. Tim Fairlight, not Eliza, met him. That puzzled him.

They walked to the house. It was indeed miniscule. The two bedrooms had scarcely room enough for their single beds. But what caught his eye was a desk and his books arranged above the table of their common room.

"Here's our new writing shop and domicile," Tim said.

"Yes. Hello, writing desk. It's good to see you," Alex said. He felt like crying.

"Now you will be able to finish your novel and start another," Tim said, eyes sparkling. "If anyone bothers us, we hardened working men can fight them off." Tim assumed a swashbuckling pose.

Something resembling a laugh came out of Alex's throat. "Don't you think it ironic that one man and a woman who dresses like a man are living together?"

"Who cares? We're a little troop. If Wolfe could capture Quebec, we can defeat the bullies. Or . . . we could be like Lincoln."

"And get assassinated?" Alex joked. "Of course, there's nothing more I would rather do than work on my novel and spend all my free time with you. You know, between us, we have enough money to move to a better domicile in Upper Town."

"We can if we can pay our living costs by working. There are lots of jobs in Ottawa now, from what I hear. With your new popularity in this town, you could get a writing job, perhaps even a reporter's job with the *Citizen*. As for me, I'm a rough character. I could work in a foundry again."

"No. You could become a detective. According to the newspaper, the police admire the work you did. Alerting them to Madeline's attempt to escape was brilliant. I'm glad you helped catch her. Otherwise, she would be a spectre out there planning to plunge a knife into our hearts."

They moved the two chairs in the room close together and sat. "You know, I'm not looking forward to Madeline's trial," Alex said. "We'll have to be there and go through all this again." How could he survive that? He would have to experience Mary's torture and poisoning over again. And, like Tim, especially after he heard what Madeline said when the police took her, he felt sorry for her. Her father started the whole cycle of violence and deception. It had bred Madeline's push for power and control. As a little girl she would never have intended all this to happen.

"The good thing is that most of the evidence against her is already on record," Tim said. "And, we'll be able to meet Benson and Victoria again before they get married and move to Kingston."

"I owe a lot to them. I hope they'll be happy together. I wonder if they'll have enough money to survive. Servants can't marry."

"Oh, I suspect they have enough money to start up a small business together." Tim gave him a knowing look; a secret Alex could explore but would not.

"You know, I could learn to like living here, especially if I could keep my promise to you after the trial ends," Alex said.

"A trip to the capitals of the world? Oh, Alex, that would be the delight of my life, but what if we run into black cats or ravens over there?"

Alex laughed. "One of the preparations for the trip will be the Alexander training project. You, sir, will be in charge of escorting me around Ottawa, where you can encourage herds of black cats to cross my trail, get me to walk under all the ladders we can find, and have staring matches with crows."

They chuckled and then sat still and thoughtfully, like an old married couple.

"Can I ask you a question about you and me?" Alex said. It had been on his mind ever since he was freed. "Are you going to continue being Tim, or will you become Eliza again?"

"I'll be Tim Fairlight to the world, but if you want to call me Eliza, you can do so here in our home."

"I'm full of questions tonight. Sorry to put you on trial. I have one more."

"Go ahead; I'm ready to give my oath." Tim was pleasant, brave.

"Will we always remain friends, or might we become something more one day?"

Tim was serious, thoughtful. Alex waited, tempted to cross his fingers.

"Let's see what time brings," Tim said, then took Alex's hand and fondled it.

The End

Acknowledgements

This book would not have been possible without the advice and support of my writers' group: Robin Boord, Maryann Kowalski, Kirsten Lind, Anne McMillan, and Rebecca Rosenberg, I would also like to thank Dinah Forbes, Bill Price, David Pratt, Ruth Stewart, Allan Cameron and Melissa Hiller. Thank you for the provision of research material to the Ottawa Public Library, the Kingston Museum of Health Care, and the City of Ottawa Archives. Last, but by no means least, I am everlastingly grateful for the encouragement and aid of my sister, Valerie Smith and my wife, Nuala O'Kelly.